NAILED

OTHER TITLES BY CORA BRENT

Worked Up

The Gentry Boys

NAILED

CORA BRENT

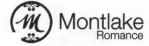

Montlake
Romance

Published by Montlake Romance, Seattle
www.apub.com

Amazon, the Amazon logo, and Montlake Romance are trademarks of Amazon.com, Inc., or its affiliates.

ISBN-13: 9781503900790
ISBN-10: 1503900797

Cover design by Eileen Carey

Printed in the United States of America

For my husband, who has given me two beautiful children and sixteen years of love and laughter.

CHAPTER ONE

"He did *what?*" I tried not to shriek into the phone as my construction foreman explained that one of the workers had decided to relieve his bladder over an empty elevator shaft.

"And unfortunately the county building inspector was standing fifteen floors below," Barnes admitted with reluctance.

"Shit."

"No, piss. But almost as bad."

I stifled another curse and pressed the crosswalk button as I headed back to the office.

"I'll be at the site this afternoon as soon as my meeting's over," I told Barnes. "I'll also call the inspector to smooth things over. The piss king is fired, effective immediately."

"Already booted him off the jobsite," Barnes assured me.

"Good. While I'm there I'll address the entire crew to remind them of the jobsite code of conduct. I'll text you when I'm on my way, so please make sure they are assembled."

Silence met my statement. Then Barnes sighed. "Whatever you say."

I knew the foreman thought I was overbearing at times, but this art museum project was extremely important. Everything needed to go well because any day now the partners of Lester & Brown were going to announce which project manager would receive the coveted downtown courthouse project.

"Approximately two o'clock," I told him. "Hopefully sooner."

"Sounds good. I forgot to ask you, did we get a plumber yet?"

"Signed Gable and Son last week," I said, slightly annoyed by the feeling that Barnes was second-guessing me. Then I reminded myself that the man was just being meticulous. There were other managers who were known to drop important balls now and then. But I never did. Yet Barnes had known me since I started with the company. As a site foreman, he managed the daily construction labor, but he reported directly to the assigned project manager, who bore ultimate responsibility for everything from scheduling to the flow of materials and the overall budget. That was me. Perhaps Barnes resented my managerial role, but he was usually the sort of guy who kept his head down and did his job. It's why I always requested him on all of my projects.

"You can always expect that I have everything under control," I added, a tad too briskly.

"Of course you do," Barnes said, with the same hint of snappishness. "I'll see you later, Audrey."

Of course you do.

"What's that supposed to mean?" I muttered as an elderly man in a red baseball cap paused to stare at me. I gave him a slight smile and started to cross the street.

Barnes's words would have been a compliment if delivered with less irritation. I tried to shove away the vague annoyance I felt over the conversation, though a nerve had been struck. I had been called a control freak at work. Hell, I'd been called a lot worse. Still, Barnes was also under a lot of pressure and probably didn't mean any harm. I wouldn't be bringing this up later. There were more important tasks to deal with, and the last thing I wanted to do was give anyone a reason to call me oversensitive. It was hard enough being the only female project manager in the firm.

I was so lost in my inner monologue that I failed to notice the light had changed. The waiting pedestrians had already crossed to the other side and traffic was beginning to move. Someone grabbed my arm and yanked me backward, pulling me out of the road.

"Shit!" I dropped my handbag in the street and went tumbling in the direction of whoever had seized me.

"I've got you," said a deep voice. An arm braced me around the waist. For one insane second I wanted to go limp against its power like a swooning virgin in an old-fashioned bodice ripper.

Then I looked up and got a load of who the voice and the arm belonged to.

All thoughts of virginal swooning evaporated as Jason Roma grinned down at me.

"Don't you know any better than to wander into a busy street?" His mouth tilted into the perpetually infuriating smirk that I'd grown used to despising after six years.

"I'm fine," I snapped, shoving him away. My heel wobbled as I took a big step back, farther away from the curb and from Jason Roma, from his strong arms and his pine-scented aftershave that always made me think of sex whether I wanted to or not. But even though I stumbled a little, I managed to avoid falling.

He calmly watched me. "You won't be fine when you turn around."

I brushed my hands over my skirt as if Jason had somehow gotten it dirty. "Why's that?"

He pointed. "Because your overpriced status symbol just got eviscerated by a city bus."

My head whipped around. The Louis Vuitton bag I'd bought for myself last Christmas was lying in a deflated heap in the middle of Third Street. A pickup truck added to the damage by running over it once more, this time managing to displace the contents, because somehow I never remembered to snap it closed. Jason Roma and every pedestrian waiting on either corner got a nice view of my crushed lipstick, scattered tampons, and the two condoms I kept in a side pocket just in case I stopped working long enough to have sex with someone.

At least I'd been holding my phone when I decided to take a stroll into traffic. It was still clutched in my palm.

The light changed again. People began crossing once more. Vaguely I recognized I was missing my brief opportunity to run into the street and collect my belongings.

Then I blinked and realized I didn't need to because Jason Roma had braved downtown traffic to do it for me.

"Here you go," he said triumphantly a moment later, handing over the sad remains of the handbag. "Looks like your wallet's still inside and in one piece, if a bit flatter."

I tried to accept it with dignity. "Thank you."

I had to cradle the handbag in my arms like a newborn baby because the seams were busted, and even though Jason had tried to stuff the loose tampons and other objects inside, they were in danger of escaping through the holes.

"I appreciate the help," I said with a bit of sincerity, which was odd for me when I was talking to Jason.

He raised an eyebrow. "You mean in saving your life? Or retrieving your purse?"

Somehow I got the feeling he was on the verge of busting out into laughter, but that was a typical impression one got from Jason. He was the type of guy who assumed constant ridicule was part of his charm. Jason Roma would probably find a reason to chuckle over a smallpox epidemic.

I looked down at the designer logo now sporting tire tracks. "Both," I mumbled.

He leaned forward, too close. "You're welcome, Audrey."

I tried not to take notice of the fact that Jason looked like he'd just stepped away from a modeling shoot. How the hell did he manage to appear cool and freshly pressed on a grimy urban street beneath the

Arizona sun? His almond-shaped dark eyes raked me over with amusement. Those eyes of his looked for a long time and lingered in places they shouldn't. I fought the urge to press my thighs together in order to quell the rush of heat. He'd notice, I was sure of it.

"Let's go get a drink," he suggested with a jerk of his head. "The Cobalt Room is just down the street."

"A drink? It's not even one o'clock in the afternoon."

"Good. Then they won't be crowded."

I glared at him. "I have a meeting."

He grinned. I never knew a grin could really be devilish until I met Jason Roma. But his grins were full of trouble and sex, especially when they landed in my direction. "Skip it."

"I can't and you know it."

Jason dropped his usual smirk and a concerned expression crossed his face. He reached out to brush a nonexistent object from my shoulder. "I think you've had a hell of a scare. You should sit down for a few minutes and collect your thoughts."

"My thoughts are perfectly collected, thank you."

"That's too bad," Jason said, and somehow he was closer again, too close. *How had he managed to get so close?* I hadn't even seen him take a step. "I would have been willing to help you with that chore. I think we both would have enjoyed the process."

I swallowed and felt myself biting my lip, an old nervous habit.

The light changed yet again. I had to get away before I did something really stupid.

"Look, Jason, I've got to go. Thanks for your help." I pivoted and carried my ruined purse across the street in my arms like a dead animal.

"Hey, Audrey?"

I turned around.

Jason Roma held a wrapped condom aloft. "I forgot to give this back to you."

Gritting my teeth, I reversed and started marching toward the glittering high-rise that contained the offices of Lester & Brown Construction. Mercifully, Jason did not follow.

"It's okay!" Jason shouted to my back from where I'd left him on the opposite corner. "I'm sure I can find a use for it!"

Jason's words were still bouncing around my head as I took the elevator up to the eleventh floor. I felt like I'd just lost a battle in a war I hadn't even agreed to fight. It was always better to just avoid him.

Noting that I was running low on time at this point, I paused in the ladies' room for a quick check. My usually pale skin was flushed, but my hazel eyes glared back at me from the mirror without any smears of mascara. I secured the clip that kept my shoulder-length blonde hair out of my face. My lips looked rather puckered, bloodless, and I really wished my tube of Sephora lipstick was not lying in a waxy melting puddle on Third Street.

But I couldn't fix that right now any more than I could fix the fact that Jason Roma had swiped one of my emergency condoms. Knowing Jason, the thing was surely destined to be unwrapped, used, and tossed into a trash can somewhere in the Phoenix city limits before nightfall.

And that doesn't bother me a damn bit.

Less than two minutes remained before the official start of my meeting, and I hated being the last one to walk into the conference room.

"Holy shit!" gasped Helen Delflorio from the other side of the bathroom door as I flung it open.

"Sorry," I said.

She put a hand on her sizeable chest. "Almost knocked me over, doll," she said with a wink, which was supposed to be funny because Helen was a big woman—a former bodybuilder. Meanwhile, I got tired after a twenty-minute workout with a pair of five-pound weights.

Helen worked for the accounting department and was one of the few women on the management floor. I liked her. And if I had time to talk, I might have told her about my brief, humiliating encounter with Jason Roma. Then she'd tell me a bawdy story about her colorful past, and as a result I wouldn't feel so gross about mine.

"Lunch tomorrow?" she asked me as I squeezed around her.

"Sounds good," I said breathlessly, and then hustled down the long row of high-walled cubicles.

I stopped by my desk only to toss my busted purse into a drawer and grab a notebook and pen, even though I knew I'd be scribbling a grocery list while my boss prattled on about his charity golf weekend in Scottsdale.

Luckily I wasn't the last one into the conference room for the weekly project status briefing. I wasn't the first one either.

The man who had been a witness to my morning embarrassment motioned to the chair beside him, but I ignored the gesture and took an empty one at the opposite end of the long table. I primly pretended to write something just to avoid acknowledging his presence. Jason Roma seemed untroubled by the rejection and sat there casually, toying with his cell phone.

"And how is everyone's day going?" asked Elgin McCray, the chief financial officer, who often talked to the staff as if we were kindergarteners. Somewhere along the way he'd read one book about model executive behavior and had taken the contents to heart.

"Laptop had a meltdown," complained Frank Leary, a fellow project manager who always made it a point to complain about something. "Damn inconvenient."

"Everything's great. Been working around the clock to get a bid out," chimed in Mark Peterson, another project manager, one who never missed an opportunity to suck up.

"I witnessed a near tragedy a few minutes ago when a woman stepped into traffic on Third Street," said a voice that caused me to pick up my pen and begin scribbling my list in the hopes no one would notice that my face was overheating.

"Really?" asked Karen Graner. I loved her as a project assistant when it came to filling out purchase orders, but she'd probably believe you if you said clouds were made of cotton candy. "Is she okay?"

Avocados.

I looked at the word I had written. I didn't even like avocados.

"A passerby was strong enough to pull her back onto the sidewalk before she got crushed under the wheels of a bus. But as to whether or not she's okay, I'm not too sure."

American cheese.

Karen didn't have time to offer further comment, and I didn't have time to continue my grocery list, because Marty Lester walked into the room. It would be more accurate to say he sprinted into the room. He was a fast mover for such a short guy. Marty, the majority owner, chief executive officer, and president, was always referred to as The Man. He actually referred to himself that way. If you were unlucky enough to receive a call from his huge corner office, the caller ID on your dated desk phone would actually say The Man. When I told people outside the company this fun fact, they usually laughed and figured I was joking. I wasn't.

Davis Brown, a prominent shareholder who occasionally showed up for meetings and events, followed. He heaved his thick body into a chair in the corner and looked bored—his desire to keep an eye on things warred with his natural inertia.

The Man fired off questions at the project management team and awaited the answers with obvious impatience. "And the Koppling wing of the art museum?" All eyes fell on me.

"Two minor modifications, but completion will be on schedule," I said with confidence.

The Man nodded. "And the budget?" he asked the CFO.

Elgin McCray consulted a pile of spreadsheets. "Koppling is within budget for materials. And it looks like labor will likewise remain in budget."

"It will," I said, knowing I could guarantee that.

The Man was pleased by the news. "Good work, Audrey. Moving on. What's the status of the Glendale Avenue Apartments?"

"We'll be wrapping up a week early," said Jason Roma.

"Budget?"

Elgin McCray peered at his spreadsheets again. He let out a low whistle. "Under budget. Considerably."

"Excellent." Marty Lester clapped his hands together.

Jason Roma grinned at me. I did not grin back. I examined my grocery list.

Apples.

Artichokes.

Apparently I was planning to subsist solely on foods beginning with the letter *A*.

The Man described some upcoming bid opportunities around the state and prodded Elgin McCray to stand up for a moment to lecture us about containing labor costs. I thought about pointing out the difficulty of containing labor costs when the estimates we used came from the ambitious sales team's efforts to land the bid, but that would have opened up an entire barrel of worms, and anyway, this wasn't the time or the place.

I glanced across the table. Jason Roma was leaning back in his chair with his sleeves rolled up above the elbow so I had a good view of his tanned, muscular forearms. Forearms shouldn't be enough to get a girl all aroused in a crowded conference room, but in this case there was a very firm body to go with them.

Jason stifled a yawn and shifted in his chair as The Man discussed tomorrow's photo shoot for promotional materials to be used in an upcoming trade show. I returned to my list.

Almonds.

I dropped my pen.

No one had called my name or made a sound, yet some internal sense made my head snap up in the next instant. And when it did, the first thing I saw was Jason Roma. He didn't even try to hide his stare. Instead of doing the polite thing and looking away when I narrowed my eyes at him, Jason raised an eyebrow and smirked.

What the fuck do you want?

He stretched and leaned back farther in his chair. I got the feeling he was trying to send a message, but I'd be damned if I could figure out what it was.

I didn't care anyway.

I didn't care at all.

Aspirin.

"And as we all know, the big downtown county courthouse project is now upon us. I don't need to tell you again that this is the big time. We get this one right, people, and the door will be opened for state projects and maybe even federal." The Man raised his little fists in the air like he'd just won a prizefight. "I'll be needing the best for this one—the 'A team.'"

Now The Man had my full attention. I straightened up in my chair and tried to look like the most responsible person in the room. My track record could speak for itself anyway. I'd busted my ass for this company for seven years and was promoted to project manager four years ago. Since then every single one of my projects performed within budget and on time despite a number of grueling obstacles and sometimes eighty-hour workweeks. I was proud of the job I did. Hell, if project management had a rock star, then I was it.

The Man closed the meeting on that note, promising that the decision on the team for the big project would be forthcoming.

After The Man sprinted out of the room and on to his next challenge, people began heaving themselves out of their comfortable chairs to go face the rest of the afternoon.

I was capping my pen when I noticed that Jason Roma hadn't moved. He was still leaning back in his chair and still watching me. He winked, just enough for me to wonder if it was really a wink or if he had something in his eye. Then I finally picked up on his meaning.

An object peeked out of the top of Jason's shirt pocket. A silver foil-wrapped item—the very same condom that had occupied a place at the bottom of my purse a mere hour ago before it reached freedom in the middle of Third Street.

Jason waited to see what I would do, what I would say. Playing with people was his specialty, and he'd be disappointed that I wasn't willing to respond.

I wasn't in the mood to spar with him. Not today or any other day.

I capped my pen with dignity and stalked out of the conference room without looking back.

CHAPTER TWO

The next morning I wound up seeking a spot on the roof of the full parking garage. On the inside I was cursing the fact that I was five minutes late, but I'd stopped by the Koppling site first thing to reinforce the impression that I was keeping a close eye on things. Yesterday afternoon when I assembled everyone for a quick huddle to address the unfortunate incident of the elevator pisser, I was sure a few of the workers were rolling their eyes. But this morning everyone was in place doing what they were supposed to be doing, and I left feeling satisfied.

Now, as I swung my Lexus into an empty parking space, I caught a glimpse of the time and felt the satisfaction vanish.

Spitting a slew of curses, I grabbed the keys and remembered my shoes only when my feet hit the concrete. The sensible steel-toe boots didn't exactly match my power-suit ensemble, but I was a stickler for safety rules whenever I visited an active construction site. How could I expect my workers to follow the rules if I didn't?

Still, I didn't intend to go trudging into the office this morning looking so mismatched, not when I'd received a text late last night from The Man asking me to visit his office at nine a.m. because he had an important matter to discuss. Since The Man rarely sought one-on-one meetings and had HR deal with anything of an unpleasant nature, I assumed I was being summoned to receive the news that I would be the project manager in charge of the courthouse. The whole drive here I'd been silently rehearsing my response.

"Thank you so much for this opportunity. I'm beyond grateful to be trusted with this task, and I assure you that there will be no bigger priority in my life."

Yet somehow I felt less confident expressing these feelings in ugly shoes. Exchanging the boots for a pair of black pumps cost me another minute of time, but this would be a good day. Tonight on the way home I'd celebrate by ordering some takeout sushi and curling up on the couch with a steamy romance novel. Perhaps something with a sexy, smartass executive who had an appetite for riding rough and a penchant for taming uptight workaholic women. My tastes were rather specific.

Just before I reached the elevator, my phone buzzed in the old Michael Kors bag I'd dug out of my closet last night. Six years ago it had been a birthday present from my boyfriend at the time. The relationship had ended badly, but at least the handbag held up. I wrestled the phone from its depths, grimacing to see a text from my mother.

Mom: William's birthday at four o'clock on Sunday. Need you to pick up centerpieces.

I answered with a smiley emoji even though I didn't feel very smiley-faced over my brother's looming birthday celebration. With all the fuss and planning and hysteria that was going into the big event, you'd think the birthday boy was turning five instead of thirty-five. William's birthdays were always momentous occasions in the Gordon family, while my birthdays were notably more subdued, with the long-standing excuse that mine fell on the day following a major holiday and everyone was all celebrated out. Anyway, this year my mother was putting in even more effort for William, perhaps figuring floral centerpieces and an elaborate fondant cake would make him forget his freshly finalized divorce.

Not that I begrudged my big brother his birthday gala. But it would have been nice to be asked if I had other plans. Sometimes I wondered if my folks just took it for granted that I would jump when they called. Or whether they cared if I actually showed up.

The buzz of another incoming text almost made me sigh, until I saw it was The Man.

The Man: **We are waiting.**

"Shit." I broke into a run across the concrete bridge between the parking garage and the offices of Lester & Brown. Sometimes my brief stint in junior varsity track served me well because even now, fifteen years later, I could cover impressive lengths in low heels. I should have remembered that The Man expects all meetings to begin on *his* time, not yours, and if he decides that it ought to begin five minutes early, the fault lies with you for not anticipating that.

"Audrey!" Helen shouted as I sprinted past her. She was holding a pile of papers and waving them at me furiously.

"We'll talk later," I threw over my shoulder before rounding the corner to The Man's office. I came to a dead stop and took a deep breath before casually strolling the remaining few steps to the door. My knock was answered immediately.

"Come in, Audrey."

I opened the door expecting to find The Man and maybe the CFO. Perhaps even Davis Brown would be there yawning in a corner. Two faces turned to me expectantly, and I felt my smile falter.

There was The Man.

There was no Davis Brown or Elgin McCray in sight.

But, inexplicably, there was a certain difficult colleague named Jason Roma reclining in a chair with his hands casually folded as if he were waiting to be served a glass of brandy and maybe a lap dance. He waved.

"Have a seat," said The Man in a pleasant tone. He didn't sit down himself. In fact there wasn't even a chair behind his desk. A back injury sustained in a car accident years earlier made sitting difficult—he was even known to lie down on the floor in the middle of a meeting in order to stretch his back muscles.

I, however, was glad to settle into one of the cushy chairs facing him even though I was still wondering why in the hell Jason Roma needed to be here.

The Man clapped his hands together once, loudly, like a grade school teacher who wanted to ensure all eyes were on him. "I'll make this quick," he said, glancing pointedly at his silver Movado. "We all know that the courthouse is by far the largest project ever undertaken in our fifteen years. We'll be breaking ground downtown in less than a month, and I need my best project manager on the job. And that's you. The two of you. As a team you'll have equal standing and equal responsibility when it comes to managing every aspect of the courthouse's construction. Brad will be meeting with you in an hour to go over all the contract language and architectural plans. Since he was the sales lead responsible for putting the bid together, he can answer any questions you might have."

The Man paused for a breath and then beamed at us. "Congratulations to both of you. Don't hesitate to keep me informed of any complications, and always keep in mind, the future of the company rests on the success of this project."

I sat there in stunned silence and tried to absorb the jumble of words that had just been unleashed. I didn't quite realize that The Man had already dismissed us from his office until I saw Jason shaking his hand.

"Thank you for the opportunity. I'm grateful you have put so much faith in me, and I assure you the courthouse will be my number one priority from this day forward."

Bastard stole my speech.

Of course Jason didn't really steal my speech, because I'd never even spoken it out loud.

But Jason shouldn't have had the chance to make a speech in the first place.

I had a year's seniority on him and a half dozen more projects under my belt. For crying out loud, I was there his first day—I remember the arrogant party boy fresh out of Arizona State who was only hired because his father used to be in the industry. Come to think of it, I was the one who trained him.

My purse fell on the floor with a thud. I thought my lower jaw might be down there beside it. Both Jason and The Man looked at me then, and since I couldn't just sit there like a gaping fool, I got to my feet.

"Thank you," I muttered weakly, and held out my sweaty hand for a shake. The Man pumped it dutifully for half a second and shifted to impatience, like he was wondering why in the world there were so many damn people hanging around his office. Jason opened the door and kindly waited for me to walk through it.

On the other side of the door I looked at Jason. He stared back at me.

"Nice hat," he said.

"Dammit." I'd completely forgotten that I was still wearing the hard hat from this morning's site visit. I tore it off my head, realizing how weird I must have looked sitting there in The Man's office. "Conference room," I hissed through gritted teeth, marching away and pausing at my desk long enough to shove my purse and my orange hard hat underneath it.

Jason must have taken the long way to the conference room, because he didn't show up for a good three minutes while I sat there clenching my fists and trying to apply some calming meditation techniques I'd learned from a YouTube video. To no avail.

When Jason finally appeared and opened the conference room glass door, he was whistling.

"You get lost?" I snarked.

He slid his tall, muscular body into a chair on the other side of the table. "No. Nature called. It's healthy to deal with such urges when they arise."

"I don't need to hear it."

"Then why did you ask?"

"I—never mind."

"Don't you deal with your natural urges, Audrey?"

My mouth fell open. Again. "What the hell is wrong with you?"

"Nothing at all. I'm having a great day. You should be having a great day too. We just received some exciting news."

"Jason." I lowered my head and tried to focus on a response that didn't include the word *f-u-c-k*.

"We can't work together," I finally said, and raised my head to challenge him with a glare.

He shrugged, unimpressed. "We've been working together for six years."

"No, we've spent six years staying out of each other's space."

Jason grinned, waiting for me to correct what I'd just said.

"For the most part," I added miserably, hoping he wouldn't mention things that were unmentionable, hoping he couldn't discern that I was pressing my knees together beneath the table to silence the spontaneous reactions surging through my body.

Jason adopted a serious expression, which looked about as genuine as eyelashes on a chicken. "If you don't want the assignment, Audrey, I'm sure management will understand."

"Shut up."

"The time commitment will be enormous, the pressure will be . . . ah, *massive*."

"You're an asshole."

"Nobody would be surprised if you decided that you weren't up to the challenge."

I glowered. "I suppose you think you're the only one capable of handling the job."

Jason tapped his fingers on the table and looked thoughtful. "Maybe I am."

I raised a hand to my forehead to mock him. "You'll have to give me a minute. I'm blinded by your conceit."

"That doesn't even make sense, Audrey."

I took my hand away and leaned forward. "Well, I'll tell you a few things that do make sense. No other PM in the company has logged as many hours or has overseen as many successful large-scale projects as I have over the past four years."

He laughed. "Now who's conceited?"

"Not conceited, just accurate."

Jason appeared to mull this over. "Actually, you aren't."

"Aren't what?"

"Accurate."

"How do you figure?"

Jason cleared his throat. His smirk disappeared. "If you'd bothered to do a little homework before shooting your mouth off, you would have realized the total revenue of my projects in that same four-year period was five million dollars more, and all were completed under budget with an average profit margin that was six percent higher than yours."

I had no ammunition to fire in return. Sometimes I pretended Jason Roma was just a brainless ex-frat boy who couldn't keep his zipper closed. But in my honest moments I knew that wasn't true. Jason had a sharp intelligence that was difficult to match. Plus I could—though I didn't want to—admit that he was good at the job and everyone loved him. Laborers, customers, subcontractors, management, everyone. And finally, in all likelihood he was telling the truth.

"Audrey," Jason said. I looked at him, at the chiseled jaw and the broad shoulders, at the carefully slicked-back hair and the calculating dark eyes that had already seen more than I wished they had seen. "We'll be good together," he said with a confident nod. "A hell of a team."

"You mean for the project?"

His eyes strayed down to the neckline of my blouse, and even though it was too high to display any cleavage, I felt utterly exposed. He gave me a winning smile. "Of course that's what I meant."

I thought about him sitting in that same chair during yesterday's meeting, with a stolen condom in his shirt pocket. Yes, Jason was smart and charming and hardworking when it suited him. He also couldn't be trusted to tell you the correct time of day if it amused him to do otherwise. But none of that meant I wouldn't be able to effectively oversee the project with him around. Having my name attached to the county courthouse project would give me a notable résumé bullet point that even my father was bound to be impressed with. It was an assignment I could get excited about, one that would make my career. If I had to hold my nose and put up with Jason Roma in the meantime, then so be it.

"You're right," I told him. "We can get this done as a team."

Instead of answering right away, Jason had a funny look on his face. I wondered if he was counting on the idea that I'd storm out of the room and go bellowing to management. If so, then he'd underestimated me.

There was a knock on the glass and a man holding a giant camera waved from the other side. He walked right in, explained he'd been hired to take photos for the trade show materials, and asked if we would mind posing for a few photos.

"Brad told me to pull a few people off their desks, but if you have a minute to spare, I'll just take some shots of the two of you."

"I've got a minute," Jason said, glancing at me.

"Sure, why not," I said, hoping I wouldn't be instructed to smile, because phony smiles did not get along with my face.

"Great," said the photographer, already setting up his camera as if he'd never had a doubt we would agree. "Now fold your hands on the table and look as if you're having an intense meeting. Perfect. Just a few more here. Now stand up and reach across the table and shake hands. Hold it right there."

If Jason felt any discomfort that I was squeezing his hand as hard as my muscles allowed, he gave no hint.

"Uh, you can let go now," said the photographer as he replaced the lens cap.

I released Jason's big hand and flexed my cramped fingers, slightly embarrassed that I'd been holding on to him so tightly.

"Are we done here?" I asked.

The photographer assumed I was talking to him. "Yeah, all finished for now. Thanks a lot."

Jason held my gaze. "I think that's about right. We're all finished for now." He stuffed his hands in his pockets and headed for the door. "Don't forget the meeting this afternoon," he said on his way out. "I want to hit the ground running on this thing."

His last statement irked me. It was like he was adopting the role of boss and warning that I ought to be just as committed to the job as he was. I wouldn't give him the satisfaction of knowing that I was bothered. Anyone in my position must have been cursed with some shitty luck to wind up working on a project of this magnitude with such an arrogant rival.

One who also happened to be my fuck buddy once upon a time.

CHAPTER THREE

I haven't touched a drop of alcohol in years. Yet every time I approach the circular driveway of my parents' palatial Scottsdale estate, an ancient itch tickles the back of my throat.

Today was no different.

Per my mother's instructions, I'd picked up the centerpieces from a local florist because the owner had been my mother's sorority sister some forty years ago at the University of Arizona.

As I struggled with the logistics of hauling ten flower arrangements in vases filled with colored glass beads out of the trunk of my Lexus, my mother, Cindy Pennington Gordon, floated out the front door wearing a teal cocktail dress that showed she still had an enviable figure at age sixty, even if some of its finer features were of newer vintage.

"Audrey," she called, and I braced myself for some variation of the you're-doing-XYZ-wrong speech that was as familiar as the scent of the lone magnolia tree that had somehow thrived in the front yard since I was a baby. But before issuing complaints, she offered me a dry kiss on the cheek.

"Hi, Mom," I said, hugging a trio of fragile centerpieces. "Where do you want these?"

She frowned. She touched a delicate yellow rosebud petal. "This isn't what I had in mind."

"Well, this is what we have."

"Was Blanche there when you picked them up?"

"No. Her daughter."

My mother wrinkled her nose. "The beads look tacky."

My arms were starting to hurt. The damn things were heavier than they looked. "Would you like me to return them?"

She scowled. At least I think she did. Her face wasn't very elastic at this point. "No, it's too late now. The catering truck is already here and guests will be arriving in less than half an hour."

"And no adult ever celebrated a birthday without carefully crafted centerpieces," I muttered.

She narrowed her eyes. "Don't start, Audrey."

I decided to hold my tongue and keep the peace. "Sorry."

"You can bring them around back," she sighed. "The tables are all set up."

I thought my mother might grab a vase or two herself, but in her typical delegation style she figured I'd manage to take care of it. She headed back to the house, leaving me to grapple with the heavy iron gate and a precariously assembled collection of glass and flowers.

"Auntie Audi!"

Two short, blond tornadoes came careening around a corner and nearly collided with me as I eased through the gate.

"Boys, you want to help out your poor old aunt?" I asked, trying to accept hugs from my enthusiastic nephews and avoid dropping things on the unforgiving travertine.

Six-year-old Leo exclaimed, "I'll help!" immediately, while five-year-old Isaac gazed up at me with solemn brown eyes.

"Are you really poor, Auntie Audi?" he asked.

"What? No, Isaac. It's just an expression."

"Oh." He nodded with a frown. "But you are old."

"Compared to you, yes."

Leo took one of the centerpieces out of my arms. "At least you're younger than Daddy," he said with confidence, probably figuring it was a compliment.

"Yes, there is that," I said wryly.

Isaac wasn't finished with the inquisition. "Are you older than Kelly?"

"Who's Kelly?"

"The babysitter," said Leo. "She lives two houses down. She sits on her phone the entire time whenever she comes to our house, and I've heard her say that Daddy is hot."

"I'm probably older than Kelly. I'm thirty."

"Do *you* think Daddy's hot?" Isaac asked me curiously.

My mouth twitched and I suppressed a snort of laughter. "Um, no."

I was trying to nudge the boys deeper into the backyard so I could drop off these cursed centerpieces and retrieve the rest that were waiting in the open trunk of my car. After passing beneath the ornate trellises laced with carefully tended grapevines on the side of the house, I turned a corner and stopped to assess the extravagant food spread and strange table arrangement. There had to be some kind of order lurking behind the layout, but I was damned if I could figure it out. I just wanted to unload all these damn vases.

"Let me get that, buddy." My older brother materialized from the house and took the centerpiece from Leo. "Why don't you and your brother go play with your Nerf guns back there in the orchard?"

As the boys went running and hollering to the collection of citrus trees lining the south end of the two-acre backyard, William shouted, "And stay away from the pool!"

"Okay, Daddy!" they shouted back.

I set the vases down on the nearest two tables. William took a good look at the arrangement in his hands and seemed puzzled.

"What is this?"

"A centerpiece."

"It looks like it belongs at a sweet-sixteen party."

"Well, Mom spares no expense for your birthday."

William might have detected a tone of sarcasm in my words. He set the flowers down and grinned at me. "How are you, Aud?"

"I'll be better if you'll help me haul the rest of these monstrosities out of my trunk. By the way, what's up with the odd table grouping?"

My handsome big brother raked a hand through his hair and made a face. "They're supposed to form the number thirty-five."

"You're shitting me."

He laughed. "Unfortunately not. You know how Mom goes overboard on this stuff. It makes her happy."

"Sure, I know that. I considered wearing the cardigan she gave me for my last birthday, but the weather is too warm today."

"You've always suffered the short end of the stick—your birthday being the day after Christmas."

That wasn't the whole story. I knew it and William knew it, but this wasn't the time to discuss old wounds.

"We should go grab the rest of these centerpieces," I said, "before all the dignified guests begin arriving and suffer shock at the sight of naked tables."

William checked on his sons with a glance. They were darting among the citrus trees and firing little foam pellets from colorful plastic guns. Both boys bore such a strong resemblance to their father.

"I don't even know most of the guests," William admitted with a sigh. "Dad's associates and Mom's socialites, with a few fringe relations thrown in for appearances. I'm sure we'll see a mayor or three hanging around."

"Is Dad still harassing you to run for office?"

"Of course. I have a feeling that's the point behind this whole gathering, but I told him I'm already happily overworked in my courtroom."

"Dad doesn't often take no for an answer." I searched the yard for a glimpse of the great Aaron Gordon, but all I saw were nervous caterers milling around and fussing over food.

"In this case he'll have to take no for an answer," William said in a hard voice. "It's been a shitty year and I don't need any new missions at the moment. Now let's go retrieve the rest of those pastel eyesores."

"You have the boys for the whole weekend?" I asked as we headed back to my car.

"Yup."

William wasn't willing to elaborate. He kept his eyes averted and picked up the heavy box containing the rest of the centerpieces.

"Want me to take some?" I asked.

"No."

His muscles bulged inside his shirt with the effort. He must be finding time for the gym despite being a father of two and the youngest municipal judge in the county.

I closed my trunk and grabbed the wrapped gift, a gourmet salsa collection, from the passenger seat before following him silently. I wished I knew what to say when it came to my brother's divorce. We'd never discussed it.

According to my mother, William's ex-wife, Jennifer, reconnected with an old boyfriend on Facebook and decided she didn't want to be married to my brother anymore. The words *scandalous bitch* might have been thrown around, but I wasn't sure if that version of events was true. I sure as hell couldn't ask Jennifer. Even though I'd always liked my sister-in-law, I'd never betray my brother by talking about his ruined marriage behind his back.

Besides, if my mother was correct (rare but possible), then Jennifer really was kind of a scandalous bitch.

"You never answered my question," William said when we returned to the backyard.

I placed a centerpiece on a table. The head of a yellow rose broke off. I stuffed it in my pocket. "What question?"

William pulled a chair out from the nearest table and sat down. The chair was too small for his large frame. "How are you, Audrey?"

"I'm good." I smiled. "Actually, I got a promotion of sorts. I'm going to be the project manager for the new courthouse."

"The big downtown courthouse?"

"That's the one."

He grinned. "Congratulations! That's impressive. I'm really proud of you."

I blushed. Praise from William always meant a lot to me. Maybe he sensed this and that's why he gave it so freely. "Not as impressive as donning black robes and banging a gavel. But thank you."

William scrutinized me. "Stop selling yourself short. You do that too often. The courthouse is an enormous undertaking and your bosses recognized that you've got what it takes to get the job done. That means something."

"Stop." I tapped his leg with my foot. "You're going to make me cry."

But William wasn't done being my cheerleader yet. "You've come a hell of a long way since you were seventeen. I see that." He jerked his thumb toward the house. "They ought to see that too."

It was the closest he'd ever come to acknowledging that our parents had never quite forgiven me for all the grief I'd caused them years ago. I knew I had a lot to atone for. I was still trying.

I used my thumb to wipe a single tear out of my left eye.

"Thanks, Billy," I said quietly. No one ever called him that anymore, not even me. But it seemed appropriate right now, right here in the backyard of our childhood home, as I was reminded that for my entire life William Gordon was the only person who'd faithfully believed in me even when I was an intoxicated, car-stealing, sex-crazed teenage delinquent. You couldn't buy that kind of loyalty. It was only found through luck and in big brothers.

"So when does the courthouse project start?" William asked, politely ignoring my lone tear.

"Soon," I said. "But there's a lot of legwork to be done before we break ground next month. It's a good thing I'm getting to see you now, because I'll be buried in work for the foreseeable future."

My brother glanced at his sons again and his expression grew wistful. "Don't work too hard, Audrey. Time has a way of passing you by."

And with that my parents emerged from the house in all their age-less power-couple glory. Time had not passed *them* by. Aaron and Cindy Gordon would be the first to describe themselves as "pillars of the community," but the narrative wasn't far off. My father inherited a family fortune at a young age and now owned a dozen real estate agencies. He also sat on the boards of directors for seven Phoenix-based companies, while my mother had spent the last two decades as chief administrator for the county's largest hospital. They also made generous charitable contributions to causes ranging from the city zoo to the downtown homeless shelter.

When I was a kid, I used to be awed whenever I found our name etched into a prominent location. During a fourth-grade-class field trip we visited an art museum, and as we filed in I gestured to the wall featuring the names of all the largest donors. "That's us," I told my teacher, Mrs. Cook, pointing to the big letters that read "The Aaron and Cindy Gordon Family Trust." Mrs. Cook gave me a funny look and said, "I know," without smiling. It was the first time I realized that bragging about my wealthy, prominent family didn't please everyone.

My father embraced me briefly, so briefly it almost didn't happen. But then again, he was distracted because a congressman arrived. William heaved a sigh and left his chair when my father beckoned with his full glass of Scotch. I promised him I'd head over to the far side of the yard to keep an eye on the boys.

My nephews were happy to include me in their game. Ever since his divorce, William had thrown himself into his work more than ever, and with our busy schedules I hadn't seen him or the boys as much as I would like. Now, as I ducked behind a grapefruit tree, I reminded myself that I needed to make more of an effort to be around Leo and Isaac before they grew into surly teens. My heels stuck in the damp ground surrounding the fruit orchard, and the citrus fragrance was overwhelming. Memories that seemed a hundred years in the past swarmed me. This had been my playground when I was a child and my place of refuge when I was a teenager. The trees had been much smaller back then.

Leo, Isaac, and I were engaged in an all-out Nerf gun war among the thick foliage when my mother interrupted to demand that we join the party and consume some of the expensive food that had been laid out on the banquet tables.

The boys wrinkled their noses as they considered the trays of food.

"Is that chicken?" Leo asked.

I squinted at the tray. "It's fried shrimp."

"I don't like shrimp," complained Isaac.

"Well, I'm sure we can find something you do like," I said cheerfully.

"I like chicken nuggets and pizza."

My mother was standing nearby with a glass of wine in her hand. "We don't have chicken nuggets and pizza. Try some stuffed mushrooms."

"I don't want stuffed mushrooms."

My mother regarded her little grandson with some impatience. She never did relate to children well, not even when William and I were young. There was always something else, something more important she needed to be doing. "There's a lot of good food here, Isaac. If you never try anything new, then you'll never really know what you like."

Isaac pulled at his ear. "My mom keeps a bag of chicken nuggets in the freezer at home. If we don't like regular dinner, she makes them for us."

"Well, your mother does a lot of things that aren't commendable."

"Mom!" Criticizing Jennifer in a private conversation was one thing, but denouncing her in front of her children was something else. Leo and Isaac were still regarding the catered food with some consternation. Aside from my cousin Mark's fifteen-year-old daughter, who was hunched over her phone and texting furiously, they were the only children in sight.

"Hey, boys, how about we run out and get some hamburgers and fries?" William asked, and I saw from the grim set of his jaw that he'd overheard my mother's comment.

"It's your party, William," my mother objected. "You can't leave."

He waved her off. "I'll be back in a few minutes."

My mother scowled at the sight of her beloved only son walking away hand in hand with his two boys.

"Relax," I told her. "He'll return."

She sighed and refocused her attention on me as I helped myself to a plate of shrimp. "You look tired, Audrey."

I chose to ignore the critical aspect of her observation. "I've been working a lot. In fact I just received an important assignment. You're looking at the project manager of the new downtown courthouse."

My mother didn't appear to have heard me. She was looking in another direction, raising her glass and smiling at a squad of women I'd never seen before but who probably occupied some pivotal role in her vast social circle.

Annoyance pricked at me. After thirty years I ought to be used to my mother's perpetual distracted state, but sometimes it got to me.

"So I know you'll just love Diesel," I said, infusing excitement into my voice. "The odds are high he'll be paroled from prison before the baby comes."

She snapped to attention. "What? What baby? Who's Diesel?"

I bit off a piece of coconut shrimp. "My imaginary boyfriend who was spontaneously invented and now has served his purpose."

"Don't scare me like that, Audrey."

"Sorry."

Not sorry.

My mother took my elbow. "Stop piling food on your plate and come talk to Sheila Closterman."

I started choking on my shrimp. Sheila Closterman happened to be the mother of Dole Closterman, my ex-boyfriend who lived off his trust fund interest as he pursued his dream of becoming a pro golfer.

He had last been seen six years ago with his head bobbing between another woman's legs at a Fourth of July party. The two lovebirds never noticed when I opened the door to the study in search of a bathroom. I stood there for a dumbfounded second before quietly retreating, locating one of the ice buckets where champagne had been chilling, and returning to the room just as Dole's friend began squealing like a farm animal as she came. The fact that much of the ice had melted made the cascading effect particularly glorious as I poured the bucket over Dole's head. After that I turned and left the party without a word. On the drive home I wished I'd had the presence of mind to cough up a parting line, something dignified and profound like "Hope you find that special girl who lets you piss on her tits."

Dole Closterman's mother probably didn't want to hear that her beloved son was totally into watersports. There were just some things I wasn't willing to try.

"Hello, Audrey, it's so nice to see you again," said Sheila Closterman with warm sincerity as she gripped my hand. I wondered what the hell she was doing here anyway. Then I remembered that she was a long-standing member of the Arizona Fine Art Society with my mother. In fact, Dole and I had met as a result of their connection, and since he was tall, superficially polite, and from a wealthy family, my mother was exceedingly disappointed when we broke up and eliminated the possibility of handsome Closterman grandchildren with trust fund birthrights.

"It's nice to see you again too," I said, hoping that Dole wasn't lurking around here somewhere. I really wasn't in the mood for surprises. I just wanted to return to the shade of the orchard and gobble up my coconut shrimp in peace.

The two women exchanged a glance, and then Dole's mother said, "Your mother tells me how well you're doing."

Translation: *Audrey, we all know you're thirty and hopelessly single and your poor mother is starting to despair.*

Sheila Closterman wasn't finished. "And you may have heard Dole is working for his father now. He was just talking about you recently, wondering how you were doing these days."

Translation: *Dole's father gave him a pity job when the whole golf dream didn't happen, and he hasn't actually mentioned your name in half a decade but I'm trying to flatter you into thinking he's still hung up on you.*

My mother butted in. "Audrey, you and Dole were so young when you were together. I bet you'd each be pleasantly surprised to see how much the other has matured." She put a hand on Sheila's arm. "This girl works herself to the bone and her romantic life has become absolutely nonexistent. It's awful."

Sheila looked me over. "But you're so pretty, Audrey. My son would fall right over if he saw you."

"He's seen me," I reminded her.

My mother pretended I hadn't spoken. "Sheila, call me next week and we'll plan a dinner party so the two of them can get reacquainted."

Translation: *"We totally scripted every word of this conversation ahead of time in order to give our inadequate offspring the nudge they desperately need."*

"That sounds like a wonderful idea." Sheila beamed, and I could feel her gray-eyed gaze boring into me, probably trying to assess the condition of my ovaries because Dole was an only child. Future Closterman grandchildren awaited a host.

"It does sound like a great idea," I said with forced enthusiasm. "It would be nice to have something to look forward to after my upcoming surgery."

My mother jumped. "Surgery?"

Sheila's sculpted eyebrows rose. "Oh no, I hope it's nothing serious."

I waved a hand. "Not at all. According to my doctor, a tubal ligation is a completely routine procedure."

The eyebrows rose straight up to her frosted hairline. "Is that so?"

"Yes, and it's all the rage among us spinster career gals. It's better to just remove the possibility. We sleep better—*sleep around better*—that way."

My mother gripped her wineglass so hard her knuckles turned white, but I didn't feel bad. If she was determined to view me as a disappointment, then I may as well act like one.

Meanwhile, William and the boys had returned. Isaac and Leo carried colorful Happy Meal boxes and sat down at a table.

"If you'll excuse me," I said more politely than I felt. "Be sure to let me know when the dinner party will be. Tell Dole I'll bring the ice bucket."

I headed for the table where my nephews were sitting while Sheila Closterman's confused voice rang out, "Ice bucket?"

Isaac and Leo were excited to show me the little plastic toys they had received with their meals. They looked like they might be spaceships with skinny legs. William sat down with us but then was called away from the table by my father, who kept a hand firmly on his shoulder while he made a gushing, unnecessary speech about the awesomeness of William Gordon: Judge, Father, and Best Son Who Ever Lived.

People clapped. I clapped too. William smiled and waved like a broad-shouldered benevolent king. A few of the women sighed audibly.

I'd have to be a real loser to begrudge my fabulous big brother one second of the spotlight. William really *was* awesome. There was no reason to be jealous. It wasn't as if my father had never made a speech honoring me before. He had. On the night of my high school graduation twelve years ago, he stood in the same spot and tiredly thanked the guests for attending his daughter's party on such short notice when he'd received confirmation only the day prior that I'd managed to earn the right to walk with the rest of my class. It was a touching moment, one that I chose to celebrate by liberating two bottles of Dom Perignon from the wine cellar. And instead of selfishly keeping them to myself, I shared them out in the pool house with the twenty-six-year-old pothead son of the man who owned fourteen local Dairy Queens. His name was Davey, and I might have shared a few other things with him in that pool house before I wandered back to the party drunk out of my skull and wearing only a bedsheet.

People were still applauding William and shaking his hand as if he'd just accomplished something far more remarkable than coming out of the womb thirty-five years ago, when my phone buzzed.

"What's wrong, Auntie Audi?" Leo asked with concern, and I figured I must look a little alarming. I *felt* a little alarming.

But I smiled at my nephew to reassure him and said, "Nothing's wrong." Leo returned to his fries, and I returned to my phone. The text staring at me was from ED.

ED: Ran into CH architect at Diamondbacks game. We had a few drinks and he asked for a meeting. You need to be at jobsite 7am tomorrow.

I knew what CH was. Courthouse. But ED wasn't short for Edward. It stood for El Diablo, which was the identifier I'd selected for Jason Roma. My prior choice had been FuckNuts, which would give me a giggle whenever I scanned through my list of contacts, but now that Jason and I were working closely together, I had to change it to something less obvious. If someone were to peer over my shoulder and see the word FuckNuts, they might assume I was unprofessional. ED was a tad more benign.

I texted back with one word.

FINE.

It irritated me to no end that Jason was already cultivating a bromance with the courthouse architect when I had yet to meet the man. I could feel him gloating through the text. But I'd worry about Jason Roma tomorrow.

"Let's go raid that fancy cake, boys," I said to my nephews, and took Isaac's hand.

On our way to the cake table I briefly caught the eye of Sheila Closterman. She hastily looked away. Now that she knew I was either insane or soon to be infertile, I was a much less desirable match for Dole.

Funny how I hadn't really thought of Dole in years, and now his name was getting thrown in my face the same week I was partnered up with Jason Roma for the biggest assignment of my working life. The reason it was funny—and by *funny* I mean uncomfortably ironic—was because my relationship with Dole had imploded mere weeks before I began training a new employee at Lester & Brown. I had still been raw and vulnerable when Jason entered my life six years ago. Maybe he understood that about me right away, that I was desperate to put the whole humiliating Dole Closterman mess in my rearview mirror and was therefore ripe for an illicit office fling.

Isaac couldn't believe that the cake fondant wasn't actually a layer of flattened clay and insisted on having every trace scraped from his slice before he would touch it. I accepted the challenge of revising my nephew's dessert and carefully removed the offending fondant while trying not to think about how I had been seduced in my heartbroken condition.

There was a problem with that narrative, though. It was a lie.

I wasn't heartbroken over Dole at all. From the moment I shook Jason's hand for the first time and went weak-kneed over the sexual heat of his touch, I wanted him more than I'd ever wanted any man before.

Or since.

CHAPTER FOUR

"You hiding back here?" William wanted to know when he located me sitting on a stone bench deep in the orchard as dusk approached.

"Just thinking," I said.

William glanced over to the table where his sons were hunched over a tablet our mother had spontaneously produced to keep them quiet. "I've got to get going in a little while," he said. He rubbed the back of his neck briefly and then scowled. "The boys are supposed to be back at their mother's place in an hour."

My brother looked tired. The past year had been a brutal one for him, and if I could have spared him any of that pain, I would have. But William wasn't one to air his troubles out loud. We had that in common.

"You okay?" I asked. I'd asked that before. And like before, the ghost of a frown slipped away from his face and was replaced with a smile.

"I'm doing fine, Audrey."

I smiled back. "Just let me know before you leave. I want to make sure I get a chance to squeeze those precious boys one more time."

"Will do," he said. He started to walk away, then gave me one more glance. "Don't sit here all alone with your thoughts for too long."

"I won't," I promised, and watched him return to the party. I was surprised my mother hadn't come barreling over here to drag me out of the orchard yet, but perhaps after the Sheila Closterman conversation, she'd had enough of my social skills.

When I visited home my thoughts often strayed uneasily back to the ugly years when my adolescent rebellion veered off into addiction and ruin, but that wasn't where my mind was right now. Thoughts of Jason Roma kept intruding.

Not just thoughts.

Memories.

Memories that were six years old.

Memories that were now surfacing after I'd tried so hard to keep them at bay all this time. Yet they were as vivid as if they had just happened.

My fingers were still colorfully mottled from the vending machine M&M's I'd been eating at my desk, a post-breakup staple in my diet, when Marilyn from Human Resources stopped by my desk with a new employee who was introduced to me as "Jason Roma, the new project coordinator you'll be training."

I swallowed the last melted blob of chocolate that I'd been rolling on my tongue and said, "What?" in a high, surprised voice, because no one had said a word to me about training or new employees.

Marilyn immediately began to look impatient, but that might have been because she suffered from infamous bladder-control issues and needed to use the bathroom about thirty times in an eight-hour workday.

"Didn't Frank explain to you that you'd be training a new member of the project team?"

"No. Frank's been in Flagstaff since last week dealing with the university library delays up there."

Marilyn shifted her weight. "Well, it's Jason's first day and he'll be shadowing you all week. Jason, you'll be in good hands with Audrey. Please stop by my office before the end of the day and I'll issue you an employee handbook." She'd barely uttered the final syllable before scurrying away in the direction of the restrooms and disappearing around the corner.

For a second I was too exasperated to speak. As a lowly project coordinator who had been on the job for only a year and was aiming for a promotion someday, I also had to serve as backup to the frequently forgetful managers who sometimes failed to cross their own t's and wound up endangering million-dollar projects. And I was still in the process of consoling myself, because only a few weeks had passed since discovering my boyfriend with his tongue in another girl's vagina.

No, this was definitely not a good week to be trailed by some dewy-eyed trainee.

But since I was aiming for an eventual promotion to project manager, I couldn't very well refuse. I plastered a charming smile on my face and took my first good look at this Jason Roma person hovering beside my desk.

HELL-O!

He wasn't just good-looking. Jason Roma, with his thick black hair, defined cheekbones, and CrossFit kind of body, could be classified as whatever category came after "fine."

"It's Audrey, right?" He raked me over with a pair of dark eyes that set my lady parts to tingling and held out a large hand that did not wear a ring. "My friends call me Jay."

I offered my hand. "Nice to meet you, Jay."

His large fingers curled around mine for what should have been a simple handshake, but the moment of contact did strange things to me. There was his powerful hand holding on to my dainty manicured one for a heartbeat longer than necessary. There was the instant acceleration of my pulse. There was the way I boldly checked out the size of his thumb and blushed over the recollection of an old wives' tale. Then he released me and I noticed that my fingers were still coated in candy residue and were almost certainly gross and sticky to the touch.

I grabbed a tissue and handed it over as words tumbled out of my mouth. "God, I'm sorry. I was eating M&M's and I was on a conference call and they were melting in my palm. They really do that, you know. And I still ate them, but now it looks like I've been finger painting. Would you like some hand sanitizer?"

Jason took it all in stride. He balled up the tissue in his palm and fired it into a trash can fifteen feet away without looking to see if he reached the target. He was that sure of himself. I was fascinated. And when he smiled at me, all the noise in the room vanished. A man who had the power to make entire landscapes disappear with one grin was a force to be reckoned with. And even though he was obviously young, intimidatingly good-looking, and represented a very inappropriate selection as my new coworker, I couldn't deny that I had an instant crush on him.

Over the next few days as we worked side by side, I was surprised to learn that Jason was sharply intelligent with a cutting wit. He caught on to tasks with lightning speed and always seemed to know how to make me laugh. It didn't seem fair to stuff so much excellence into such a perfect package. How were ordinary people supposed to concentrate when there were Jason Romas running around in the world?

And to top it off, he was a lot of fun. Since I had a corporate credit card and received HR's blessing to have working lunches while I was training him, we hit up a different downtown restaurant every day that first week. He was a recent graduate from ASU, living with his best friend close to the university. His family used to own a local construction company, and The Man had known his father back in the day. I got the feeling things weren't all rainbows and unicorns on the home front, because he got quiet and changed the subject when it came up. I could relate to that. My own father had demanded spontaneous Breathalyzer tests until a little over a year ago, when I finally had the resources to move out. I always submitted and never argued, though I hadn't taken a drink since my last rehab stint, but it stung a little that he wouldn't recognize how successfully I'd changed.

At first Jason's questions for me mostly centered on the job, but by Friday he was getting a lot more personal. I didn't mind at all. I'd been on my guard for far too long, and something about Jason's humor and casual manner set me at ease.

"So, Audrey, you've never mentioned a boyfriend," Jason said over plates of hummus and pita wraps. He'd already told me several times that I could call him Jay, but I couldn't get used to the nickname. A man like this deserved more than one syllable.

I looked him in the eye. "Neither have you, Jason."

He hadn't mentioned romantic entanglements of any shape. I thought I saw him glancing at a few tits and asses during our lunch dates, but that might have been my paranoia. Honestly, I was half hoping at this point that I was barking up the wrong tree with my newfound infatuation.

But Jason laughed loud and hard. When he was finished, he crossed his arms over his chest and peered across the table at me. "Boyfriends have never been in the picture."

"Girlfriends?"

"They think so."

"What does that mean?"

He shrugged. "It means I'm into having a good time. Not really looking to slap a label on anyone's ass."

"That was blunt."

"Yep." He leaned forward and playfully tapped my hand. "So are you going to tell me if there's a boyfriend worth mentioning?"

I sighed and told the story of Dole. How we'd been together for about nine months, practically an eternity on the Audrey Gordon Relationship Scale. But now when I thought about it, I realized that near the end we weren't really feeling the heat anymore. Still, that didn't mean Dole was free to go shoving his patrician nose into the first willing crotch that came along.

"So you caught him?" Jason asked.

"In flagrante delicto."

"That sucks."

"Yes, it does."

"'Cause if I was planning to go down on a girl at a party, you'd be my first choice, Audrey."

I dropped the pieces of pita bread I'd been tearing up as I talked about my asshole ex. Jason took a casual sip of his water.

I must have heard him wrong. I had to have heard him wrong.

"What do you think about that?" he asked.

I thought I might like to shove my panties down, stand on the table, and swallow Jason's absurdly handsome face between my thighs.

"Um, I'm not sure." I picked up a new slice of pita bread and began savagely shredding it.

"What can I do to make you sure?" His deep voice was velvet and butter—all things sinful and delicious.

I was having a whole lot of trouble sitting still. "You can tell me what you want."

He chuckled. "That would be a hell of a filthy conversation to have here among the lunch-hour crowd."

I looked him in the eye. "Then let's have it later, Jason."

He nodded with approval. "Later works."

"I have my own apartment, no roommate."

"Good."

I felt drunk, reckless, irresponsible. The way I used to be. The way I'd stopped being some time ago. "I should tell you that, while there's no official policy, I get the feeling the company frowns upon romantic connections between coworkers."

Jason's sexy grin practically melted my panties. "Then we won't brag about it."

That evening Jason knocked on my apartment door, and I'm not over-stating when I say we screwed each other's brains out. Jason was a year younger than me, but someone—or multiple someones—had given him a hell of an education. There was no boundary he shied away from pushing, nothing he didn't want to try. I didn't kid myself that we were having some great affair. I knew it was just sex. I knew it would end sooner rather than later.

Helen from the accounting department was the only friendship I'd developed in the year I'd been working at Lester & Brown. And even though I'd told her all the dirty details of Dole, I told her nothing about Jason, not even when she went fishing.

"So the new boy seems like he's fitting in real well," she said over lunch plates of Thai food.

"Is he?" I asked, struggling to keep a straight face as I poured an excessive amount of soy sauce over my food and tried not to think about all the exotic ways Jason had been "fitting in" to my body lately. I had the delightfully sore muscles to prove it. But I wouldn't admit it to Helen. Or to anyone.

Three weeks passed and I'd been fucking Jason nearly every night. With him everything happened in the moment. I didn't think about the past or the future.

Then one afternoon he crept up behind me in the copy room.

"Hey, pretty girl," he whispered as his hands circled my waist and traveled lower. "Want you."

"Me too," I whispered, dropping a few contract pages on the floor as Jason ground his hips against my ass. We'd been good at work, so stoic and professional no one seemed to suspect what was going on. But keeping up the façade was getting tough. I glanced over my shoulder at the closed door of the copy room. "Is it locked?"

He looked. "Now why the hell does the door to the copy room have a lock on it?"

I giggled. "For moments like this."

He swiftly turned the lock and then hiked my skirt up. "And this."

I dropped to my knees and unfastened his belt. "And this."

He held my face in his hands, then sucked in a breath as my lips closed around his swollen dick.

"*Why is this door locked?*" *The door handle rattled as the shrill voice of The Man penetrated the haze of lust in the tiny room. "Who locked this?" There was loud, semi-hysterical banging. "Who's in there?"*

I was already furiously smoothing my skirt down while Jason tucked himself back inside his pants. In order to look busy and not even vaguely sexual, I grabbed a stapler and started stapling together the sheets I'd been copying, while Jason opened the door.

"Beg your pardon, sir. I was just cleaning the knob and must have accidentally flipped the lock."

The Man didn't care. He conducted a brief, frenzied search for green Post-its in the supply cabinet and left.

I cared, though. I cared a lot. There was a time when I would have found the entire situation uproariously funny, to be nearly discovered by an authority figure as I gave head in a bizarre location because I was almost certainly drunk out of my skull. I enjoyed shocking my parents. The only time I felt like I had their attention was when I was behaving badly. And then there was the added bonus of upsetting their orderly world of status and privilege. Once my mother caught me getting high in the garage with a naked father of two who was ten years older and a sports coach at my high school. When she started screaming at me, I decided to remove myself from the situation by stealing the keys to my father's Porsche, which I promptly crashed into the neighbor's front-yard fountain.

But that was a long time ago, and since then I'd worked hard to shed all traces of my bad-girl persona. I'd grown up. And even though I wouldn't admit it out loud, I desperately wanted my folks to have a reason to feel half as much pride in me as they did in my brother. More important, I wanted to be proud of myself. I'd never get there by giving Jason Roma blow jobs in the copy room.

It was time to put an end to whatever this was.

Since Jason was trained and busy with his own work, there wasn't much reason for us to interact throughout the day. We were both present in an afternoon department meeting, but I sat way on the other end of the conference table and tried to avoid catching his eye. I wasn't blaming him. Every time Jason showed up at my apartment door, I'd practically pounced on him. It was my own sorry-ass fault that I now found myself in a less than desirable position of having fucked my new coworker a few dozen times. Now I just needed to tell him that all this reckless screwing needed to end. He'd understand.

I stayed at work an hour late to finish completing an extensive materials order. When I finally left I was startled to find Jason there in the parking garage, leaning against my car as if he were having his picture taken. He flashed his trademark devastating grin when he saw me, and my resolve to inform him I couldn't take my clothes off for him anymore almost vanished.

I set my bag on the hood of the car. "I thought you left."

"I did. Went down the street, grabbed some tacos, and came back." He held up a white paper bag. "You hungry? I picked up a few extra."

I slumped beside him against the car, lowering my head. "Jason."

He let out an exasperated sigh. "You're mad, aren't you?"

"No."

"Bullshit. You've been bent out of shape ever since that jackass came pounding on the copy room door."

"Quiet," I hissed, and looked around furtively. But there was no one else to hear except for some scattered vehicles still waiting for their owners to call it quits for the day. "That so-called jackass happens to be the owner of the company, and I can't justify being on my knees in the copy room in the middle of the day."

His arm nudged me. "It's not the middle of the day now. There's probably hardly anyone left up there. Let's take another crack at it."

"Not funny."

"Not trying to be." He faced me, bracing his palms on either side of me against the frame of the car, issuing the kind of seductive challenge that weakened every argument. "And you know whatever I get I'll give back just as good."

"Jason."

"Audrey."

"I can't," I whispered. *"We have to stop this."*

He nipped at my neck. *"Why?"*

Because you're like a drug, one I can't get enough of, and I have a rotten history with addiction.

"Because it's going to mess things up at work," I told him, pushing him away.

He took a step back and raked his hand through his hair. *"I swear I'm not trying to screw things up for you. We're having fun. Nothing wrong with that."*

"I shudder to think what would have happened if we'd been caught today."

"You mean caught with my dick in your mouth."

My jaw clenched. *"Yes."*

He laughed. *"I would have liked to see the look on the old man's face."*

"Shut up," I spat. *"Can't you take anything seriously?"*

He pretended to think about it. *"It's Thursday. Gravity is reserved only for Monday, Wednesday, and sometimes Friday."*

"You're such a child."

Jason rolled his eyes. *"Look, Audrey, I like hanging out with you, and we have a good time together. Not looking for something permanent."*

"Neither am I."

"Good, then let's go back to your place and spend some time reenacting the copy room scene. It was hot. I've been thinking about it all day. We can pretend that boss man busts through the door just as I come in your mouth."

"Jason!"

"It would have added to the shock value if you'd had your tits exposed."

"Grow the fuck up," I said, annoyed he still was making this a joke.

Jason looked at me. There was a flash of something in his dark eyes—irritation or anger or hurt; I couldn't tell the difference when it came to him.

His voice was tight. *"Rest assured, I'm fully grown, Audrey."*

"You're a twenty-three-year-old man-child who thinks with your dick and apparently couldn't give two shits about your job, a job only acquired because someone in management knows your father, who ran his own company into the ground."

This time there was no mistaking the anger in Jason's dark eyes. Immediately I regretted what I'd said. I knew very little about Jason's family—it was bitchy of me to lash out like that when all I wanted was to end things on an amicable note. I started to apologize but Jason cut me off.

"Give me a fucking break, Audrey Gordon. You think there's a single damn person in that building unaware of who you are? Your father and his cronies probably run half the city. And you can fuck right off with your conceit over the job. I asked around. I know you didn't even bother to finish college, probably never had a steady job before working here, and you have a few legal demerits on your permanent record. Your family name and maybe a timely phone call from Daddy opened the door for you, sweetheart, and you damn well know it."

"You asshole," I whispered, balling my fists up. It was the truest and most devastating speech anyone had ever flung in my direction. Jason thought he'd cut me down, but he didn't know me at all. He didn't know how hard I'd worked since I started at Lester & Brown, how badly I wanted to forget about the reckless girl I'd been. Jason didn't know these things because we didn't usually have meaningful conversations. And there was certainly no point in having one now.

Jason was smirking, triumphant, probably figuring he'd bested me with a few harsh observations. He'd done nothing of the kind.

I straightened my back and glared at him. "Go fuck yourself, Jason."

He snorted. "Nah. But I'll have no trouble finding someone else to do the job."

On that note he turned his back and walked away.

"Jason, wait!"

He turned around, annoyance written all over his face.

I twisted my hands and blushed, hating every second of needing to ask him for a favor. I took a deep breath. "Please don't say anything. About this. Us. Please don't tell anyone at work."

He took his time about answering. Then he said, "I won't. I'm not as much of an asshole as you think I am, Audrey."

Then he resumed his walk in the opposite direction. I didn't stop him a second time.

I kicked aside the bag of dropped tacos and retreated into my car, pounding the steering wheel once with my fist before starting the ignition. On the drive home I comforted myself with the fact that Jason wouldn't last long at Lester & Brown. He'd get bored and move on or else he'd get fired when he screwed up something important, as he was bound to do. That frat-boy mentality came with a short attention span. Jason would almost certainly be gone in another six months.

"Auntie Audi?" said a sweet voice, shaking me out of my reverie.

My youngest nephew stood three feet away. He yawned. "Daddy said to tell you that we're leaving now."

I stood up and held out my hand to Isaac before walking across the vast yard toward the party tables, which were littered with used plates and napkins. While I was out brooding in the orchard, nearly all the guests had departed.

William seemed distracted when he gave me a brief farewell hug. I cuddled the small bodies of my nephews close for a long moment, silently promising once again that somehow I'd find the opportunity to spend more time with them.

"That went well," my mother commented in a bright tone as we watched William and the boys leave through the gate.

"The centerpieces made all the difference," I said.

My mother threw me a look, as if she was trying to guess whether I was full of shit or not. I grinned and she laughed.

"They worked out fine after all," she said.

"It was a nice party, Mom. I'm sure William was pleased."

I wasn't really sure about that at all. It was more likely William had simply endured the event. But my mother would be happier if she thought otherwise.

She looked in the direction of the wrought iron gate William had just exited. "Do you think so?"

I plucked one of the flowers out of the nearest centerpiece and sniffed it. "Sure. Who wouldn't be delighted by a gala event celebrating the day you were born?"

Her eyes scanned me, and her brow wrinkled just a little. "You wouldn't. Would you, Audrey?"

She sounded uncertain, as if she truly didn't know one way or another. It struck me how little we really knew one another. This should not have been a revelation. And I knew I was as guilty of avoiding important topics as she was.

"No," I told her honestly. "I wouldn't."

I started to help with the cleanup until my mother scolded me, insisting that the catering staff would take care of it. She handed me a tray of leftovers that I was happy enough to take. My father had already decamped to his study and I planned on saying goodbye, but when I reached his door, it was closed. I hovered on the other side for a moment, debating whether I ought to interrupt his probable liaison with a bottle of expensive Scotch, and then just left, clutching my foil-wrapped package of congealing mushrooms and shrimp.

On the drive back to my apartment, the things I'd been fretting over in the orchard resurfaced. I hoped that wouldn't be happening every day now that I'd be constantly working with Jason.

I could admit I'd been wrong about him in some ways.

Jason didn't get bored with the job and he didn't screw up. Management loved him, and his promotion to project manager happened mere months after mine. Avoiding him completely was out of the question since we worked in the same department, but I found it was easy enough to limit contact since we were never assigned to the same projects. Jason cheerfully moved on to a variety of other conquests, and when I happened to see him around town, I always pretended I didn't notice the youthful eye candy dry-humping him in plain sight while I clutched the arm of whatever responsible fellow I was currently seeing.

After that big blowup in the parking garage, I was afraid he'd betray me by engaging in some locker room talk with some of the guys around the office who had lunch at Hooters every day. They seemed like Jason's crowd.

But to his credit, he proved to be discreet. He might get a kick out of subtly mocking me when the occasion arose (e.g., the Third Street handbag mishap) until I wanted to throttle him with one of his designer neckties, but to my knowledge he'd kept his word about keeping the details of our sexual exploits to himself.

In all this time I'd never heard so much as a whisper indicating he'd ever said a single gossipy thing about me. Of course I preferred things this way, even as I wondered if he thought about our time together anywhere near as much as I did.

CHAPTER FIVE

The day after William's party, I arrived at the courthouse jobsite twenty-five minutes early and somehow Jason still managed to beat me. He was walking around in the flattened dirt and he stopped to watch as I approached.

"I thought you said the meeting was at seven," I said a little huffily.

"Good morning to you too, Audrey," he replied, and held out a brown paper bag. "Would you like a buttered muffin?"

"What is that, a sexual innuendo?"

"No. It's a polite statement. You ought to try it now and then. Politeness."

"I don't want your buttered muffin, Jason."

He crumpled up the bag. "Too bad. It was tasty."

"How do you know if you didn't eat it yourself?"

He shrugged. "I took a bite."

"You took a bite of the breakfast you were planning to offer me?"

"Sure."

"What if I'd decided I wanted it?"

"But you didn't." He hurled the bag into a nearby open dumpster.

I looked around. "Where's this architect?"

"He's not here yet. You're half an hour early."

"Then why are you here?"

He breathed in deeply as the sounds of Phoenix traffic rattled past. Soon it would be rush hour.

"What can I say? I love the smell of the asphalt in the morning," Jason said. "What do you love in the morning, Audrey?"

"Jason," I said a little sharply.

He looked at me. "What's up?"

I took a breath. "Is this going to be a problem?"

"Of course not. You're more than welcome to hang out here until the meeting starts."

"You know what I mean."

He grinned, obviously enjoying himself. "No, enlighten me."

I took a deep breath and reminded myself that I might have some explaining to do in the office if I broke Jason Roma's nose. "Is there going to be a problem with us working closely together on this project?"

Jason appeared to consider the question carefully. He tapped his chin and gazed out at the ten-acre city plot where a derelict hotel had been razed to make room for the courthouse. "I'm not sure. Just how *close* are we going to get?"

"You're ridiculous," I huffed. "I'm going to get a cup of coffee."

"Does this mean you're blowing off the meeting?"

I glared. "No. I'll be back in fifteen minutes."

Once I had consumed a few ounces of caffeine, I felt a little less on edge. Maybe I was overreacting when it came to Jason. He liked to get a rise out of people, that's all. It wasn't best to contend with that in a colleague, but I could handle him. I could keep things professional. And when Jason realized I could no longer be baited, he'd get bored with trying and just do his job. And the best way to embark on this new era was by marching back to the jobsite, coolly ignoring any mocking remarks, and having a successful meeting with this architect whose name I wished I'd inquired about. I assumed it had to be Mike Destin, the original chief architect at Lollis Architecture Group, the Phoenix firm that had been hired to draw up the plans even before bids were made on the project. I couldn't really picture old stern-faced Mike yapping over beers at the Diamondbacks game with Jason Roma, but I knew Jason well enough to figure he could probably nudge the pope out of his comfort zone if he set his mind to it.

When I returned to the site, I saw that Jason was no longer alone and I cursed myself for taking off in the first place. Jason and the man who was presumably the architect were walking inside the perimeter of the heavily roped-off jobsite. I squinted at the man. From a distance I could tell he did not have the stoop-shouldered look of Mike Destin, yet there was something familiar about him.

I pasted a smile to my face and hoped it didn't look too ghastly. An ex-boyfriend once complained that I was terrible about keeping my heart off my sleeve and ought to figure out how to fake it like the rest of the world.

And speak of the devil.

There had to be some kind of cosmic force that rounded up bad liaisons and dumped them on your head. That was the only way to explain how the past week had coughed up an encounter with Dole Closterman's mother, an involuntary partnership with Jason Roma, and now this.

"Are you having a stroke?" Jason asked from ten yards away, after I'd stopped in my tracks and cupped a hand over my mouth when I realized he was in the company of Lukas Lund, ex-boyfriend, Nordic god, brilliant architect, and currently ranked number two on my Best Sex list.

And to add to the irony of this strange scene, Lukas was unknowingly standing beside number one on that same list.

Both Lukas and Jason were staring at me at this point, so I forced myself to resume walking and pretend there was nothing odd about this.

"Lukas," I said with forced enthusiasm. "Wow, it's nice to see you again."

"Good to see you too, Audrey," he said. Everything about Lukas was cool, from the sweep of his unblinking glacial blue eyes to the way his large body occupied space with a kind of imperial detachment.

"I take it you've met before?" Jason said, and I noticed that he seemed honestly surprised. Surprised and not altogether pleased.

"We've run into each other a few times around town," Lukas said evasively, and looked away in the direction of Chase Field as if the subject already bored him. We weren't together that long, only for about four months, more than two years ago. Lukas was gorgeous, intelligent, and fantastic in bed, but I never felt quite comfortable around him. Particularly because I'd seen how quickly that cool, calm veneer could vanish if something really pissed him off.

"I take it you're not at Stern and Foster anymore?" I asked Lukas, referring to the architecture firm he'd been working for when I met him.

"No, I'm not. I've been at Lollis for nearly a year." He gestured to the expanse of open dirt. "I just took over this project from the original architect."

"What happened to Mike Destin?"

"He's dead. Massive heart attack three weeks ago."

"That's sad," I said, knowing it sounded lame. I couldn't think of anything else to say.

"Yup."

I swallowed. "So how have you been?"

"Can't complain. And you?"

"I'm good."

Lukas zeroed in on me with his intense stare. He held it for a long time before he said, "You certainly look good."

It was an inappropriate thing to say. And Lukas had already demonstrated to me just how terribly unpredictable his moods were. Yet I found myself unable to do more than mutter "Thanks," and look away.

Jason cleared his throat, maybe to remind us that he was still around. "It might be easier to conduct this meeting at the diner across the street. Anyone up for breakfast?"

"I thought you already had a buttered muffin this morning," I said with sarcasm.

"Only a single bite," Jason replied, blinking at me. "And it wasn't nearly enough. Let's get something more substantial. Come on, my treat."

"You mean the company's treat," I countered.

"I wouldn't mind some breakfast," Lukas said in his silky baritone.

On the walk over to the diner, Jason started chatting with Lukas about baseball. Lukas was a huge baseball fan. It made sense that he would have run into Jason at a Diamondbacks game, especially after I gleaned from their conversation that during yesterday's game they happened to be guests of a valley land developer.

After the recent shock of finding Lukas Lund at my jobsite this morning, I wasn't particularly hungry, but I ordered a cheese omelet to be cooperative. Jason and Lukas had ended their discussion of pitching rotations and moved on to the groundbreaking ceremony in a few weeks. I should have been contributing to the conversation and, in fact, Jason tossed me curious glances a few times, but I was too busy consuming copious amounts of coffee and reflecting on how disconcerting it was to be sitting at the same table with two men whose dicks had been in my mouth.

"What do you think, Audrey?" Jason asked me suddenly.

I set down the coffee cup. I had no idea what I was being asked to think about. This was not the scenario I envisioned when I woke up this morning.

"I think the courthouse project represents an opportunity for us to showcase our best work and make an enduring contribution to the city," I told the men.

There. A very benign, if slightly cloying, bullshit answer to whatever question had been asked.

Jason and Lukas glanced at each other.

"That's great," Jason said with his telltale smirk, "but I was really asking for some input on Lukas's idea of expanding the lobby. He thinks the original design will prove inadequate once the courthouse is in use."

"We can find the space if we cut out some of those useless decorative pillars and move one of the jury-duty rooms," Lukas said, eyeing me. "I was playing around with it last night and can get the proposed revision over to your team by tomorrow."

"And then we can present it to the county." Jason nodded. "I think they'll like the idea."

"That sounds great," I said with a little too much enthusiasm.

Jason and Lukas didn't appear to notice, however. They returned to discussing the project and assorted progress benchmarks. I paid attention and made the appropriate comments, but all along I couldn't shake the surreal sense that this was a dream.

"Wait, you have one of those condos in the high-rise next to the ballpark?" Jason asked Lukas.

"Moved in last year," Lukas confirmed. "It's nice to be able to see the games going on even when I'm not inside the stadium. Plus, the commute to work is pretty sweet."

"Man, color me jealous. I bought a house in Chandler a few months ago and I miss the easy commute. That I-10 is the devil."

"You bought a house?" I asked Jason with surprise. When he first started working for Lester & Brown, he was living in some mancave close to the chaos that was Arizona State University. Since then I'd heard he moved up to a nice downtown place, and I had just assumed he was still there.

Jason nodded. "Yes, I bought a house."

"Why'd you move out to Chandler?"

He looked down. It was uncharacteristic of Jason to look uncomfortable, but he hesitated for several long seconds before he spoke again. "You get more bang for your buck in real estate out there, plus I'm dealing with some family issues."

"I'm sorry," I mumbled. All I'd ever known about Jason's family was that they'd once been wealthy but their fortunes changed when his father's business failed. I'd be curious what kind of family issues would motivate a player like Jason to settle down out in the stucco suburbs of the East Valley. But he didn't look as if he was in the mood to talk about it. Instead of asking for details, I took a bite of my cheese omelet.

Lukas left a few minutes later to deal with some architect emergency, but before he walked away, he handed me his card and fixed those startling blue eyes on my face with hypnotic intensity.

"I'm glad we'll be working together, Audrey," he said in a tone that was actually pretty inviting. "Reach out to me anytime if you want to discuss the project. Or anything else." He nodded to Jason. "See you, Jay."

"So long," said Jason, but he was looking at me.

"What?" I snapped when Lukas was out of sight.

He sighed and whipped out his corporate credit card. "That was awkward."

"For who?"

"For everyone, I think. So, you and the Viking architect . . ."

"Do not finish that sentence."

Jason leaned forward. "Then finish it for me."

I cut the remains of my omelet with the side of my fork. "Yes, Lukas and I used to see each other. It was a little over two years ago. He was one of the architects on the Samaritan Hospital project, and when it wrapped up, he asked me to dinner."

Jason broke into a nasty grin. "And did you, ah, have dinner with him more than once?"

I glared at him. "Don't venture into perverted territory. I won't follow you."

"Then you've changed, Audrey," he said with a nasty grin that reminded me we'd spent a lot of time naked together.

I sat up suddenly and angrily, nearly toppling my chair. "You never stop."

"Hey, I'm sorry," Jason said, and he actually did look kind of sorry. His usual smirk had disappeared. "Please sit down and finish your breakfast."

"I'm done anyway," I said, but I sat. "It's really not a big deal. Yeah, Lukas and I dated for a few months, but it was several years ago and we haven't kept in touch. I had no idea he'd wind up being the chief architect on the courthouse. I can't say I had a strong desire to run into him again."

"It doesn't seem like he feels the same way. Poor boy was practically drooling."

"Lukas . . ." I started to say but didn't know how to continue. Jason didn't need to know the rest. Lukas Lund was a great lover and always paid for dinner, and sometimes that icy calm dissolved without warning.

Somewhere in the back of my mind I had suspected something was off with him even before he seized a drunk bar patron and slammed him into a wall after the guy taunted that I had a nice ass. Yet his temper didn't flare often, and I began to think my worries were all in my head. Then came a night when he became annoyed that I kept answering work emails at dinner, and out in the parking lot he grabbed my phone out of my hand and hurled it against a brick wall.

That only happened once.

I made up my mind to break things off with Lukas the instant I saw the spider-web cracks on my iPhone. Maybe he only threw a phone, but who does that? And could that escalate to something else? There was no way I was going to stick around for that shit no matter how sexy he was or how profusely he apologized. But Lukas didn't even try to argue. He accepted the fact that it was over between us and he wished me well. It would have been a very dignified breakup if I weren't clutching a small can of pepper spray in my sweater pocket just in case he got out of line. Luckily he didn't.

"Audrey?" Jason's voice was gentle. "It's really none of my business. And I don't care how gifted an architect the guy is. If he broke your heart, then he's a douchebag."

It was a silly thing to say, but he was trying to be kind for once. I just didn't have time to deal with Jason's abrupt transformation into a caring human being.

"He didn't break my heart." I stood up and collected my purse. "I've got to head back to the office. Remember, we have that conference call at eleven."

He nodded. "I remember."

I left him there to finish paying for breakfast. Before I returned to my car, I paused by the empty space where a stately modern courthouse would someday stand. If I closed my eyes, I could see it as if it had already been built. When I opened my eyes, there was nothing to see but dirt and possibility.

I hadn't lied to Jason. Lukas never broke my heart. And Jason never broke my heart. My heart hadn't even been cracked by Dole Closterman or any of the handful of other names that had been important to me for a little while.

No, the only person who's ever really broken my heart is me.

CHAPTER SIX

When you're the only daughter born into a wealthy family, life comes with certain advantages. It's like being born on third base. I didn't appreciate that fact of life until I'd already managed to waste a lot of those benefits.

Throughout my childhood I was a good student and a decent athlete, although nothing remarkable like my big brother, who never glanced at a trophy or a medal that didn't end up in his possession. My family was a collection of diehard overachievers. My mother spent hours at the hospital or engaged with one of her various committees, leaving the big house always feeling empty. As for my father, he was always working hard at something very important, which I didn't fully understand at the time. All I understood was that it was better to stay out of his way when he walked through the door until he had a chance to visit his study and suck back a highball. Or two. Or five. He couldn't seem to handle being home for more than fifteen minutes without nursing a drink.

Aaron and Cindy Gordon weren't naturally affectionate people, but I can't say that I felt unloved. I attended great schools, owned fantastic wardrobes, and received the keys to a BMW convertible before I even officially had my license. But all that privilege can have its pitfalls, especially if no one ever explains that it's a bad idea for a sixteen-year-old girl to drink a bottle of schnapps and play Lipstick Dick at a party. I quickly discovered that I liked drinking. I liked sex. And I wasn't going to let anyone stop me from doing either one.

As it turned out, they didn't even notice at first. Unless there was a high-profile event where I could be trotted out as the perfect daughter, my parents barely acknowledged my existence. I hadn't realized how unhappy I was until I found some terrible distractions to dull the ache of their benign neglect.

Now when I think about those days, I'm horrified. I deserve to be horrified, deserve to wince as I remember my brother picking me up out of a puddle of vomit after Brynna Cole and I combined a bottle of tequila with some painkillers stolen from my mother's medicine chest. No one was home at my house, as usual, so we had invited Clark Lutz over to party, whom I vaguely remember humping in my canopied bed before I started puking everywhere. Clark and Brynna got spooked and took off. So it was William who found me, William who drove me to the hospital, William who tried to convince my folks that I was at the point where I needed help.

But they weren't convinced despite William's pleas. Having a daughter go through rehab wasn't an item on their bucket list. Plus, even though the Phoenix metro area is huge, all the rich people seem to know each other. The country club crowd would have found out and it would have been a source of humiliation for my parents. And as I sat there picking at my scratchy paper gown in a hospital bed while my mother stared out the window and my father angrily signed the discharge paperwork, I understood that potential gossip meant more to them than I did.

And so I responded as any petulant teen would.

I became even worse.

I ignored curfews. I stole from my brother's wallet to supplement my new drinking habit. I nearly flunked out junior year and nearly flunked out senior year as well. My father must have made a payoff or called in some favors, because there was no way I earned that high school diploma. I was too busy getting drunk in the school parking lot and then riding good old Clark or his buddy Max Levine in the front seat of my BMW while waving to passersby. College wasn't even on my radar. William was excelling at Stanford Law School and I was surrounded by bright young things who couldn't wait to sprint into their exciting futures. Yet the future sounded boring to me; it sounded like some bullshit that parents and teachers spat at you to keep you in line. I'd stepped out of line a long time ago. I was a hot mess. And I knew it.

I couldn't guess what my parents were planning to do with me at that point. My father slapped me across the face when I told him to go fuck himself after he presented me with an ASU catalog. He apologized. His big hands shook as he pressed a towel filled with ice cubes to my bleeding lip. I remembered thinking that it was weird how he was more upset than I was. I was so wasted at the time that the blow had scarcely even hurt.

Then William came home for a visit and put his foot down.

"Goddamn it, I don't fucking care how it looks. We're getting her some help *now*, because I swear I'm not fucking going back to school until I know Audrey's being taken care of."

Even though I was sleeping off a hangover in my bed, I could still hear him yelling from the other side of the house. William was shouting, but he was shouting *for* me, not at me. Someone cared. Someone was on my side. Someone didn't hate me even though I hated myself most of the time. And I drifted back to sleep feeling a little less empty than I had in a while.

I awoke to daylight and the noise my mother made as she rummaged through my dresser.

"What's going on?" My throat was so dry the words emerged as a croak. For the past year my mother had visited my bedroom about as often as she ventured into the gardener's shed in the backyard, which was next to never. So the sight of her handling my underwear was a little unusual.

She glanced at me long enough for me to see that she was not wearing her usual mask of perfectly applied cosmetics. "We found a place for you," she said in a bright voice that sounded too high pitched, artificial.

I yawned. "A place? Can I expect to see bars on the windows?"

I took note of the open suitcase on the floor. It was part of an old set that I last remembered using for a tenth-grade school trip to Washington, DC. My mother dropped a pair of bras into it and then opened my T-shirt drawer.

"Don't be dramatic, Audrey," she said with a sigh. "I just mean that you're going to a place where you can get well."

"Am I sick?" I asked. Stupid question, because I really did feel sick. I needed my mother to leave so I could reach into my nightstand and find the unopened bottle of vodka I knew was hidden beneath some old empty journals. After a few sips I would feel better, more clearheaded. I could talk my mother out of whatever plan she'd made.

But she wouldn't leave. She closed the suitcase and approached my bed, reaching out a hand that seemed about to caress my check before it was abruptly pulled back. There was sadness in her eyes when she said, "Yes, you're sick. Now get up. Your father is waiting in the car and we are leaving right this minute."

Typical rehab wouldn't do for a member of the Gordon family. No, a cot in a sterile building was for the unwashed addicted masses. My folks found a place that was equal parts resort and rehabilitation center in the pinewoods outside Prescott. The first time I was there I stayed for a month, suffered terrible withdrawal, and endured countless therapy sessions where I learned my promiscuous tendencies were connected to my addictive personality. The drinking, the sex. I had tied them together, and I needed to stop doing that or I would never have a meaningful relationship. But the caring counselors assured me I could overcome those things. I didn't need to be a prisoner to my worst urges, and I agreed. I returned home and enrolled in a few classes at community college. I went on normal dates. It seemed like a happy ending. And I'd like to say that everything went smoothly from there on out, but life isn't like that. As it turns out, I relapsed several times before I was sent back to the pinewoods.

My defining moment came one sunrise when I arose from bed as if someone had called me out of a deep sleep. Pushing aside the curtains of the private room's lone window, I stared out at the magnificent green landscape as the sun stubbornly rose over the mountains.

"I don't want to be here anymore," I said out loud, and I wasn't just talking about rehab. I didn't want to be this person I'd become—this callous, self-hating brat who pissed away everything she'd ever been given just because she could.

My parents accepted me home with wariness. I was lucky they allowed me back into the house at all. By that time I was twenty and they were under no legal obligation to keep me any longer. My sorrow over everything I had put them through the past few years hung over me. They didn't seem to believe my heartfelt apologies, possibly figuring they were just another manipulative tactic. I didn't blame them. But I was confident that I'd win them over in time. They were my parents. They loved me, even if sometimes they couldn't stand the sight of me.

Over the next two years I continued to attend classes at a nearby community college, earning my associate's degree in business management. William, big brother and eternal champion, was in the audience for my graduation right beside his new fiancée, a pretty brunette named Jennifer who planned to be a psychologist.

William tried to convince me to continue and earn that coveted four-year degree, but I didn't feel completely comfortable in school anymore. And besides, I'd spent so long in a fog of self-destruction, I wanted to work hard. I wanted to be like my big brother and be worthy of my own last name.

A series of temporary office positions around Phoenix gave me valuable experience, and then my father mentioned how he'd heard the prestigious construction firm Lester & Brown was searching for entry-level project assistants. The speed of my hiring stunned me a little, but I instantly loved the work. It took so much multitasking, so many things to be responsible for. I thrived. For the first time in my life I was actually participating in something that would yield a tangible result. Visiting the completed projects would actually bring tears to my eyes. These buildings all had a purpose. And I'd helped create them.

Shortly after I began working for Lester & Brown, I got my own apartment in Phoenix. My very first night there I wandered around the small, quiet rooms congratulating myself on finally reaching adulthood at age twenty-three. I was resolute. Never again would I allow such self-destructive impulses to consume me. I didn't expect that it would be easy every day, and it wasn't. In the beginning I struggled a lot. Sometimes I still did. Sometimes I was tempted to take a bottle of wine to bed and remain there for twelve hours. But I stayed clean. Some alcoholics find salvation in AA meetings with sponsors and sobriety coins. There was nothing wrong with that. I'd even tried going to meetings now and then, although I tended to stay in the back and say little as I wondered what I was doing there. Work was my salvation. Work was my constant when the old demons beckoned. I didn't turn into a nun, but I did stop drunkenly screwing around with inappropriate partners. Other than the notable—and sober—Jason Roma blunder.

I dated occasionally and even had a few relationships. And if I never fell in love with any of them, then that was all right. I was busy enough with work. Wiser to avoid risking my heart after I'd so carelessly bruised it myself for so long. Even after all this time I wasn't sure how fragile the thing was.

Now at age thirty I was able to look in the mirror and marvel over my reflection. I was a model employee. A satisfactory daughter, a devoted sister, and a loving aunt. I hadn't done anything I was ashamed of in a very long time.

In fact, since I stepped out of that luxury rehab facility for the last time, determined to reform, I could think of only one thing I'd done since then that was reckless—a three-week fling with a colleague. It still bothered me because I was pretty sure I'd do it again. Jason had tapped into something basic and primal inside of me. I didn't love him. I didn't even really like him. But I still wanted him. Bad. Maybe even bad enough to toss away caution and my career in the process.

I was still stewing about the unexpected surprise that had been delivered at this morning's meeting when I returned to the office. Lukas didn't drive me crazy the way Jason did, but seeing him again had caught me off guard, and not in a good way.

Someone had made coffee in the break room, so I paused to indulge in a cup. Helen passed by with a pile of papers in her arms.

"Should I even ask about lunch?" she said with a laugh. "Or will you blow me off again like you have twice in the last week?"

I grimaced as I swallowed the last of the coffee. "I'm sorry. Got a ton of work to take care of today. Maybe next Wednesday?"

"Maybe nothing. Wednesday it is. I'm holding you to it, doll, and if you are nowhere to be found Wednesday at noon, I will enlist Jason Roma's help to track you down." She cocked her head and eyed me. "How are you guys getting along? Word around the office is there's been some tension between you two."

"There's nothing between me and Jason," I insisted. "Nothing but work anyway."

Helen raised an eyebrow. I had never admitted to her that Jason and I had hooked up years ago, but I wondered how much she suspected.

"Okay," she said. "But someone might wonder why you spit out the boy's name like he's a type of dangerous reptile."

"I didn't mean to," I sighed. "I'm just in a bad mood. Jason definitely isn't a reptile. And he isn't dangerous."

Helen dropped the subject and waved her papers at me before she said she needed to run because the CFO was waiting.

I waited until she was gone and then I crushed the paper coffee cup in my hand.

"Jason's only as dangerous as the devil," I muttered, still troubled by the private knowledge that I remained extremely attracted to him. I didn't want to know what I'd be risking by going down that path again.

Maybe nothing.

Maybe everything.

I fired the cup at the wastebasket on my way out.

CHAPTER SEVEN

ED: You are late.

I groaned when I saw the text come through. I didn't need El Diablo to remind me that I was late. After checking my mirrors, I'd floored the accelerator on the freeway, hoping to make it by the end of the brief groundbreaking ceremony. Unfortunately, a motorcycle cop with a handy radar gun caught me doing eighty-five in a sixty-five-mile-per-hour zone and took his time writing out a ticket.

By the time I got to the courthouse site, the groundbreaking ceremony had ended and everyone was packing up their cameras and retreating to their expensive vehicles. None of the press or preening politicians cared to hear what the behind-the-scenes project staff had to say, but I was expected to be present. I'd planned to be. But hints of a late materials delivery obliged me to drive clear across town and personally remind one of our suppliers of their contractual obligations.

As I eased my way through what was left of the crowd, I tried to appear nonchalant, as if I'd been right here all along. I saw The Man shaking the hand of a longtime business associate of my father's. He'd been to my parents' house a number of times when I was a teenager, but when I attempted to catch his eye as he walked briskly to his car, he looked away and didn't appear to recognize me. Or maybe he did and that was the problem.

"Think you need this more than I do."

I jerked my head around at the sound of his voice and caught the small silver object flying my way. It was a watch. It was Jason's watch.

"You know why I was late," I said, my face growing hot.

Jason was chewing gum. I could smell the spearmint from here. He appraised me from behind his dark sunglasses. "Yeah, you needed to go on a wild goose chase out to Glendale."

"It wasn't a wild goose chase." I tossed his stupid watch back to him. "Breckel was making noises about not being able to make the delivery tomorrow even though they charged us a fortune for expedited shipping. I said since everything is just sitting in their warehouse, they'd better move heaven and earth to get it on-site tomorrow morning as planned."

Jason chewed his gum some more and stuffed his hands in the pockets of his light gray trousers. He lowered his voice. "We could have dealt with that on the phone, Audrey."

"I didn't want to take any chances," I said with a sniff. "It's imperative that we stay on top of things at all times."

"And all I'm saying is that I'm perfectly capable of helping the team stay *on top* of things. That way you don't have to go tearing around the valley at breakneck speed and show up late, with your hair looking like something a sparrow might lay eggs in."

I scowled and touched my head. A few loose hairs had escaped the clip, but I'd be willing to bet no bird would find it nest-worthy. Jason was just being Jason. I should be getting used to him in our parallel roles. Yet somehow he always managed to get under my skin. As far as splitting up the job tasks more equitably, I didn't mistrust Jason's abilities. On the contrary. I'd observed him long enough to understand that even though he seemed to fly by the seat of his pants half the time, he always came out ahead.

As much as I would like to chalk all of his success up to luck, I had to admit that wasn't the case. Jason possessed a blend of magnetism and managerial prowess that fit the job perfectly. He trusted that when he handed down an order it would be followed, and it was. Contractors and colleagues wanted to please him. Clients loved him. It galled me. But the man got shit done.

"How was the ceremony?" I asked.

He took off his sunglasses. "It was fine. Relax, Audrey. No one was searching for a photo op with you."

"Always a charmer," I muttered.

"A man can be honest or charming," Jason said. "Not both."

I scowled. "You steal that from a fortune cookie?"

Whatever blazing retort Jason planned on firing back was cut off by The Man's sudden appearance.

"That went well," he said. "Did you two get to meet the mayor?"

"He looked pretty busy," Jason said. "And we were standing all the way in the back."

"Right, we didn't want to get in the way," I said, glancing at Jason and wondering why he chose to cover for me.

The Man didn't seem to care. "Well, kids, I'll be in the office this afternoon for the obligatory project kickoff meeting now that the labor is about to begin. From this point forward everything will be in your capable hands. And I expect it will all go smoothly."

He walked away without saying goodbye.

"That sounded semi-ominous," Jason said when he was gone.

"There's a lot at stake here. The reputation of the firm. Our careers." I yanked my hair clip out since it was loose anyway. Jason watched as I ran a hand through my hair.

"Take it easy," he said. "I understand all that."

"Good. Then I guess I can count on seeing you at the meeting this afternoon."

"Of course. Why wouldn't I be there?"

"I don't keep track of your plans, Jason."

"I'll be there," he said firmly.

"And I don't know about you, but I plan on being here at five a.m. tomorrow when the crew shows up."

"I have similar plans," Jason said. He put his sunglasses back on.

"Glad to hear it." I started digging around in my purse to locate the car keys I'd hastily tossed in there.

"Hey, Audrey."

I looked up at the sound of my name. "What?"

Jason leaned in. "You're not the boss. We're partners here."

I rolled my eyes. "I am well aware of that."

"Are you? Then how about you quit snapping at me every chance you get? And learn how to delegate the small things or it'll take us a decade to get the damn building up."

Instead of answering him, I stalked away. On the walk back to my car I caught a glimpse of Lukas Lund, who must have been here for the groundbreaking ceremony as well. Since he was on the other side of the street, I thought he didn't notice me, but he raised a hand in greeting. I stopped at the intersection and waited for him to cross at the green light.

"I looked for you this morning," he said as he stepped onto the sidewalk.

"Sorry, I was running a little late. Did you need something?"

Lukas leaned against the light pole. His eyes matched the color of the sky above. "No. But I'd love to buy you a cup of coffee."

When I hesitated, Lukas raised an eyebrow and clarified. "To discuss the project, Audrey. I'm just interested in hearing about what happens now on your end."

"Oh. Right." I had a million things to do back at the office. This afternoon Jason and I would be standing in front of management, laying out the timeline. Tomorrow morning a crew of fifty construction workers were going to show up and begin work. Several enormous material deliveries were taking place overnight. But suddenly all I wanted to do was sit down for a few minutes and recharge with some caffeine.

"Sure," I told Lukas. "I'd love a cup of coffee."

He smiled.

A few yards away was a small, independent place called Brewer's. I deliberately stood in line before Lukas because I didn't want him offering to pay. Since that awkward early morning encounter weeks earlier I'd seen him a few times, but we hadn't had much reason to chat one-on-one. Our communications took place mostly via email.

I was already seated and sipping my iced coffee when Lukas approached with his drink in hand.

"I knew I'd get you with coffee," he said.

I raised the cup as if I were offering a toast. "My one vice."

Lukas set his cup down and briefly drummed his strong fingers on the table. "Audrey, do I make you nervous?"

"What? No, not at all." I fidgeted, wishing I were somewhere else, anywhere this conversation wasn't happening. There was too much going on right now. I didn't need complications like sexy, possibly dangerous exes who wanted to rehash the past.

Lukas didn't blink. "You're still a terrible liar."

I smiled. "Is that really a character flaw?"

"No." He sighed, and for a second he looked sad. "I know why you didn't want to see me anymore."

"I was busy with work."

"I scared you." His mouth was set in a grim line. "That night when we argued."

"You apologized."

"But it wasn't enough."

I squirmed again. "No, it wasn't."

"I've thought about you, Audrey. I've thought about you a lot over the last two years." His hand grazed mine. "No pressure, but I'd like another chance."

I picked up my cup of coffee and took a drink, partly to hide my face and partly to remove my hand from Lukas's reach. His touch wasn't unpleasant. Just the opposite. In spite of everything, I could still be wildly physically attracted to him if I let myself. But I wouldn't.

"Well, Lukas, the thing is, I'm crazy busy right now with work. I'm not seeing anyone and I don't anticipate that changing anytime soon."

He sat back in his chair. "You were always ambitious," he said a little wistfully.

"I still am," I told him. "And this is a huge opportunity for me."

"You're right," Lukas said.

My phone buzzed.

ED: Where the hell is the materials spreadsheet?

Lukas kept his eyes on me while I read the text and then read it again. The spreadsheet Jason was searching for was on the common drive in a folder labeled *Courthouse*. It would only take me a few seconds to answer his text and be done. Instead I saw an opportunity to escape my current situation, so I tossed my phone into my purse and stood.

"I'm sorry, Lukas, there's an urgent work matter I need to deal with."

Lukas didn't ask what it was. The corner of his mouth tilted for a split second as if he were amused, and I recalled his accurate observation that I didn't know how to lie very convincingly.

"All right," Lukas said. "But I still need to ask you for a small favor."

I looked at my wrist as if I were checking the time. Unfortunately, I wasn't actually wearing a watch, so it probably looked odd. "What's that?"

He got to his feet slowly, came around to my side of the table, and set his hands on my waist, reminding me how tall, powerful, and absurdly hot he was.

"Think about it," he whispered. "Think about giving me another chance, Audrey. I don't need an answer tomorrow. But think about us. How good we were together." Then he kissed me on the forehead in a move that was somehow both sweet and erotic.

Then I shut my eyes for an instant and remembered the flash of fury on his face when he hurled my phone into a wall.

I remembered the way my heart had leapt into my throat that night when I realized we were alone in a dark parking lot and I had no idea what Lukas might do next.

"I can't," I whispered.

Lukas took a step back with a sigh.

I did not say a word or look him in the eye again before I ran out of Brewer's.

CHAPTER EIGHT

"Did you submit that purchase order?" I demanded.

Jason looked up from across the office we were now sharing since management decided to use our partnership to free up an office for Davis Brown, of course, whenever he dropped in.

He'd been staring at his phone, probably playing Mortal Death or whatever kind of video-game crap people like him entertained themselves with, while I scoured the approved purchase orders for the one I needed.

"What purchase order?" he asked in all innocence.

I gritted my teeth. "The one I told you to submit on Wednesday before you took off early. Where the hell did you go anyway?"

He looked annoyed. "I came in at six, didn't take a lunch, and left at four. As for where I went, call it a family obligation."

I paused. Jason didn't often mention his family. I was having some trouble imagining him as emotionally available in that way. He'd always struck me as proudly selfish. "Was that really it?" I asked. "A family obligation?"

He leveled me with a hard look before answering. "Not all of us live and breathe the world of Lester & Brown."

My defenses rose. "I don't appreciate being attacked for prioritizing my job."

Jason rolled his eyes and heaved a sigh. "I'm not attacking you, Audrey. You're the one who questioned whether my family obligation was real."

He had a point. I was out of line questioning his other commitments. Jason was a hard worker. Just because I was singularly focused on work didn't mean I could expect everyone to follow suit.

"I'm sorry," I said. "Now what about the invoice?"

He shook his head. "Your estimates were excessive."

"Who says?"

"Everyone I showed it to."

I considered throwing my desk lamp at him. "Everyone you showed it to? Are you going behind my back?"

"I'm perfectly willing to go in front of your back. Seriously, Audrey, we've got to be conservative or we'll wind up over budget before we're halfway done."

"Fuck, Jason!" My head went down on my desk. Since the courthouse had broken ground two weeks ago, I was getting an average of three hours of sleep a night. And I couldn't even turn around in my own workspace without running into the wall of resistance that was Jason Roma.

"Hey."

Something tapped my arm.

"Audrey."

I curled my arms more tightly around my head.

"Go away."

I just wanted to sleep. I didn't have time for sleep anymore. I didn't even have time to play around with my vibrator for ten minutes. Once I hit the bed, I was unconscious. But in the daylight hours when I needed to be at the top of my game, I was ready to explode. Or pass out. Either one would be fine right now as long as I didn't have to look at Jason for a little while.

"Audrey, sit the fuck up and read this." His voice sounded tight, angry, and since Jason's usual response to my distress was laughter, I raised my head with curiosity. He shoved his phone in my face and I could feel the blood draining from my head as I read the text from the foreman.

"Oh my god."

"Let's get down there." He slid the phone back into his pocket.

Once management caught wind of an accident down at the jobsite, they'd demand answers immediately. All we knew at this point was that a crane had tipped over and a man was trapped. We needed to get on top of this.

"We'll take my car," Jason said when we reached the parking garage. Another time I might have argued with him, but since we were traveling to a potential tragedy, it didn't seem appropriate.

I had my phone on speaker, trying to get ahold of Barnes, the foreman. "Why aren't we moving?" I snapped.

"Seat belt," Jason snapped back. "I don't feel like dealing with more than one disaster at a time."

I huffily clicked it into place as Barnes answered.

"Emergency crews are on their way," he assured me.

"Is the man conscious?"

"Yeah, but I can't tell how badly he's stuck," Barnes hissed. "He's just a kid, nineteen years old. Started two days ago. He shouldn't have been driving the damn thing."

I could hear the sirens in the distance as we left the garage and headed for Central Avenue. I'd left my closed-toe shoes and my hard hat in my own car, but it didn't matter right now. Covering the two-mile distance in record time, Jason pulled right into the dirt by the construction vehicles. The bones of the future courthouse building were beginning to take shape, and on the far north side a crowd of people clustered around the fallen crane. Jason and I hurried over as the first fire truck arrived. The crane lay on its side like a crippled yellow dinosaur. I shuddered as I thought about the boy pinned beneath that mess.

Barnes hailed us from his position beside the crane. "We were just about to call it a day," he said as he ran a hand across his sweaty forehead. "Needed to move a pair of trusses, but I still have no idea what the kid was doing running the crane."

"Where were you?" I asked.

Barnes lowered his head a little. "Signing for a materials delivery. I never gave the green light to start up the crane. I'm sorry."

Jason patted the man's shoulder. "Don't beat yourself up. Can't have eyes in the back of your head."

Another fire truck and an ambulance arrived.

"You said he just started?" I asked.

Barnes nodded. "Two days ago."

"Who went over the safety protocol with him?"

The big man thought about it. "I believe he . . . had a brief orientation."

"Brief and apparently inadequate," I muttered.

"Audrey," Jason warned. "Not the time to point fingers."

"I'm not pointing fingers," I argued. "I'm trying to figure out why we have a nineteen-year-old new employee trapped underneath a crane he shouldn't have been driving."

Barnes looked miserable as he nodded. "I take full responsibility."

"Maybe you shouldn't," I said. "After all, you're not the one who insisted that I cut back on visits to the site to address safety issues with the workers." I turned my glare on Jason.

Jason heaved a sigh of annoyance. "You want to come down every day and deliver the same harsh lecture. It's demoralizing for the crew."

I got in his face, challenging him eye to eye. Well, eye to collarbone since he stood about seven inches taller than me.

"It's demoralizing to learn about safety standards? Or only demoralizing when the information is delivered by somebody without a dick?"

"Oh, for fuck's sake." Jason rolled his eyes. "Give it a rest, Audrey. Everyone is aware that you have a vagina. That's not why they all fucking cringe when they see you coming."

"What the hell does that mean?"

"It means you're an overbearing, anal-retentive pain in the ass."

"Well, you're a shiftless, two-faced, conceited pig."

Barnes cleared his throat loudly. It was enough to pull Jason and me out of our public shouting match and make us realize every word was being overheard by the workers, the first responders, and the news crew who had just shown up. The only good news I could see was that the pinned man had been unpinned and now rested on a stretcher.

"That's enough, both of you," Barnes warned us with quiet menace, as if he were the parent in this situation. He left us and walked over to kneel beside the injured worker, who moaned as a paramedic checked his vitals. The only visible injury was his bloodied right leg, but with an accident of this magnitude, there would be good reason to worry about internal damage.

Jason and I watched as the paramedics began to lift him into the waiting ambulance. A blonde reporter in a flashy, short red dress walked around with a microphone trying to get information from whoever was willing to talk to her.

"Shit," Jason said.

"For once we're in agreement," I muttered.

My phone had been going off inside my purse, but I was afraid to look and see who it was. Yet the inevitable can only be postponed for so long, and I pulled it out, feeling dread as I saw The Man was calling.

"We're down at the site now," I told him. "The worker has been extricated. I'm not sure how badly he's injured. The ambulance is getting ready to drive away."

The Man barked something into my ear and I swallowed hard.

"I understand. We've got to deal with things here, but we will be there as soon as we can."

Jason watched me as I ended the call.

"I take it we're being summoned," he said.

My stomach was starting to hurt. "Yes, we are."

The first priority, of course, was finding out the condition of the injured worker, Jonas Ramirez. Barnes had traveled to the hospital with him and texted to say Jonas only had a fractured and lacerated right leg that would require surgery. Anyone who took one look at that toppled crane would come to the conclusion that Jonas Ramirez must have had a guardian angel on duty today.

Jason dismissed all the workers for the day while I answered questions from a police officer who'd arrived on the scene. After getting a few eyewitness accounts, he assured me that he understood the event had been an accident; however, we would likely face a fine from the city in light of the fact that a worker was operating equipment without sufficient experience.

When everyone had finally cleared out, Jason met my gaze.

"Ready to walk the plank?" he asked.

"After you," I said.

When we returned to the office, most of the staff had either gone or were getting ready to leave. Jason and I trudged down the hall in morbid silence, bumping into Helen on her way to the elevator.

"Everything okay?" she asked, glancing from me to Jason. "I hear you guys had a scare over at the courthouse."

"We're told he's in stable condition," I said. "That's what matters." My tiredness weighed so heavily, I felt like I could see through time.

Helen squeezed my arm. "That's good news."

Jason was looking toward the long, empty corridor. "They're waiting for us, aren't they?"

"Yes," she confirmed. "They've been waiting for a while."

Jason nudged me. "No reason to put this off. It's not like they can kill us."

"No, they can only fire us," I said miserably.

"Accidents happen," Helen assured me. "Especially on construction sites. This isn't the company's first accident, Audrey. It'll be okay."

But it was the first accident on any of *my* projects. It was the first accident on the most important project the firm had ever undertaken. It was an accident that could have been avoided.

"Don't beat yourselves up over this," Helen instructed. "Get some rest this weekend."

"Is it really the weekend?" I asked tiredly.

"It's Friday," Jason said. "Most people consider that the start of the weekend."

"Great. Let's get this over with."

We knocked on The Man's door together and walked in to find half a dozen members of Lester & Brown's senior management awaiting our arrival. The Man was standing behind his desk, his ferret-like face flushed with anger.

"Sit down," he ordered.

The only available seating was a leather couch where supposedly The Man took a nap now and then. Personally, I couldn't imagine him sitting still long enough to sleep.

We dutifully sat down on the couch, the cushions pushing us intimately together. There was something unnerving about the grim expressions confronting us. Every eye in the room was focused in this direction, and there was nothing friendly about the vibe. I was reminded of this low-budget horror movie I'd seen years ago and could easily imagine that any second The Man would begin chanting and throwing animal blood at us.

"Is something funny?" The Man shouted as he threw his pen, and I realized I'd giggled out loud over my fleeting horror fantasy. I was cracking the fuck up. I had to be. Because there was nothing funny about any of this at all.

"No, sir," I said, and tried to look properly contrite.

"I'm not going to mince words here," said The Man. "I'm sick of your shit. I'm sick of getting calls from subcontractors complaining that the two of you are at each other's throats and giving conflicting information half the time."

Jason kept his eyes focused on The Man. I folded my hands in my lap.

"I'm disappointed in you two," our boss went on to say. "It seems your egos are getting in the way, and I expected a hell of a lot better. You're the best we've got. The best project managers in the whole company. And you are both one fuckup away from getting tossed right off the largest project we've ever had. Do I need to remind you what a career killer that would be if you plan on remaining in the Phoenix area?"

He glared as he awaited our answers.

"No," Jason and I replied in unison.

"Fix this," said The Man as he pointed a finger first at me and then at Jason. "I don't know what your problems are, and you've both worked with me long enough to realize I don't give a shit. Get the job done or get the hell out of the way. Now get yourselves back on track, because you'd better believe we'll be keeping a close eye on you."

The Man crossed his arms and waited for us to leave. He didn't want to hear any mumbled apologies, so we didn't give them. We crept out of there like two kids leaving the principal's office, and we didn't say a word until we were back in our own office with the door closed.

Jason broke the silence. "That was brutal," he said as he leaned back in his desk chair.

I smoothed a few stray strands of hair back. "It sure as shit wasn't fun."

"Did you think it was creepy as fuck how no one else in the room so much as breathed too loudly?"

"Seriously. I was wondering if they were going to start performing some kind of satanic ritual."

"Is that why you laughed?"

"Yeah. Plus I might be a little lightheaded because I haven't eaten since breakfast."

Jason was rocking back slightly in the chair and gazing at me closely. "That can be easily remedied."

"What exactly are you offering to remedy, Jason?"

"Dinner. Everyone deserves dinner, Audrey."

"I suppose they do."

Jason changed positions and leaned forward, setting his palms flat on his desk. His large, rough hands looked like they were capable of doing hard work. I remembered how they felt on my body.

His handsome face turned earnest, apologetic. "I know you think I don't care enough about work, but I'd like to prove otherwise. I really don't want to fuck up this project. Why don't we go out to dinner and see if we can clear the air?"

"Clear the air?"

He grinned. "Yeah. Just a casual dinner between two long-standing colleagues who possess a sort of resentful respect for one another."

With my stomach growling, I got to my feet. "That doesn't sound half bad."

CHAPTER NINE

"You like pizza?" Jason asked, playing the gentleman and opening his passenger door for me. He'd offered to drive to dinner, and I was too tired and hungry to put up an argument. It was kind of nice, actually, just settling in to the leather upholstered seat and allowing myself to be transported.

"I love pizza," I told him as he got behind the wheel.

Jason's best friend was the owner of the famous Esposito's, an old-fashioned, wood-fired pizzeria in downtown Phoenix. The original restaurant was out near the university, and ever since they opened up this downtown location, I'd been meaning to go but somehow never quite got around to it.

Esposito's didn't take reservations, and since it was Friday night the line was considerable, but Jason led me around the back of the building to the kitchen.

"Yo, Dominic!" he bellowed into the chaos of activity.

A tall dude with Italian good looks was tossing dough in the air. He looked over and smiled broadly as he caught the shaped pie with expert flair. "Jay—didn't know you were coming tonight."

"Hope you can find some room for us," said Jason.

"Of course." Dominic set his work down and approached his friend. I marveled to myself that the two of them must turn some heads when they hit the town. They bumped fists and then Dominic noticed me.

"I'm Audrey," I said, holding out my hand.

"I'm covered in flour," said Dominic, shaking my hand anyway and presenting a smile nearly as dazzling as Jason's. Dominic had a rougher look about him, though—unshaven, with worn jeans, and tomato-sauce stains decorating his white Esposito's T-shirt. Jason, on the other hand, always looked like he'd been professionally dressed moments earlier, even when he was standing in the middle of a construction zone beneath the blazing sun. And unfortunately, I'd always been a sucker for boys who are nicely put together.

Dominic called, "Hey, Stevie, I'll just be a minute."

A man who vaguely resembled an older and slightly out-of-shape Dominic closed one of the mammoth brick ovens and waved a hand. "Take your time. I've got everything covered."

We followed Dominic out into the restaurant. The place was pretty packed, between the customers dining at the tables and those lined up at the takeout counter. Dominic spoke to the college-age girl who was at the hostess podium. She squinted at her seating chart and checked off a box with a marker.

"Come on," Dominic said, waving us over with two menus in his hand, "I've got the best table for you."

He wasn't kidding. The far corner booth was probably the quietest and most private location Esposito's had to offer.

"I feel kind of bad putting you to some trouble when the place is this busy," Jason said, sliding in.

Dominic snorted. "No, you don't," he said, tossing the menus on the table. "And it's no trouble. I'll let Mel know you're here. She'll probably want to take your order herself."

"Thank you, Dominic," I said.

"You are very welcome, Audrey," Dominic said. I caught a glance between him and Jason and wondered if they were communicating in bro code to deduce if anyone was going to get fucked tonight.

Nobody was.

At least, nobody currently sitting at this table.

"How long have you guys been friends?" I asked when Dominic was gone.

Jason looked over the menu. "Since we were teenagers. I was about to start my senior year of high school when he moved in next door."

"Was he the same friend you were living with when you began working at Lester & Brown?"

Jason looked up with surprise. "Yeah, that's him. Surprised you remember that kind of detail."

"In our line of work, it's always good to be in the habit of remembering details."

Jason lowered the menu. "I completely agree," he said.

The words sounded casual, yet when our eyes met I felt a rush of heat that sped up my heart.

I swallowed and shifted in my seat. "So what's good here?"

His grin came slow and sexy. "Everything's good."

A gorgeous black-haired woman wearing the same Esposito's T-shirt as the other employees slid into the booth beside Jason. "I just heard you were here," she said, and gave him a side-hug.

A small twinge of unwanted jealousy bubbled in my gut until I saw the woman had a big diamond ring on an important finger.

Plus, Jason's smile was friendly, not the kind of smile that promised a variety of dirty outcomes. I could tell the difference, especially where he was concerned.

"Melanie," he said, "this is Audrey."

"Hi, Audrey," she said cheerfully. Then her eyes widened. "Wait, is this *Audrey* Audrey?"

"Audrey Gordon," said Jason quickly, shooting Melanie a warning glance. "Audrey, this is Melanie, Dom's fiancée. Audrey and I are colleagues; both of us are managing the courthouse project."

"Oh, right," said Melanie, but she blushed a little and I wondered if Jason had been complaining about me to his friends. Either that or there was a significant second Audrey in his life.

"Nice to meet you," I said politely, because none of this was Melanie's fault.

She smiled. If she and Dominic had children, they would be stunning. "Nice to meet you too."

"You've got a great place here. I always meant to try it," I said, glancing around to admire the rustic, Mediterranean-style décor. My stomach was also plotting a full-scale revolt over the insane smells that were coming out of the kitchen.

"You look hungry," Melanie said with a laugh.

"I'm tempted to steal a slice of pizza from the next table," I admitted.

"Do you take your pizza with toppings or just cheese like this dull character?" She tapped Jason's arm.

"I like pepperoni, but cheese is fine."

"Half cheese, half pepperoni it is," Melanie said, easing out of the booth. "I'll send over some garlic knots right away so you guys don't start eating the napkins. And I'll also bring out one of our best bottles." She put a finger to her lips. "Don't tell Dom."

"Um, thank you, but no wine for me," I said a little awkwardly, caught off guard by the offer. "I can't."

Melanie tilted her head, most likely wondering why I'd turn down a glass of wine on a Friday night, but she was kind enough not to push the issue. "I bet you would love a glass of our home-brewed iced tea."

"I would," I said gratefully. "Thank you."

Melanie smiled one more time and hurried away. But when my eyes returned to my dinner companion, he was looking at me a little oddly.

"What's the deal?" he said. "Is it a religion or are you allergic to alcohol?"

"Neither," I said. "A bottle of wine just seemed a little romantic for a work dinner."

Jason frowned over my answer. "No, that's not it."

"Who says?"

"I do. Your eyes shift around like a cornered animal when you're not telling the truth."

"And of course you know me *so* well," I muttered, wishing there was some food on the table so there would be something to distract Jason away from this conversation.

"Not as well as I'd like to," he said in a phony flirtatious tone.

I glared. "Cut the shit."

"No thanks. That sounds messy."

"We've known each other for six years, Jason."

"And yet we hardly know each other at all. Isn't that right?"

I smoothed my napkin on my lap so I would have a reason to look down.

Jason had apparently realized he'd hit a nerve. So of course he kept hitting it. "So what's the deal? Do you think I can't keep my hands to myself after a few glasses of wine?"

"You're not the problem," I said bluntly. "I am."

He ran a hand over his smooth-shaven square jaw. "Now you're being cryptic."

The words were hard for me to say. I never uttered them if I didn't have to. And when I did, such as right now, I uttered them in a whisper.

"I'm an alcoholic, Jason."

He blinked. "I'm sorry. I didn't know that."

"I don't tend to broadcast it. I haven't had a drink for many years, not since before I started working at Lester & Brown. I started early, though, when I was a teenager. Put my parents through a hell of a lot of grief. Put myself through even more." I still couldn't look at him as I spoke.

A moment of silence followed. My face burned and I wished I hadn't unloaded so freely, but I was grateful that Jason had enough sense not to follow up with a sarcastic quip.

"Audrey," Jason said.

I finally looked up. His face wasn't full of laughter or pity. Either one would have been too much to take right now. His eyes, so dark they were nearly black, were actually gentle. He held my gaze for a moment before he spoke, as if he were sorting through the words in his head first.

"When I was growing up, my father used to beat the hell out of me," he finally said. "In fact I have a scar on the back of my right shoulder that looks like a crescent moon. He was old-fashioned, used a belt with a thick monogrammed buckle. One day he went a little too far and broke the skin. When I reached my teens I started mixed martial arts training, mostly in order to learn how to punch back. After that he made do with telling me what a worthless piece of shit I was every day. But he's always been a great guy, my dad. Just ask anyone, except me, and they'll tell you so." Jason sighed and laced his hands together on the table surface before continuing. "In my teens I started responding by behaving as badly as the old man already thought I was, getting booted from two of the best prep schools in the state. I'm not proud of that history. But I can't pretend it's not true either."

I don't even think I breathed while Jason narrated this sad tale. I never had any idea about this piece of his background. I thought he was exactly like the guys I knew growing up: rich, arrogant, spoiled. But I didn't doubt the truth of his words for a second. Back in the day, I hadn't given that scar any thought.

Perhaps the two of us—with our private shame and scars hidden beneath shiny layers of affluence—were more typical than anyone guessed.

"I didn't know," I told him.

He shrugged and shifted his eyes as if he might be a little embarrassed. "It's not really a topic I enjoy bragging about."

"I get it." I nodded. "I don't regularly disclose my stints in rehab or the fact that I'm a source of shame to my parents."

Jason looked surprised. "Even now?"

Actually I wasn't sure how my parents felt these days. We weren't in the habit of having frequent honest conversations. But there were no mind-reading abilities required to understand that they gazed at me with caution, even during those family times like my brother's birthday. I'd disappointed them for years. I could do it again.

"I was . . ." I said to Jason, my voice trailing off as I struggled to find the words I was looking for. ". . . a mess," I finished. "For a long time. It was years ago, but families have long memories."

Jason touched his chin in a thoughtful pose. "Can I tell you something, Audrey?"

"Sure."

He took his hand off his chin and leaned forward. "I've known you for six years and I think you're one of the hardest-working, most reliable people I've ever met. I also think that anyone who feels differently ought to have their fucking head examined."

Jason was a well-known bullshit artist, but there was nothing insincere about him right now. It wasn't his fault that I couldn't seem to answer, that hearing such praise from a man I'd been at odds with most of my professional life had meant the world to me.

Luckily I was spared the chore of responding right away, because Melanie returned with a pair of iced teas and a basket of garlic knots.

"Pizza will be out in a few," she said cheerfully, and turned to the elderly couple at the next table to inquire how they liked their meal.

I bit into a buttery garlic knot—the tastiest thing I'd eaten in a month. "She seems nice," I said, hoping to steer the conversation in a more casual direction.

Jason stirred some sugar into his iced tea. "Mel? She's freaking amazing. Dom hit the jackpot. They're getting married in a few weeks."

"Are you going to be the best man?"

"I'm afraid that honor goes to Dom's brother. I'll be a lowly groomsman."

I grabbed another garlic knot, looking around. "This was a good idea."

"What?"

"Sitting down to a friendly dinner and trying to evolve into something better than mortal enemies."

Jason stopped stirring his tea. "I don't think of you as my enemy, Audrey."

"So you don't tell your friends that I'm some kind of imperious she-devil?" I asked, thinking of Melanie's surprised comment when she heard my name.

He shook his head. "Not that I can recall."

"Well, if I'm not the enemy, then what am I?"

He grinned. "A habitually painful challenge."

I kicked him under the table. "There's some more pain for you."

"Didn't even hurt. Kick harder. Use your heel."

"I honestly can't figure out if you're being perverted or not."

"The safe assumption is always yes. Speaking of perverts, how's the Viking king?"

"Lukas?" I was startled. Jason hadn't mentioned him since the morning the three of us shared a slightly awkward breakfast. And Jason wouldn't know about the coffee-shop encounter with Lukas a few weeks back or how he'd asked me for another chance. If I'd really wanted to be with Lukas Lund, I would have been tempted to think about him a little more. Instead I hadn't thought twice about rejecting him, although I was aware he kept hanging around more than he needed to in the hopes I would change my mind. There was no need for the chief architect to hand deliver minor plan revisions to the jobsite, yet Lukas had shown up twice in the past week alone.

"Yeah, *Lukas*," Jason said, and even though he looked amused, he practically spat the man's name.

I shrugged. "You know about as much as I do about the status of Lukas Lund. You're copied on all the emails he sends."

He shrugged. "Okay, shifty eyes."

I kicked him again. This time he grabbed my foot and plucked my shoe off.

"Jason," I hissed. "Give me my damn shoe back."

"Later," he said. "Pizza's here."

I sat there and ate two slices of pizza with one shoe on. I didn't really have a choice unless I wanted to make a scene, and I didn't want to make a scene. To my amazement I realized I was having fun. The only time we discussed work was when Jason checked with the hospital and found out Jonas was out of surgery and doing well. I made a note to send something to the kid's hospital room tomorrow.

"We're pigs," I said, nodding to the pizza. "Can't believe there's only two slices left."

"They're yours," Jason said, pushing the tray over. "I'm not a fan of pepperoni."

"Hey, I have to use the restroom."

"Do you need my permission?"

"No, I need my shoe."

He crooked a finger. "Come here."

"Where, in your lap?"

"If you'd like. Or you could just give me your foot underneath the table and I'll replace your shoe."

I could have just stood up and stubbornly demanded my shoe. But there was a big part of me that was enjoying this game. Despite the fact that I'd spent the last six years trying to deny that I was still extremely physically attracted to the man across the table, I wanted to keep play-ing. I rested my bare foot on his knee and it felt good, it felt reckless, it felt daring.

Jason didn't keep his word. Instead of replacing my shoe, he gently took my foot in his hands and rubbed the pad of one thumb over the arch. "You're ticklish," he observed.

I *was* ticklish. But that wasn't the reason I was having trouble sitting still. Every erogenous zone in my body instantly awoke and throbbed the instant Jason touched me.

"Knock it off," I said, my voice squeaking.

He smirked and treated my foot to a deeper massage. "Why?"

I swallowed. "Because we're having a rather X-rated moment in the middle of a family restaurant."

"No, it would only be X-rated if I pressed my rather sizeable erec-tion into your heel."

My mouth fell open. "You're nuts."

"And yet you still want me." He raised an eyebrow. "Right?"

I did. I really did. Whether it was because I hadn't had sex with another breathing creature in many months or because I was sick of work or because six years of simmering sexual tension had reached a boiling point, I wanted Jason Roma bad. Or maybe the biggest reason was because I'd already had him. And I knew exactly what I was missing.

Jason's hands were now circling my ankle, kneading the joint and slowly working higher. "Audrey, I like you. Always have. I genuinely respect you as a partner. And right now, I want to take you back to your apartment and fuck you every which way until the sun comes up. Would that really be the end of the world?"

My heart was pounding. Slowly I retracted my foot from his grasp. He let me. He even handed over my shoe.

"I've still got to go to the restroom," I muttered, fumbling with my shoe.

"I'll be waiting," Jason said casually. "Will you do one thing for me while you're gone?"

I stood up and gathered my handbag, holding it over my chest like a shield. "What's that?"

He winked. "Think about what I said."

I didn't promise one way or another. This was all too similar to my talk with Lukas. Only Lukas was asking for a lot more than Jason was. And I had a much bigger reason to refuse him. Jason only wanted some fun—some relief from the push and pull of physical attraction that we'd been fighting all this time.

After dealing with my bursting bladder, I stood at the mirror washing my hands and examined my face. My skin was flushed, my hair slightly messy. I looked like I'd already been doing something to feel guilty about.

"Audrey," said a voice at my side. I'd been so busy staring at myself that I hadn't noticed there was another woman in the restroom. And that the other woman was my ex-sister-in-law.

"Jennifer," I said, feeling strange about not greeting her with a hug like I did for years. But I couldn't very well hug the woman who had wrecked my brother's life.

Jennifer tucked her light brown hair behind her ears. She was as petite and pretty as ever, still looked the same as the vibrant girl my brother had brought home for the first time eight years ago. But now she also looked nervous.

"How are you?" she asked. "I saw you across the restaurant and I was trying to get up the nerve to come say hello."

I took note of her flashy red dress and careful makeup. "I'm fine. Are you here with someone?"

She looked away for a second and then nodded. "Yes."

"A date?"

"My boyfriend."

"The same one you left my brother for?"

She winced. "It's not that simple, Audrey."

"It never is," I muttered, and searched my bag for some lip gloss. If Jennifer was waiting for me to make her feel better about ditching my brother for Mr. Fabulous from Facebook, then she'd be waiting for eternity.

"I've been meaning to call you," Jennifer said. "I thought we could have lunch sometime."

"Are the boys with William tonight?" I asked, ignoring her suggestion and the earnest tone in her voice. Before the divorce, planning a lunch with Jennifer wouldn't have been at all out of the ordinary. We'd been friends. I had thought of her as my sister. It hurt that I couldn't think of her that way anymore.

She looked down. "He's working. They're with a sitter."

"Great. This has been a nice chat, Jennifer, but I really do need to go."

Her unhappiness drove lines into her face. "I don't blame any of you for despising me."

"Okay."

"I just wish you didn't."

Instead of answering, I leaned toward the mirror and applied the lip gloss. The thing is, I didn't really despise Jennifer. She was the mother of two incredible little boys whom I loved more than the world. I just couldn't forgive her for hurting my big brother. I knew instinctively he'd never forgive anyone who hurt me. And after everything he'd done for me, I owed him that.

"You have a good night, Audrey," Jennifer said before she walked out.

"I will," I said, even though she'd already left. I stood in front of the mirror alone and wondering what the hell the point of it all was. What was the sense in being chronically ethical and upstanding like William when all it got you was a cheating spouse and a broken family? The answer suddenly wasn't clear to me.

The only thing clear to me was that no one really had their shit together. No one had all the answers. And in the meantime, I didn't need to deny myself every single bit of irresponsible fun.

Jason was out there in the dining room waiting for me. He'd been blunt about his intentions. My heart pounded as I remembered his direct, unabashedly erotic words.

"Would that really be the end of the world?"

The question had come from Jason, but I knew the answer.

"No," I said out loud. "It wouldn't be the end of the world at all."

I smiled at myself in the mirror. I'd been good for far too long. It was time to be a little bad, just for one night.

Jason smiled when he saw me returning to the table. He really was outrageously sexy. I couldn't wait to tear that Armani shirt off and feel those broad shoulder muscles underneath my hands. It was almost intoxicating, this feeling. I needed this, needed him. I wasn't really breaking any rules. And the courthouse be damned. Just for tonight. No one would ever know.

He waited for me to sit back down, but I didn't sit. I stood beside him and slid my fingers up his muscled arm. He watched the progress of my hand and a look of comprehension dawned. He hadn't really expected me to say yes to his proposition. But I just wanted him to take me out of here before I did something sensible and changed my mind.

"Let's go," I said.

CHAPTER TEN

My right arm was being crushed. From the elbow down it was wedged beneath the frame of a tiny toppled crane that looked like it had been built for Barbie dolls yet was substantial enough to keep a piece of my body pinned. There was no pain, but my attempts to yank the arm out from the maw of the Barbie crane were fruitless. Then a wave of thunderous applause erupted and I looked up to find my fellow Lester & Brown employees gathered around in a thick circle, all clapping like mad and wearing orange hard hats. I looked down and idly wondered if my coworkers were applauding because I found myself trapped by a tiny crane or because I was completely naked.

With a gasp, I opened my eyes and saw my bedroom ceiling.

Then I realized that the bedsheet had slipped down and my left nipple was exposed. That was odd. I didn't usually sleep in the nude.

But my right arm was indeed pinned by something, but the something in question did not resemble a Barbie crane. It looked like a naked Jason Roma.

With a groan, I covered my eyes with the hand that wasn't stuck underneath Jason's firm, still-sleeping body, and everything came back to me.

We'd left Esposito's in a hurry, driving straight to my apartment with Jason's hand on my thigh. Once when we paused at a red light I glanced at his calm profile and thought, *"What the fuck am I doing?"* But then he turned my way and flashed a smile promising sex and sin. And instead of demanding to be returned to the parking garage so I could retrieve my car and go home to a boring, lonely night with some ice cream and *Game of Thrones* reruns, I parted my legs and moaned slightly when his hand slid under my skirt, his large, sure fingers boldly searching higher.

"Goddamn, you're so fucking sexy," he swore hoarsely, and then the light changed.

By the time we reached my apartment three miles away, I was so into this I was no longer having second thoughts. Like a drunk, I staggered a little when I stepped out of Jason's car, but he was there instantly, wrapping an arm around my waist. At my apartment door I fumbled with the key until Jason took it from me and unlocked the door with one confident twist.

I reached for the knob but he stepped in front of me, circling each of my wrists in his big hands. He pinned them above my head and I felt the stucco scratching the back of my wrists while he peered down at me. He wasn't smiling anymore. The look in his eyes was nearly savage with lust, as if he might tear my clothes off and fuck me right there in the corridor. I can't say I would have objected.

Jason didn't rip my clothes off, though. He leaned in and kissed me with a slow, tantalizing sweetness that left me melting into the wall. His breath tasted like the mints we'd been offered at the restaurant. Jason had always kissed like he knew every secret of the deed, and I was almost panting by the time he withdrew his tongue.

"You want more?" he asked, pressing into me so I could feel the rock-hard proof of his desire.

I nodded.

"Say it."

"I want more."

He nodded with approval. "Because for six years, you've been dying for this."

"Yes."

Jason released my wrists and opened the door. He held out a hand to me. I took it.

The door was barely closed before we were all over each other. Jason was unapologetic when he ripped my blouse in his haste to get it off. I didn't care because I was too busy enjoying the feel of his mouth devouring my lace-clad breasts. My bra was pushed down, my skirt pushed up, and my legs went around his waist when he lifted me. We wound up on the couch with me half-naked and straddling him. I felt some mild pressure and a snap. Jason came away with my torn panties and tossed them somewhere unseen. Meanwhile, I was working hard to get the buttons of his shirt open, but they weren't cooperating fast enough so he ripped it open the rest of the way with a porn-movie-worthy move.

I gasped, pretending to be shocked as I ran my hands over his tanned, muscular chest. "I bet that shirt was expensive."

He grinned and grabbed my naked hips. "I bet your panties were too."

I nodded. "They were."

Jason yanked on the skirt that was bunched around my waist. "Take this off."

I couldn't oblige from this position, so I stood up, unzipped, and slid the skirt down. Jason watched.

"Leave the heels," he ordered, idly rubbing his hand over his cock, which looked ready to bust through the zipper of his pants.

"Now you," I said, feeling slightly self-conscious about standing in front of him completely naked and wondering if everything looked as good as it did six years ago.

Jason let out a low whistle, quelling my concern. "Just a minute. I want to look at you. You're as goddamn gorgeous as I remember."

I climbed into his lap once more, straddling him, feverishly beginning to work his belt and feeling frustrated when he stopped me.

"Not yet," he said harshly, instead wrapping his hands around my waist and settling me right over his cock.

"Oh, fuck," I whispered, my body beginning to rock back and forth of its own free will as it sought a release from the frantic throbbing between my legs. I was desperate to feel more than the friction from his zipper, but between the restaurant flirting, my own sex deprivation, and the fact that I'd been aching to screw Jason Roma again for years, I was seriously close to the brink. He had me decoded all right. There was no denying how much I'd wanted this for years.

"Jason," I panted, grinding on him in earnest now, bracing my palms on his strong shoulders just like I'd envisioned in the restaurant. I was on the cusp of dry-humping my way to a hard climax on his pants, and I was just fine with that scenario. The wave crested and then broke with a furious crash that left me shaking and groaning and ready for more, because my orgasms always conquered me in clusters of three.

I was still quivering and half out of my mind, but when I looked down and saw the bald triumph on Jason's face, I was determined to have him at my mercy as much as I was at his.

"Audrey," he said sharply when I dropped to my knees from his lap and struggled with his belt and his zipper until there was nothing in my way except a pair of black silk boxers. Jason could have stopped me if he'd really wanted to. He was far bigger and stronger, and he seemed determined to call the shots here. But once I shoved the flimsy fabric aside and had my lips on his dick, he unleashed a colossal groan, tangling his hands in my blonde hair for leverage to push deeper into my mouth. Jason was larger than average and I ached to have him inside me in the old-fashioned sense, but I was also relishing the power that came with controlling his pleasure.

But Jason wasn't going to let me have my way on this. After less than a minute he grabbed a handful of my hair and pulled back, not roughly, just hard enough to get my mouth away from its target audience. I didn't have time to voice an objection, though, because his mouth immediately collided with mine in a kiss that could only be described as fierce. My eyes closed, my arms slid around his shoulders, and I allowed myself to be carried somewhere, anywhere. It didn't matter to me, and I only vaguely recognized that mere seconds later I was being deposited on the wide suede-covered chaise lounge that had once sat in a scarcely used room in my parents' house.

Once I was flat on my back, I opened my eyes to find Jason looming over me. His shirt was off completely. His pants were down. And he held an object aloft with a wry grin.

"Told you I'd find a use for it," he said, and tore open the foil of the condom that had been carried at the bottom of my purse. I heard myself giggling over the absurdity of all of it, but seconds later when Jason rolled on the condom and parted my legs, I was done laughing. The chaise lounge was lower to the floor than a standard couch, and he knelt at the far end and seized my hips, pulling me closer.

"Audrey, did I mention you're fucking perfect?" Jason asked, but he must not have wanted an answer because an instant later he plunged into me with enough force to make me cry out over the shock of being stretched so abruptly. Jason responded by pushing deeper, harder, ruthlessly, until I was arching my body to give him maximum access and clutching the frame of the chaise lounge. I came and then came again, shrieking Jason's name the second time. I clutched at his muscled arms, whimpered into his chest, aware that I was utterly at the mercy of his body and loving every minute of it.

Suddenly he paused, pushed the sweaty hair out of my face, and peered down at me. "I want to hear it again," he said in a gruff voice.

"What?" I whispered.

His grin was triumphant and he bucked his hips slightly. "That you've wanted this for years."

I swallowed. "I've wanted you for years, Jason."

He didn't answer. Instead his mouth crashed into mine, and the pace of his pounding thrusts grew so frenetic I thought the furniture might crack beneath our bodies. Jason broke the kiss and unleashed a deep moan while I strained to pull him in as deep as possible. He shuddered as he came and I welcomed every furious spasm until he was spent.

"Holy shit, that was good," he gasped from where his sweaty head was resting on my chest.

I ran my fingers through his short black hair, an unfamiliar feeling of tenderness rising in me as we breathed hard together in the aftermath.

Then I remembered Jason telling me he never had girlfriends.

I remembered he'd been my constant workplace opponent for six years.

I remembered the variety of gorgeous women I'd seen him with, none of whom he ever seemed to take seriously.

I couldn't afford to forget who I was dealing with. I stopped stroking his hair.

"I hope you brought more condoms than just that one," I said.

He raised his head and grinned. "I have three more. After that we'll have to get creative."

I grinned back. "Challenge accepted."

We didn't really have sex till sunrise. The sky was still dark when we finally collapsed in each other's arms amid the wreckage of my bed.

But now that I was awake, my arm was becoming numb. I had no choice but to shove Jason in another direction. Using the heel of my free hand, I pushed at his back. He didn't move. I pushed again. He flinched, but my arm was still trapped beneath his hard body.

"Jason," I hissed.

"Just give me five more minutes," he groaned, burrowing his head into my pillow. "I'll eat breakfast at school."

Where the hell does he think he is?

I cleared my throat. "Jason, it's me. It's Audrey. You're in my apartment."

He rolled over. Luckily he rolled away so I was able to extricate my deadened arm. And he should feel lucky that my huge California-king bed saved him from rolling right onto the floor.

I rubbed my tingling arm while Jason propped himself up on one elbow and gave me a lazy grin. With his tousled black hair hanging in his eyes and his torso all tangled up in my sheets, he looked like the definition of Sex God. And if there was any doubt that he deserved the title, I now had a bunch of supremely dirty new experiences and a pronounced soreness between my legs that would erase the uncertainty.

"Good morning, beautiful," he said, and yawned. "Had a dream I was in high school."

"That sounds even worse than my dream," I said.

Jason's eyes were scanning the exposed parts of my body with interest, so I wrapped myself in a sheet.

"You're free to make yourself some coffee," I tossed over my shoulder before escaping to the bathroom and locking the door behind me to make it clear he was not welcome to follow. After languishing beneath a hot shower for a good ten minutes, I dressed hastily in a pair of yoga pants and a T-shirt, tying my wet hair into a messy topknot.

Part of me wished Jason would already be gone when I opened the door. And then I realized that was an impractical wish because I needed him to drive me to the parking garage where I'd left my car. I also needed to make sure he understood that the events of last night were just between us. It wasn't that I was ashamed.

Okay, maybe I'm slightly ashamed.

But it was over. We both got what we wanted. This wouldn't be happening again.

After a deep breath, I opened the door. Jason hadn't left. He was sitting at my kitchen table drinking from my green jadeite coffee mug and reading a newspaper.

"Where'd you get that?" I asked.

He pointed to a cabinet. "From there."

"I meant the newspaper."

"From outside."

I crossed my arms. "Jason, did you steal a newspaper from one of my neighbors?"

He turned a page and took a loud sip from my mug. "I'll put it back when I'm done."

I rolled my eyes and searched through the cabinet for another coffee mug.

"I already made you a cup," Jason said. He gestured to my Phoenix Art Museum mug that was waiting across the table. "I added an excessive amount of cream and sugar just like you do at work."

"Thanks," I said, feeling strangely caught off guard by the fact that Jason Roma had ever paid attention to how I prepare my coffee. On the counter was a cinnamon coffee cake I'd picked up at the grocery store the other day. I brought it to the table and cut a few pieces with a butter knife.

Jason wore only his boxers, and I tried to swallow some breakfast without staring too hard at all the masculinity taking up so much space in my small kitchen. Meanwhile, Jason ate his cake, drank his coffee, read someone else's newspaper, and seemed perfectly unbothered by this situation.

"What are you doing today?" he asked.

"Thought I'd go into the office and then stop by the hospital to see Jonas."

Jason looked at me. "Jonas doesn't know who you are. You didn't know who he was until he got wedged beneath a crane."

"So what?" I snapped. "Maybe he'd like a visitor. Maybe he's just sitting there all alone in his hospital room and wishing—"

"That a strange woman dressed in yoga pants would darken his doorway and nervously ask after his welfare in the hopes he won't sue the company she works for?"

Instead of firing back, I smiled. "I was going to change out of my yoga pants first."

He set the newspaper down and boldly checked me out. "You should. Actually, you ought to do that right now. I'll help you search for something more appropriate. I don't even believe you're wearing panties, Audrey."

I *was* wearing panties. And they were seconds away from being at risk because I was tempted.

Enormously tempted.

But this could too easily become an everyday thing. And getting too attached to the likes of Jason Roma would be a hazardous proposition. Not to mention the fact that we'd already muddied our working relationship more than enough. There was still a courthouse to build.

"Do you think you could drop me off?" I asked.

He frowned. "Where?"

"I told you, I want to go into the office."

"It's Saturday. No one will be there."

"The engineering department will be there. And there's bound to be one or two salespeople lurking about the premises."

Jason stared at me for a moment. Then he shrugged. "All right."

"Do you think we could leave soon?" I asked.

It was a not-so-subtle way to let him know that carnal pursuits were currently off the table. I only hoped he wouldn't want to go hang out at work with me.

"Give me five minutes," Jason said a little gruffly. He folded the newspaper, slapped it down on the table, and began hunting around my apartment for his scattered clothes.

He disappeared into the bathroom and emerged five minutes later fully dressed. Well, nearly fully dressed. His shirt hung open due to the fact that half the buttons had been ripped off in a lusty frenzy twelve hours ago.

"Jason?" I said gently as he fished his car keys out of his back pocket.

"Yeah?"

"I really had a great time last night."

He paused and looked me in the eye. "I did too, Audrey."

The walk from my apartment door to Jason's car felt off. Perhaps the awkwardness was solely on my end. Jason was whistling a Jimmy Buffett tune. He stopped when we reached his car and opened the passenger side door for me before climbing behind the wheel.

We passed the courthouse site, which wasn't nearly as busy as it was during the week, but there was still work going on.

"Do you want to stop?" Jason asked.

I would have if I were alone. But I looked at my yoga pants and Jason's torn shirt and figured that it would be better if we didn't show up looking like we'd just rolled out of bed together.

"I'll swing by there later," I said, knowing that although Barnes wasn't there today, the second foreman would be on-site at least until noon.

There weren't many cars in the parking garage. Later it would fill up when the baseball fans were searching for a place to park close to the stadium.

Jason pulled into the empty space beside my Lexus. He shut off the ignition.

"Are you staying?" I asked.

He looked at me. "Do you want me to?"

I didn't. I needed at least a few hours away from Jason and his smile and his banter and his magnetic sexuality.

"It's your office too," I said, and started to open the door.

Jason hit the lock button.

"Is this the way it's going to be?" he asked. He didn't sound angry. Just curious and maybe a little baffled. "Are we going to pretend last night never happened?"

"Yes. I think we need to."

Jason looked straight ahead at a concrete garage pillar. "I see."

"I'm not complaining," I said. "And I don't regret it. We already agreed we both had fun."

"What if it was more than just fun?" He took my hand.

"But it's not." I withdrew my hand. "Is it?"

He didn't answer. He didn't try to take my hand again either. But he did press the unlock button.

"You know how to reach me if you need to," he said, and looked in the opposite direction.

I hesitated before getting out of the car. Somehow I felt like I'd hurt him. I hadn't meant to.

No, Jason wasn't hurt.

The idea was ridiculous. In all the time I'd known him, he was never anything but sarcastic and proudly corrupt. And he was the one who had suggested a night of uncommitted fucking. That was what he got.

"I'll text if anything urgent comes up," I said. "Otherwise I guess I'll see you Monday."

"Hold on a second," he said.

I stayed where I was while Jason walked around to the back of his vehicle and pulled an object from the trunk. I couldn't see what it was until he opened the passenger door and handed it to me.

"You might want to put this on before you go in," he said.

I unfolded the ASU sweatshirt. "Why? It's not exactly cold."

He revealed the know-it-all smirk I'd seen a thousand times and couldn't stand. "Because you forgot to put on a bra this morning and your nipples are at full salute."

I leapt out of the car and almost threw the stupid sweatshirt back at him. Then I thought better of it. I didn't even say goodbye to him before I pulled his sweatshirt over my head and stalked into the office building in dignified fashion with my hidden hard nipples.

CHAPTER ELEVEN

Monday morning seemed like business as usual. Jason made no reference to the weekend, and two minutes after he walked into our mutual office, he asked if we could go over the monthly invoice we'd be sending over to the county. I resisted the urge to fidget in my chair when he came around and looked over my shoulder at the spreadsheet on my screen, but after surveying the numbers he just said, "Let's add another five percent to the construction labor."

I chewed my lip. It was important to get the details right since we had to rationalize percentage of completion on the billing.

"I stopped by the jobsite this morning," I told Jason.

"So did I," he said. "Right after you. I got there just as you were driving away. Lukas was left behind in the dust, mooning over your tire tracks."

"That's ridiculous," I scoffed, although I'd been a little unsettled to find Lukas there this morning. He appeared to be waiting for me to show up and then asked me a simple question that could have been easily dealt with via email or text. I knew that sooner or later I needed to address the issue with a follow-up conversation. The doubts that were born the night he lost his temper wouldn't disappear. Nor should they.

Jason snapped his fingers loudly and I broke out of my trance.

"What did you do to your hand?" he asked, and I looked down to find I'd been subconsciously rubbing my palms together as I recalled the way Lukas had snatched my phone away because I wasn't paying enough attention to him.

I shook my wrist out. "Nothing. I was just thinking about an unpleasant event."

It was a mistake to divulge that kind of information and I knew it right away. Jason was shrewd. He would guess that something was wrong.

"Does he scare you?" Jason asked suddenly.

"Who?" I said, claiming ignorance.

Jason rolled his eyes. "Your flaxen-haired boyfriend."

"He's not my boyfriend," I spat. "I told you we only dated for a few months and that ended abruptly when he—" I cut myself off mid-sentence. I hadn't confessed to anyone why I'd broken up with Lukas. Luckily we hadn't been together long enough for anyone to ask too many questions. But Jason wasn't just anyone.

"What did he do, Audrey?" Jason asked, and his voice was gentle, full of concern.

I slumped in my chair and started peeling off pink Post-it notes. "Lukas has a temper sometimes. We had an argument one night and he grabbed my phone and threw it against a wall."

Jason said nothing. I put my Post-it notes down and glanced over at him. A moment ago his voice had been calm, but now his face looked thunderous.

"Did he hurt you?" Jason asked in a tight voice. I saw his fist closing.

"He went a little nuts," I admitted. "The screen cracked, and for a second I thought he might go for me next." I paused, remembering. "The thing about Lukas is we had fun together. And he never openly threatened me. But it's weird when I see him now, so reserved and upstanding, I can almost convince myself it didn't really happen. But I know it did. And I know I'd be a fool to trust him."

"Your instincts are correct," Jason said. "Audrey, I want you to tell me if he does anything to make you uncomfortable, okay?"

"I'm really not worried about being attacked at the jobsite by Lukas Lund," I said. A thought occurred to me. "Jason, please don't say anything to him. Don't say anything about this to anyone."

He snorted with brief laughter. "Haven't I proven to you yet that I know how to keep a secret? I'm on your side, Audrey. We're partners. Don't forget that."

It was probably the nicest thing I'd ever heard Jason say, but I was too surprised to respond. He got up to leave, saying he had to get to the far west side of the valley to see about one of the pre-courthouse projects that was still wrapping up.

"Remember we've got the meeting with Mark Bracero down at the courthouse at two o'clock," I said.

He glanced at his watch. "I'll make it."

"You'd better," I warned. "He's Davis Brown's BFF, so that's one subcontractor we especially need to keep happy."

Jason grinned. "I'm good at keeping people happy. See you on-site later."

I found myself staring at the door after Jason exited, feeling conflicted. On the one hand, I was glad to see him go. He was still Jason Roma, still the same guy I'd been avoiding like rabies for the past six years, the guy who stole condoms and made maddening observations about hard nipples. On the other hand, despite my best efforts, I couldn't stop thinking about Friday night's erotic details. And then today he had to go and say something like "I'm on your side, Audrey." Even if he didn't mean it or if he only meant it in the most professional sense, I couldn't get the words out of my mind.

Helen knocked on the door a short time later carrying a stack of materials invoices she needed me to sign off on.

"How is he?" she asked.

"Jason's just fine," I said, looking over the quantities and pricing and then signing off with a flourish.

Helen's dry chuckle was loud. "I know *Jason's* fine, doll. And if I were a few years younger, I'd be trying to check him out up close. I was talking about the kid who got hurt on Friday."

"Oh." I blushed over the error. "Jonas Ramirez is his name. He was released from the hospital yesterday morning. He may need another surgery and is definitely facing months of rehabilitative care, but the doctors expect he'll recover."

"That's a relief," Helen said. She looked pointedly at the empty side of the office. "And where is Mr. Roma right now?"

I inspected another invoice. "He had to take a drive to the west side. I'll see him this afternoon."

Helen fell silent and I looked up. Her smile nearly reached her ears.

"What?" I said.

"What?" she mimicked me. "You're blushing."

"It's hot in here."

"If you say so," Helen replied, but she was still smiling.

"I do."

"And I suppose it has nothing to do with the fact that you and a certain sexy project manager have been circling each other and panting like animals in heat." She laughed at my shocked face. "Don't look so alarmed. Some people have a sixth sense. I have a sixth sense."

I chose not to acknowledge her bawdy declaration. "Here are your signed invoices," I said sweetly.

Helen winked at me on her way out the door. "I plan to trap you at some point and force some details out of you. In the meantime, say hi to Jason for me."

When Helen was gone I tried to concentrate on work once more, but I felt a bit unsettled. Helen was my friend and I felt pretty sure she wouldn't run around gossiping, but I didn't feel comfortable confirming any of her suspicions where Jason was concerned. It was true that I didn't want our indiscretions to become water-cooler conversation, but beyond that I didn't want to examine why I spent so much time thinking about Jason Roma.

My phone buzzed with Barnes and a small emergency that took the rest of the morning to resolve. I ate lunch at my desk and kept my mind on the job until it was time to leave for the meeting.

When I reached the jobsite, Jason was already there, just beyond the dust and the activity. He was shaking hands with a man sporting a shock of white hair who must be Mark Bracero, the owner of the company that was going to be handling the bulk of the electrical work. Given his friendship with Davis Brown, we'd have to stay on our toes around him lest he start making complaints to the bosses.

"Hello, I'm Audrey Gordon," I greeted him, holding out a hand.

He shook my hand with a frown. "I assumed standard protocol was in place for visiting a jobsite," he said.

I was a little nonplussed by the statement until I saw Jason glance down at my feet.

Shit.

Not only was I still wearing my open-toed sandals, but I had forgotten the hard hat that was required when visiting a construction zone.

"Forgive me," I said. "I'll just run back to my car and then we can proceed with the meeting. Unless you would like to speak off-site. There's a fabulous diner across the street."

His frown deepened. "The meeting is supposed to take place at the jobsite and I expect it *will* take place at the jobsite. If you can't handle a construction zone, young lady, then perhaps you'd be better off in a different line of work."

111

Jason broke in. "I think Audrey's right. It makes more sense to hold the meeting off-site. We've got a lot of ground to cover and it's loud and hot here."

Mark Bracero's scowl disappeared as he regarded Jason. "Perhaps you're right, Jason," he said warmly. "Let's go have a seat inside that restaurant over there."

Jason flashed me an apologetic look and I tried to stop seething over being insulted and called "young lady." I'd run into worse than Mark Bracero in this industry, and I was sure I could win him over if we all sat down and discussed more practical matters.

It turned out I was wrong. With a glare, Mark Bracero dismissed everything that came out of my mouth and instead would ask Jason what he thought. My anger surged, nearly getting the better of me, so I sat in my chair and sipped my soda in order to avoid doing something stupid, like calling the man a chauvinist pig.

To his credit, Jason realized what was going on and refused to use it to his advantage. "Audrey, what do you think?" he kept asking every time Bracero would talk right over me.

It didn't seem to matter. At the end of the meeting Mark Bracero shook Jason's hand as if he were his son and told him he was glad to know the project had such a conscientious manager in charge. I received nothing but a cool nod before he walked out.

When the waitress brought the check for the drinks and appetizers we'd ordered, I grabbed it first. "I've got it," I said grumpily, pulling out my corporate card and slapping it down on the table.

"I'm really sorry, Audrey," Jason said. He sounded angry. "You didn't fucking deserve to be treated like that."

"I did forget my hard hat," I grumbled, because I didn't really want Jason's pity.

He put his hand over mine. "The guy's an asshole. We're stuck working with him, but I want you to know that I've got your back."

I shrugged and slid my hand out from beneath his. "Thanks for trying," I said.

The waitress returned with the credit card slip. I left her an enormous tip and signed my name with an angry flourish.

"I'm heading back to the office." I stood. "You?"

He nodded. "In a little while."

I turned and began walking away.

"Hey," Jason called.

I turned around and looked at him. He'd left the table and was following me. Jason stopped about two feet away and gazed at me with earnest sincerity.

"I meant what I said."

"Thanks, Jason," I mumbled, and then walked out before he could add anything else. The heat outside was punishing even though it was barely the beginning of spring. I hurriedly crossed the street and returned to my car. Barnes talked nearby to some of the workers. He gave me a friendly wave. Maybe he was willing to forget about the unprofessional way Jason and I had been bickering at the jobsite on Friday following the crane accident. I waved back.

In the refuge of my car I blasted the air conditioner and tried to dissolve my irritation over Mark Bracero's bullshit attitude. Everyone had their own shit to deal with, and occasionally running into scowling sexist dinosaurs who didn't believe women belonged on construction sites was mine. It wasn't the first time I'd been treated unfairly and it wouldn't be the last.

"I'm on your side."

"I've got your back."

Remembering Jason's words had a calming effect on me. I hadn't expected such loyalty from him. But knowing that it was there when I hadn't even asked for it helped. It helped a lot.

Before I backed up and drove away, I noticed that Jason himself was standing about ten yards away beside his car. He must have left the restaurant immediately after I did, but maybe he understood that I needed some space so he didn't try to catch up with me. He was staring at the hive of activity in the middle of the jobsite. I watched him for a moment, and as I headed back to the office, something occurred to me for the first time.

I liked working with Jason. Strangely enough, I was starting to feel grateful we'd been partnered together.

CHAPTER TWELVE

One proverbial fire after another required extinguishing on the court-house project over the next two weeks—a problem with one of the material suppliers, a problem with the concrete crew, a problem when an unseasonable heavy rainstorm cost a few days of progress. Somehow in the midst of all the hectic day-to-day activity, Jason and I had settled into a comfortable routine. He hadn't once mentioned our night of sexual abandon. I had little doubt that to observers we appeared nothing but professional. Helen still badgered me with claims about her "sexth sense," but I always changed the subject and hoped she'd get the message.

The Friday before Easter, William surprised me by calling and asking if he could take me to lunch. He also mentioned he'd love to see the courthouse site up close, which made sense since he was a county judge. I offered to meet him somewhere, but he said he was just down the street and would be right over. The second the call ended I began feverishly tidying up my desk, even though it was already quite neat and I highly doubted William would care if a few things were out of order anyway.

"Hot lunch date?" Jason asked from across the room, smirking as he watched me stuff some loose papers in my desk.

I rolled my eyes, because even though Jason and I were not at each other's throats, he still managed to get on my nerves now and then. "Very funny. And no, it's just my brother."

"The great William is coming here?"

"I don't think I've told you very much about William."

"I make it my business to find things out. He's a judge, right?"

My desk phone buzzed and I pressed the speaker.

"You have a visitor," chirped Marnie, the receptionist up front. I could tell by her voice that she found the visitor in question quite intriguing.

"Thank you, I'll be right up," I told her, trying not to picture the free-spirited Marnie engaged in her typical greeting of attractive male guests. It involved lunging forward over her desk to give the observer a nice view of her ample cleavage. So far no warnings from Human Resources have tempted her to change. Normally I didn't give a damn if Marnie wanted to show her boobs to the world, but I felt a little queasy about subjecting my brother to that kind of attention.

"So you're a judge," Marnie was purring when I reached the lobby. "That must be so exciting."

"It has its moments," William said, easing back. Then he saw me and grinned. "Hey, Aud."

"William, I see you've already met Marnie." I shot her a look. She shrugged and smiled. "Why don't you follow me back to my office and I'll grab my purse?" I was trying to spare William further exposure to Marnie's charms.

He dutifully followed me back to my office, where no one would be leaning over the furniture practically naked. However, there was still a certain complex coworker delighted by my brother's arrival.

"I'm Jason Roma," he said before I had a chance to squeeze a word in. "I'm glad to finally meet a member of Audrey's family."

"William Gordon," my brother said, pumping Jason's outstretched hand and looking him over with curiosity.

I cleared my throat. "Jason and I are sharing an office while we manage the courthouse project together," I blurted. "Now where do you want to go have lunch?"

William didn't answer the lunch question. "So you're a project manager too," he said to Jason. "I asked Audrey if we could stop by the site of the courthouse."

"Which must interest you more than the average person," Jason said. "I imagine you'll be working in the building when it's finished."

"I will be," William agreed. "How long have you and my sister been working together at Lester & Brown?"

"There's a new sushi bar down the block," I broke in. "But they get crowded at lunchtime, so we should get going."

Jason stepped to my side. "Audrey and I have been working together for years," he said. "Long enough to become great friends. I'm glad to have this chance to collaborate with her on a project of this size. She's brilliant."

William smiled with pleasure to hear me being praised. "Yes, she is. I always tell her that, but somehow I think it means more coming from someone with no genetic link."

"She's the best there is," Jason confirmed. He gave me a friendly squeeze and paid no attention to my subsequent glare.

Unfortunately, William was always the essence of manners, so I knew what would come next. "You busy for lunch, Jason? You're welcome to join us."

"Thank you, I'd like that," said Jason, and I had no idea if he was sincere or if he was just hoping for an opportunity to subtly torment me. True, we were getting along better these days, but just because I had stopped having fantasies about throwing staplers at Jason's head didn't mean I wanted him cozying up to my family. Some worlds just shouldn't collide.

"Is that okay with you, Audrey?" Jason asked in a tone that indicated he couldn't imagine why it wouldn't be okay.

I shot him a look that warned that he shouldn't disrupt our fragile peace by making oblique references to my nipples in front of my brother. "Yes, that's fine."

Behave. Please behave.

The sushi restaurant already had a line twenty deep, so we opted for a trendy pita-wrap place around the corner.

"How'd you get off work early?" I asked William when we sat down. As far as I knew, he never took a day off from the bench. He routinely put in twelve- to fourteen-hour days even when court wasn't in session.

"It's Good Friday," William reminded me. "The building closed down early, and I wanted to get some shopping done for the boys this afternoon."

"Are Leo and Isaac all ready for the Easter bunny?" I asked, smiling at the thought of my rambunctious nephews.

He nodded and set down his glass of water. "Jen has them Easter morning," he said with a hint of dejection. "I'm planning to get them around eleven and bring them to Mom and Dad's house. By the way, you're coming on Sunday, right?"

"I wasn't aware I was invited."

My brother raised an eyebrow. "It's Easter, Audrey. Standing invitation."

More than likely I'd receive a text from my mother sometime tomorrow afternoon, an afterthought. After all, that was what had happened last year and the year before.

"Come on," William prodded. "Mom is ordering one of those two-hundred-dollar gourmet hams for dinner, and the boys will be crushed if their Auntie Audi isn't there."

"Auntie Audi?" Jason chuckled. "I kind of like the sound of that. How old are your boys, William?"

"Isaac's five and Leo's six," William said, immediately whipping out his phone to proudly display a picture of his smiling sons.

Jason examined the image. "Damn, they sure look like you."

"That they do," William said as he pocketed his phone once more.

Suddenly I was reminded of my little run-in with William's ex-wife a few weeks back. I hadn't mentioned that encounter to him yet. I wouldn't be mentioning it now. More than a few times since then I'd thought about Jennifer's words, remembered her eager plea to meet for lunch sometime. But my loyalty was to William first, and it felt too soon to start socializing with his ex-wife. Someday the raw wounds might heal enough to reconsider. There were still the boys to think about, and it was in their best interest for all the adults in their lives to be on good terms. Plus, I genuinely missed the easy friendship Jennifer and I had once shared. I missed the way she would call me out of the blue just to tell a funny story about Leo giving his pet turtle a bath in the toilet or inform me that I simply *had* to meet her for lunch on Friday at the new Thai restaurant on Central. I liked the idea that at some point Jennifer would somehow be part of my life again. It couldn't happen yet, but there was plenty of time to sort it out.

Jason wanted to hear more about William's work as a judge. When William talked, it was difficult not to be awed. Not many people had the responsibility to decide the fate of their fellow human beings.

After an hour William glanced at his watch and said he had to get going. His briefcase was full of paperwork he needed to deal with if he wanted to have some time with the kids this weekend.

"But you wanted to see the courthouse site," I reminded him.

He glanced at his watch again. "Let's make it another time. Can I tell the boys you're going to be there on Sunday?"

I sighed. "Yeah, I'll be there."

William flashed a confident grin. "Good. What are your plans for the holiday weekend, Jason?"

For a horrifying second I wondered if William was inviting Jason to my mother's would-be Easter celebration. The lunch with William hadn't turned out so badly, but I couldn't quite handle the idea of

Jason Roma grinning as he observed the upper-class dysfunction of the Gordon family.

"I'll be spending most of the weekend with my father," Jason said.

"Your father?" I was startled. I'd wondered about the "family obligations" Jason had cryptically mentioned. In six years, the only time I'd ever heard him mention his father was that tragic story of abuse he related at dinner. And he never said that his father was still living around here. Once he'd stated that his mother lived in Europe now, but there was never a word about his father. I hadn't even realized the man was still alive. I felt bad I'd ever questioned Jason's honesty about his personal commitments.

Jason nodded and looked away, and I took that as a hint that he didn't want to discuss his family matters with me, which was fine. He and William shook hands before my brother offered me a quick hug and hurried out.

"The office is closing early today," Jason told me when we were out on the sidewalk. "I just got the email."

"Good, then it will be nice and quiet this afternoon while I'm trying to work," I commented, to no response. I waited until we'd walked about twenty more yards before I said, "What?"

"I was thinking."

"About . . ."

"You. It's no wonder."

I stopped walking. "What's no wonder?"

He looked at me as if I were a puzzle he'd just brilliantly solved. "It's no wonder why you're driven at work to the point of obsession. Now that I've seen what you're trying to live up to."

I didn't appreciate the remark, no matter how true it was. I didn't even like admitting to myself how much I wanted to live up to William's example. Even at a young age I'd longed to have my parents look at me with the same kind of pride they reserved for their son. I never held that against my brother, though. It wasn't William's fault he was practically perfect.

"Jason, do me a favor and keep your asinine little observations to yourself."

I stalked back to the office and buried my face in my work until it was dark outside. Jason remained for a few hours after most of the staff had cleared out in anticipation of the holiday weekend. When he told me to have a nice weekend, I nodded and said, "You too," but I didn't even look up from my computer screen.

CHAPTER THIRTEEN

Easter actually turned out to be a nice day. As expected, my mother texted me at six p.m. the night before and informed me that I could show up for an early holiday dinner at two o'clock.

The boys practically tackled me when I showed up with two towering baskets full of candy and other goodies. My mother greeted me with a glass of wine in her hand. She started to offer me one but stopped before she finished her sentence, looking embarrassed. At least this time I didn't have to remind her that alcoholism was a lifelong addiction. My father emerged from his study alongside my brother and I expected to be offered the usual polite, stiff hello due a distant third cousin.

Instead Aaron Gordon smiled when he saw me and said, "William and I were just talking about your success at Lester & Brown. According to your brother, you're doing great work on the courthouse building. Keep it up."

"Thanks," I said, trying to overcome the mild shock I felt at receiving a semi-compliment from my father. The last such occasion I could recall was after my performance in *The Nutcracker* at the age of eleven.

My father nodded and wandered over to the minibar. Then he nudged William over to the corner of the room, probably so he could harass my brother about running for city council again.

Leo and Isaac wanted me to help them put together a puzzle featuring a cartoon rabbit carrying a giant egg. To my mother's chagrin, we cleared a space at the immaculately set dining room table.

We'd never been a church-going family, but while the boys and I were piecing together the puzzle, Leo mentioned that his mother had taken them to a morning service.

"So Jennifer goes to church now," my mother sniffed as she nibbled on a stuffed mushroom appetizer that the housekeeper, Luanne, had prepared the day before. "That's rather ironic, considering."

"Mom," I hissed, glancing around and feeling some relief that William was out of earshot, still on the far side of the dining room and being lectured by my father. William looked bored. Or annoyed. And luckily the boys didn't think anything of their grandmother's sarcastic comment. This morning I'd thought about texting Jennifer, just a short and sweet "Happy Easter" to dissolve the icy distance between us a little. She probably would have answered, maybe sent some photos of the boys discovering their Easter baskets this morning. I realized the next move should come from me, that she might have been waiting for it ever since we ran into each other at Esposito's, but I couldn't bring myself to do it quite yet.

My mother's cutting remark about her ex-daughter-in-law turned out to be the only briefly uncomfortable moment in an otherwise pleasant afternoon.

Spending time with my nephews put me in a good mood that was still going strong on Monday morning. My phone went off when I was driving over to the courthouse site.

ED: Did you receive a voicemail from Bracero on Friday?

I frowned. I hadn't actually spoken to Mark Bracero since the day he haughtily called me "young lady" and suggested that I find employment in an alternate industry. But I checked my voicemail anyway before responding to Jason, just in case. There was nothing there, and when I stopped at a light I texted to Jason that there had been no voicemail from Mark Bracero. Jason didn't follow up with another message until I was pulling into the construction zone at the courthouse.

ED: Don't worry about it. Dude probably can't remember what he was doing an hour ago.

I suspected that wasn't true, but I wasn't going to waste the morning worrying about whether Mark Bracero thought he had called me. It didn't make sense anyway. Whenever he sent an email he addressed it to Jason, and Jason had to forward it to me so I would know what was going on. That's work life with the bosom buddy of one of the names on the company masthead.

Work at the site was humming along like it should. There hadn't been any mishaps since the crane accident. I was walking along the perimeter when a shadow crossed my path.

"Good morning, Audrey," boomed a deep male voice, and I found myself looking up into glacial blue eyes.

"Lukas." I blinked, a little surprised to encounter him here at this hour. He'd texted me on Saturday and asked me to dinner, but I had declined.

He gazed out at all the activity, squinting in the sunlight. "I like to stop by here if I happen to be in the neighborhood," he explained. "I never get tired of the sight of something created out of nothing."

"I see." I stared down at the sturdy shoes I was required to wear when visiting a construction zone.

"I'm lying," Lukas said.

When I looked up, he had an eyebrow cocked and he was staring down at me intently.

"You're lying?"

He nodded. "Most of the time I stop by here hoping to run into you."

"Lukas, I'm sorry but—"

He cut me off. "It's okay, Audrey. You don't have to say it. Shit." He shifted his weight, and his handsome face winced. "I've become a creepy stalker, haven't I?"

"You're not a stalker or creepy," I said, even though I didn't entirely mean it, because loitering around my work zone in the hopes of striking up a conversation seemed juvenile and, yes, a little creepy.

"But you don't want to date me," Lukas said with a half smile.

I shook my head. "No. I guess I should have been more clear."

Lukas's customary aloof mask had slipped. He actually appeared vulnerable as he lowered his head for a moment and said, "My loss."

I hadn't realized how tense I'd grown during this conversation until he said those sad words, admitting defeat. Then I managed to exhale the breath I'd been holding. I didn't know whether Lukas had it in him to be a good man, but I did know it wasn't my job to find out.

"Audrey!" That voice didn't come from Lukas. It was even more familiar to me.

I looked up, surprised to see Jason Roma barreling in our direction. I found myself admiring the broad lines of his shoulders and the powerful strides of his strong legs even as I wondered why he was practically sprinting over.

"What's wrong?" I shouted, having panicked visions of falling cranes.

Jason stepped in front of me. "What the hell are you doing here again?" he challenged Lukas.

"What's your fucking problem, Roma?" Lukas growled back. "For weeks you've been giving me the side eye. In case you forgot, I'm the goddamn architect on this project."

"I didn't forget," Jason said, and got right up in Lukas's face. Jason was about two inches shorter, but all the hours he obviously logged in the gym, combined with the fact that he had spent years in mixed martial arts training, made him a worthy opponent even for Lukas

Lund. What I didn't know was why the hell he was suddenly spoiling for a fight.

"I'm only gonna say this once." Jason closed in. "Leave her the hell alone."

Oh. That's why.

"Jason," I started to say, but he ignored me because he was busy pushing a finger into Lukas Lund's chest.

"Stop shadowing her," he warned. "Stop showing up out of the blue and pretending like you have a fucking reason to be here. I know what your fucking reason is, like I know you can diddle with your blueprints a lot better back at your drafting table."

Lukas's hands had tightened into fists. His jaw was set so hard he could probably crack diamonds in his perfect teeth.

"Touch me again"—the look in his eyes was nothing short of homicidal—"and I'll fucking break that pretty-boy face of yours into sixty separate pieces."

"Eat shit, asshole," Jason scoffed. "You won't connect one swing before I flatten you in the fucking dust."

Lukas scowled. Jason glowered. I knew I ought to try to separate them, but I couldn't even believe this was happening. Two well-dressed, highly successful men about to brawl in the dirt?

"Just keep your fucking distance from now on," Jason warned, and started to turn his back.

A frightened cry escaped my throat because I saw what Jason hadn't. Lukas had reached full-wrath mode and he was rearing back for a hell of a punch.

But I underestimated Jason. He sidestepped as the powerful fist came sailing his way. Everything seemed to happen in slow motion as Lukas stumbled when his assault was thwarted. Jason took advantage and delivered one mighty, impressive kick that swept Lukas Lund right off his feet.

"Stop!" I yelled, finally finding both my voice and the presence of mind to get between them and start handing out lectures like a teacher at the schoolyard. "Knock it off, both of you. You're being ridiculous."

Given that we were on the far north perimeter of the site, we weren't within view of most of the workers. Only a few curious stares came our way.

Lukas got to his feet and brushed the dirt off his knees. He looked disgusted. With me, with Jason, maybe even with himself.

"Fuck this shit," he said, and stalked off in the opposite direction.

Jason touched my arm. "Are you okay?"

I shook him off. "I'm fine. What the hell was that all about?"

He narrowed his eyes at Lukas's departing figure. "Tired of seeing him lurking around here. Like a goddamn spider hunting its prey."

"And so you opted to go full alpha-male idiot and assault him in broad daylight? What the hell makes you think I need your protection, Jason? Did I ever once fucking ask for it?"

He shook his head and gave me a stubborn glare. "No, Audrey, you've never asked for a damn thing. You've certainly never asked for protection. But you have it. Whether you want it or not."

"That's fantastic, Jason. You sound just like a Neanderthal."

"Neanderthals didn't have advanced language skills."

"Shut up. You know what I mean."

To my chagrin I saw that several workers had wandered away from their posts and were openly observing the entertainment.

"We're making a hell of a scene," I said, feeling extremely tired all of a sudden. But I still had enough fire in me to fix Jason with a severe glare. "Let's get one thing straight. I don't need to be guarded as if I'm some breakable treasure. I'm every bit as capable as you are."

"Really?" Jason challenged. "And what the hell would you have done if that dickhead had made a grab for you? You think you could have defended yourself and taken him down, all hundred and twenty pounds of you?"

I crossed my arms and stood my ground. "Jason, right now I'm going back to the office, but I want you to listen to me carefully first. Do not come busting into situations you know nothing about to offer any more of your so-called help. I am *not* yours to defend."

Jason didn't blink. "Noted, Audrey."

He didn't follow me when I walked away. In fact I did not see him at all for the rest of the day.

CHAPTER FOURTEEN

Three days later as I drove to work, my annoyance at Jason still swirled. Who did he think he was, charging into a conversation and tossing threats around? The fact that I'd already confessed to him that Lukas possessed a frightening streak of violence was irrelevant.

Except it isn't.

I sighed as I turned off the ignition. In my heart, I knew Jason and I would never be regular coworkers. We couldn't be friends either, not in the traditionally platonic sense. I didn't know what the hell we were.

Before I exited the car I checked my phone. Jason had sent me a text late last night to remind me he had a personal issue to take care of first thing this morning but he'd be on the jobsite by ten, and then he'd take the cluster of supplier meetings scheduled for this afternoon. I had stared at the text for a long time with my finger hovering over the screen, my pride warring with my inclination to reach out. We had traded some devastating truths about ourselves over dinner at Esposito's. I wondered about the family obligations Jason had referenced before and if that had something to do with his personal mission this morning. I wondered if it was all linked to anything he'd told me about his past.

Would he tell me about it if I asked?

But I didn't. I simply tapped out the word "Fine" and plugged my phone into the charger for the night. Yet as I stared at my bedroom ceiling in the dark, I remained troubled by the idea that I'd missed an opportunity.

Since I couldn't sit in the parking garage all morning brooding over Jason, I headed for the office.

"There you are," Marnie greeted me when I walked into the lobby. "Marty Lester said to send you into his office as soon as you arrived."

"What does The Man want this early?" I asked.

She shrugged. "He didn't say. Better go check it out, though. He was in kind of a state this morning."

A soft, involuntary groan escaped me as I headed for my office to drop off my purse before facing The Man. The fact that my high-strung boss was "in a state" could be the result of anything from running out of cups in the break room to a catastrophic jobsite explosion.

Of course I'd already known Jason wouldn't be in our office. I suddenly wished he were. I knew I could face our boss without him, but I'd grown used to the idea that we were a team, at least where the project was concerned.

"Come in, Audrey," said The Man when I knocked on his door.

I had a flashback to the day I entered this office expecting to be rewarded with the courthouse assignment. And I was. But so was Jason. That day he was already sitting there in all his gorgeous glory waiting for me to show up. He was not waiting for me today.

Instead I saw only The Man, Marilyn from Human Resources, and a very pissed-off-looking Davis Brown.

"Have a seat," ordered The Man, and I noticed he didn't meet my eye when he said it. Marilyn was gazing at me with open pity. Davis Brown threw me a disdainful glance and then looked away.

"Good morning, everyone," I said nervously as I sat. Whatever happened next was not going to be to my liking.

The Man actually looked apologetic as he addressed me. "Audrey, as of today, you are removed as the courthouse project manager."

My jaw didn't drop. I didn't jump to my feet and start shouting. I gazed at him calmly, thinking I must have misunderstood his meaning. "I beg your pardon?"

Davis Brown spoke up. His voice sounded like it had somehow been mixed with shards of glass. "Your obvious incompetence has become apparent to one of our most important partners."

Marilyn spoke up. "I think the point can be made without insults."

Davis Brown didn't agree. "Well, I think Ms. Gordon requires a strong dose of the truth. Not only has she repeatedly dropped the ball, but she gets hysterical every time someone rightfully questions her competence level."

Lukas? Was Lukas angry enough to lodge some wild complaint?

"Am I being fired?" I asked.

"No," The Man answered immediately. "Of course not."

"But you are jeopardizing the largest project the firm has ever undertaken," Davis Brown continued, addressing me directly now. "And so from now on the county courthouse will be solely managed by Jason Roma."

His words kicked me in the stomach. I didn't know what distressed me more, the fact that I was being unfairly removed from a project I was working my ass off for or that Jason might have been told that I'd be blindsided this morning.

"Does Jason know?" I managed to croak.

The Man nodded. "I informed him."

I couldn't take a breath right away. Somehow the fact that Jason knew and hadn't seen fit to warn me stung even more than the demotion.

Marilyn cleared her throat. "Audrey, you're still a very valued employee here. We want to make sure you're aware of that."

I looked at her. Her words were gentle but something in her eyes blazed. Whatever was happening here was bullshit and she knew it.

Davis Brown heaved his heavy body to his feet, his knee joints popping audibly. "Now that this has been handled, I've got someplace to be." He held out a hand to The Man. "Marty, now that we all understand each other, I'll leave the situation in your capable hands."

"I'm afraid we don't," I said, my loud voice echoing in the conference room.

The two men looked at me—The Man a little uneasy and Davis Brown irritated that he was required to waste another word on me.

"Don't what?" he said rather crossly.

I rose to his level and tipped my chin up. "We don't understand each other," I said. "I deserve to know who has been slandering me so I can decide how to proceed from here."

Davis Brown's beady eyes narrowed. "Mark Bracero's word has been good in this industry since before you were born," he sneered.

"Mark Bracero." I chuckled in spite of the situation. "Mark Bracero is a condescending, sexist pig who has probably been searching for a way to kick me off the project since the moment we met."

"Okay now," Marilyn said, trying to inject some peace into the room before the situation grew explosive. "Let's all sit down and discuss this calmly."

But no one was going to be sitting down and discussing anything calmly, because an instant later Jason Roma flung open the office door.

"Well, look who's decided to join us," I snapped. "I assumed you were just taking the coward's way out with your so-called personal issues."

"You assumed wrong," he said. And that's when I noticed that the fury in his expression was even more pronounced than it had been the moment he charged Lukas Lund. But it wasn't directed at me.

Jason stopped in front of The Man's desk. "I received your gutless email," he announced, tossing his phone on the desk. "You really didn't think something of this magnitude rated a fucking conversation first?"

"The decision has been made," Davis Brown declared. "You ought to be grateful for the opportunity, Jason."

"Grateful?" Jason snorted. "To work for a company that would toss one of its most dedicated employees under the bus? And on the word of an idiot like Mark Bracero?"

I got up and stood beside Jason with a glower at my boss. "You might have bothered to ask a few fucking questions before accepting Bracero's version as gospel." Normally I would never use profanity to make a point in front of management. But there was nothing normal about this situation. I cast a sidelong glance at Jason, our eyes locked, and he gave the slightest of nods. He hadn't betrayed me. We were on exactly the same page.

The Man looked uncertain. Davis Brown looked thunderous. Marilyn nervously glanced at the open door and started to get up, presumably to close it.

"Leave it open," Jason demanded when he saw where she was going.

Marilyn sat back down.

Davis Brown panted like a bulldog, his florid face a doughy blob of anger that was now directed at Jason. "You little shit. Mark Bracero has been my friend for over thirty years."

"I don't give a fuck," Jason fired back.

"You should," Davis snarled. "If you give a damn about your career."

"I don't, not if it means enduring this garbage. Mark Bracero has treated Audrey with an abominable lack of professionalism since the moment he met her."

I broke in. "It's true. The man has made openly sexist remarks, belittled me, and he has consistently refused to communicate with me directly, for no legitimate reason."

"I should have mentioned it sooner," Jason said. "I never believed he would take his grudge as far as demanding Audrey's removal from the project. I owe her an apology for my silence." He looked directly at me. A tinge of regret flecked his expression. "I'm sorry, Audrey. This is bullshit and you don't deserve to be treated this way."

I suppressed a smile as relief continued to flood through me. We really were a team, Jason and I. Bracero and his bitterness didn't stand a chance against us. "It's okay, Jason. It didn't occur to either of us that management would be so easily cowed."

"Now you listen here," Davis Brown spat, but Jason shouted over him.

"No, *you* listen, asshole. Audrey Gordon is a brilliant project manager and the most dedicated employee you have. I am confident anyone who has ever worked with her will say the same if testimony is required."

Davis Brown blinked. "Testimony?"

I knew where Jason was heading with this. "For the costly discrimination lawsuit I plan to file if you don't immediately reverse your terrible decision," I said.

"And as soon as I leave this office, I plan on sending a detailed email to every member of the Lester & Brown Board of Directors to ensure they have an *honest* version of events," Jason added.

For a moment utter silence reigned in the room and in the office beyond. I fought the urge to smirk in triumph. The Man now looked contrite while Davis Brown had deflated, his fat shoulders drooping noticeably.

Marilyn, however, was sitting upright in her chair and smiling. I was tempted to smile with her, despite feeling choked up. No one except my brother had ever gone to bat for me the way Jason just had.

"Audrey," The Man said with an apologetic grimace, "you have my very personal and very heartfelt apology. The decision to remove you from the project was made too hastily and without all the facts. You are reinstated on the project, and I will be speaking to both our lawyers and the board about nullifying Mark Bracero's contract, given his conduct." He glared at his associate. "I think we can agree these actions are all in the best interest of the firm. Right, Davis?"

"Agreed," Davis mumbled in the tone of a man who knew he'd been defeated.

"Good," Jason said as he picked up his phone from the desk. "Now let's stop wasting time and get back to work."

He stalked out of the room without waiting for anyone to respond. I wanted to break into applause. I was sure a few people listening in the gray cubicles beyond the door would have joined in. Instead I shook The Man's hand, shot Davis Brown one final glare, and left with Marilyn.

"Congrats," she whispered after we closed the door. I wasn't sure it was the right sentiment in this case, but who wouldn't get a big kick out of watching the evisceration of the corporate bosses? Then she gave me another smile and hurried off in the direction of the ladies' room.

Helen popped her frizzy head up over a cubicle on the other side of the room and gave me a thumbs-up. I wanted to run laps around the office in celebration, but there was something I needed to do first.

When I walked into the office Jason and I shared, he was sitting at his desk typing away like he was finishing a novel. He didn't look up when I entered.

"Jason," I said, approaching his desk and flattening my palms on the surface.

"Just a minute," he said brusquely, continuing to type. He was quick, attacking the keys with a purposeful vengeance.

I waited for several minutes, pulling up a chair as he finished pounding on the keys. This must be that email.

"You could have just taken the golden opportunity and run," I told him. "But I really appreciate what you did in there. Thank you."

Jason looked up at me. He hadn't shaved today, unusual for him. I liked it, though, liked the dark scruff around his jaw. I wouldn't have minded feeling it against my skin.

"You shouldn't thank me," he said. "It's a shitty world when people have to thank each other for doing the decent thing. I should have mentioned to management weeks ago that Bracero was a problem. It never occurred to me he'd pull a stunt like this. I meant it when I said I was sorry."

I digested that. "I hope this little sideshow didn't interfere too much with your plans this morning."

"My plans?"

"Yeah." I cleared my throat. "Whatever personal obligations you had to deal with."

I wasn't trying to pry, but I could admit to being a little curious. Maybe Jason had had a job interview. The idea unsettled me.

"My father had a doctor's appointment," he said. "That was my personal obligation. Taking my father to the doctor."

I was surprised. From what Jason had told me about his father, I wouldn't expect them to have a great relationship. I tried to imagine bringing my own father to the doctor and I couldn't. He would balk at the idea that anyone ought to miss a morning of work to help someone else. My father's work ethic had always been rigid, uncompromising. Somehow over time I'd begun to adopt the same principles. And I was discovering I didn't much like the idea of turning into my father.

"You're wrong about something," I blurted to Jason, and he raised an eyebrow, waiting for me to continue. "You're wrong that people shouldn't acknowledge when someone goes out on a limb for them." I shifted in my seat, struggling with how to express myself. "Jason, what you did today, standing up for me even knowing it might hurt the career you've worked so hard for . . . I don't have a long list of people who would do that for me."

"That's a damn shame, Audrey," Jason said, leaning closer until less than a foot separated us across the desk. His shirtsleeves were rolled above his corded forearms, and I remembered too well the feel of his strong hands on my body.

I swallowed, then shut my eyes briefly, trying to banish a sense of dizziness. I was glad I didn't have to fight for my job every day before nine a.m. But I was well aware that the early confrontation in The Man's office wasn't the reason my pulse was racing now.

My hand landed on his. "Can I buy you lunch today?"

He looked down. "As a way to express your gratitude?"

"You might say that."

"No."

"Oh." I started to withdraw my hand but he took it and laced our fingers together.

He exhaled. "Audrey, I don't want to spend a casual lunch with you today, trying to be repulsively professional and refusing to say what's really on my mind."

I raised an eyebrow. "When have you ever shied away from saying what's really on your mind?"

He slowly brought my knuckles to his lips. "All the time where you're concerned."

"I'd never guess it from all the sexually charged one-liners."

He squeezed my hand and flashed his bad-boy grin. "Make this at least a little easier on me, okay?"

"You're the one who turned down my lunch invitation," I sniffed.

"Only because I want more."

His thumb was idly stroking my wrist, making concentration difficult.

"How much more?" I whispered, already guessing. And my guesses were all distinctly X-rated.

But the answer was unexpected.

"I want you to be my date Saturday night."

"Your date?" *Huh?* "Where would we be going?"

"A wedding."

"Whose?"

"Dom and Melanie's," he answered, as if it should have been obvious.

The heat of a blush unfurled across my skin. Jason wasn't suggesting a night of emotionally detached sex. He wanted to bring me to his best friend's wedding.

"Um, I'm pretty sure you need to clear it with the bride and groom weeks ahead of time if you plan on bringing a guest."

He nodded. "True. And I did."

"You already told them you were bringing someone?"

"I told them I was bringing you."

I gaped at him. "But it's two days away and you hadn't asked me yet."

Jason shrugged, unconcerned with the details. "I was waiting for the right time. This is it."

"Jason Roma." I shook my head, startled by how pleased I was over the invitation. "You are full of surprises."

"So you'll come to the wedding on Saturday?"

"I'll have to find a dress."

"You're beautiful no matter what you wear, Audrey."

I'd never taken compliments well and my face grew even hotter. Jason was still holding my hand and I had an irrepressible urge to kiss him. If someone happened to be watching through the tiny square of glass on our office door, I didn't give a damn. I reached across, intending to give him a quick peck on the lips, but Jason had other ideas. He must have been anticipating my move because his free hand seized the back of my neck and pulled me into a deep kiss full of heat and tongues and unyielding demands. I wasn't complaining, not even when his unshaven jaw scratched against my smooth skin. In fact I moaned into his mouth and nearly cried out in frustration when he pulled back.

"Say you'll come," he whispered, inches away from my face, his tongue teasing my bottom lip.

I was surprised I could form words. "I'll come," I whispered back. *Actually, I might come right here and now.*

"Good." Jason released me and settled back in his chair with a small, victorious grin. He was proud of himself. Yet the fact didn't trouble me in the slightest.

I had a rather goofy smile on my own face as I made my way back to my desk.

"Hey, Audrey?" Jason said from his chair.

"Yeah?"

"Been meaning to ask you, why the hell did you name me ED on your phone?"

Heat rose in my cheeks. "What?"

"There was a day at the jobsite a few weeks ago when you were so engrossed in your phone you didn't notice that I was standing right behind you. Not thirty seconds later I received the message you'd furiously typed and addressed to ED. Does it stand for something?"

"Uh, no," I stammered. "Just a mistake."

Five minutes later, when his attention turned elsewhere, I swiftly grabbed my phone and reclassified ED.

CHAPTER FIFTEEN

Half a dozen gowns in my closet would have sufficed, but I wanted to wear something new to the wedding. Jason had really thrown me for a loop. Not only had he proved to be my most avid defender in the workplace, but he'd surprised me with this invitation. It was sweet and somehow far more intimate than an ordinary night out. And if all that wasn't enough to make me a little weak-kneed, he turned out to be the kind of guy who would escort a father he did not like to the doctor when he was needed. There were moments when I was beginning to wonder if I was actually starting to fall for Jason Roma.

After scouring the mall on Saturday morning, I returned to my apartment with only a few hours left before Jason was supposed to arrive. Once I'd showered and applied my makeup with care, I curled my hair, which was now past my shoulders, longer than I'd kept it in years. The floor-length black gown with a low neckline and a daring slit up the right leg felt sinful sliding over my body, and I stood in front of the mirror, pleased at the effect.

Jason was pleased too. I could tell as soon as I opened the door.

"Come in," I said, stepping back.

He shook his head. "Hell no. If I take two steps right now, that dress will be on the floor and we won't be going anywhere until tomorrow. Dom will never forgive me."

I laughed and allowed my right leg to creep out of the side slit. Jason noticed and his hot gaze ran slowly up my leg. "You're so beautiful," he said in a husky voice.

The intensity of his gaze took my breath away for a few heartbeats.

"You look amazing too," I said, drinking in the sight of him in his black tuxedo.

Jason crooked a finger, backing up. "Let's go."

I grabbed my clutch off the couch and followed him into the corridor, locking the door behind me. I'd known this man for six years and detested him for large swaths of that time. And then he held out his arm, flashed his incomparable smile, and my infatuation with Jason Roma kicked up a few notches.

Both the wedding and reception were being held in a historic downtown hotel that was built in the twenties. Jason explained to me in the car that even though Melanie wanted to have the wedding at Esposito's, it was ultimately decided to be impractical.

"I have to ask you something," I said.

"Ask away."

"What did you really tell your friends about me?"

He focused on the traffic straight ahead. "We should have that conversation later."

"Why?"

"Because I have a few ideas about how this night will go," he said.

"What ideas?"

He nodded and zeroed in on me. "You'll see."

I wasn't sure what he meant, but the possibilities sent my pulse racing. Every time Jason's sexy dark eyes glanced in my direction, I was a little more excited to find out exactly what kind of so-called ideas Jason was keeping to himself.

The old hotel was classy and perfect and exactly the kind of place where I would have wanted to get married if I had ever thought about it. Normally I wasn't a hopeless romantic, but my throat felt a little tight as I watched Dominic and Melanie exchange their vows. Melanie looked nothing short of dazzling in her sleeveless full-skirted dress, and Dominic was the second-hottest guy in the room, after Jason. Whenever my eyes strayed from the blissful couple, I focused on Jason standing there in his tux as he watched his friends make an enduring commitment. His broad shoulders projected strength, and his smoldering good looks set him apart from every other man in the room, at least in my eyes. At one point he turned my way, searching for my face among all the other guests. When he found me, he winked. My heart fluttered in response.

When Melanie and Dominic kissed for the first time as husband and wife, I was taken back with a jolt to another time, another wedding. My brother had been so in love with his bride the day he married Jennifer. Despite the bridesmaid tulle scratching my legs then, I remember being awed at the way William's large hands trembled with emotion as he placed the ring on her finger. I'd already started to think of Jennifer as my sister, a permanent addition to the family. At the time I'd been sure they would be together forever. Some people were lucky enough to have that fate. But not them. Eight years and two kids later their love story was over.

I shook the melancholy off. It didn't seem fair to obsess over sad endings at such a happy beginning. This was Melanie and Dominic's day. I hoped with all my heart that they'd remain every bit as in love as they were right now.

After the short ceremony, we were all herded into an elegantly appointed ballroom. Jason returned to my side and slipped his arm possessively around my waist.

"I swear I didn't hear half the ceremony," he murmured in my ear. "I was too busy staring at you."

I smiled as his arm tightened around my waist. "Likewise," I whispered back.

When we reached the bride and groom, Jason presented me as "The gorgeous and incomparable Audrey Gordon, whom you've met before and hear me talk about all the time."

Melanie embraced me with a friendly hug. "I'm so glad you came, Audrey."

Her new husband, who was a little more reserved, settled for a handshake, but he did smile. I didn't miss seeing how he also raised an eyebrow at his best friend.

Dominic's brother and business partner, Gio, was the best man, and Gio's very glamorous, very pregnant wife, Tara, served as a bridesmaid. They'd also obviously known Jason for a long time—Tara nudged her husband with amusement when she noticed how Jason kept his arm around me at all times.

A beautiful woman who could have been Melanie's slightly taller twin was the maid of honor. She was the bride's sister, Lucy, and she made the first toast after we all sat down. Then Gio got up and made a second heartfelt toast to "My big brother, my hero. And to Melanie, my new sister. May every happiness on earth belong to you. I love you guys."

But it was Dominic's toast that had everyone dabbing their eyes with their linen napkins. When he rose and held up his glass, he looked very grave, and I would guess that he wasn't a man who enjoyed speaking in front of people.

"Melanie," he said to his bride, "I'm going to steal a few words from William Shakespeare for this occasion. 'My heart is ever at your service.'"

Then he bent down and kissed her gently. She closed her eyes as his lips lingered on hers. The room went utterly silent as Melanie and Dominic shared their perfect fairy tale moment.

With only around fifty wedding guests, the seating seemed somewhat informal. Jason and I had found a table with Dominic's cousin, Steven, whom I had glimpsed briefly in the kitchen the night Jason took me to Esposito's. His youngest daughter sat to my left.

"I like your dress," she said shyly.

"Thank you," I replied. I pointed to the silver unicorn that stood out against her light pink dress. "I like your necklace."

"Alice," her father prodded gently, "eat your vegetables, honey."

The girl, whom I would guess to be around ten years old, wrinkled her nose as she popped a single pea in her mouth. It was the sort of thing my nephew Leo would have done.

I nudged Jason. "How's your father? I kept meaning to ask."

He looked up from his plate. "My father?"

"You mentioned taking him to the doctor the other day."

He took a sip of wine, and I thought a shadow passed over his face. "Just a routine appointment," he said, and I could tell from his voice that he didn't want to talk about it anymore.

I touched his hand. "Thank you for inviting me tonight, Jason."

He grinned. "It never occurred to me to invite anyone else."

As soon as the music started, Jason grabbed my hand and tried to pull me to my feet. "Dance with me."

"I'm still eating," I objected, reluctant to leave the eclectic mix of delicious food that included pizza, tamales, and an assortment of side dishes. It was the strangest, and tastiest, wedding meal I'd ever been served.

But Jason wouldn't be deterred. "If they take it away by the time you get back, I'll get you more."

I hadn't danced with anyone in a long time, but Jason was a fantastic partner, whirling me around with expert precision, and I laughed as I tried to keep up. Yet as much as I enjoyed being spun around by him, I was glad when the music slowed. Jason pulled me close, and a brief shiver rolled through me as I thrilled to the feel of his hard muscles and relaxed into his arms.

I reached up to touch his smooth-shaven face. "I kind of liked the beginnings of that beard."

"Then I'll start growing a new one tomorrow," he responded.

"I've never seen you with a full beard before."

He shrugged. "I've never grown one before."

"And now you will?" I couldn't quite figure out if he was joking or not. "Yes, I think I would like to see that."

"Then I'll do it."

"Just because I'd like it?"

He grinned. "Just because you'd like it."

I slipped my arms around his shoulders and gazed into his eyes. Pure sincerity stared back at me.

"I can't figure you out," I admitted.

He tightened his arms around my waist. "I'll tell you anything you want to know. Just ask."

"Okay. What did you tell your friends about me?"

His expression grew mischievous. "I said you were a pain in the ass with nice tits."

"Jason, if we weren't at a wedding, I'd knee you in the balls."

"Doubt you could pull it off in that dress. Anyway, you didn't let me finish."

"I'm afraid to hear the rest."

Jason pressed his forehead to mine. "I also said you're brilliant and dedicated, that you're the sexiest woman I've ever met, and that even when you're driving me nuts, I still want you so badly I can hardly concentrate."

The sound of other people in the room faded. There was only Jason. I wanted to believe him. But I'd thought of him as an obnoxious adversary for so long. I figured he always thought of me the same way, no matter what went on in the bedroom.

"And you've felt this way all these years?" I said, my tone doubtful.

"No." He shook his head emphatically. "I feel this way now, Audrey. *After* all these years. In all this time, I never would have turned down the chance to get you naked again, but that's not all I want anymore. That's not why I invited you to my best friend's wedding. That's not why you're always on my mind. That's not why I'd be tempted to savagely crush the windpipe of any fucker who might hurt you and why I won't step aside when you insist you don't need my help. And, dammit, I wish I'd had the balls to tell you all this before we went back to your apartment a few weeks ago."

He tipped my chin up and stared into my eyes for a long, powerful moment before delivering his most important declaration. "There was a time when I was happy enough just to have your body for a little while. That's not enough now. I want all of you."

We had stopped dancing altogether. We were just standing there in the middle of the dance floor wrapped up in each other and probably attracting a few stares, but I didn't care.

"You told me once you didn't have girlfriends," I reminded him.

He raised an eyebrow. "I think I was twenty-three at the time. I'm not twenty-three anymore."

"No, you're not."

Jason's hands slid down far past my waist, pressing me against him. "Audrey, I don't want girlfriends. Just you."

Most of the time he didn't appear to take life seriously, and he could beat a person's last nerve to death with his caustic commentary. But I also knew he was loyal and funny and wildly sexy. I didn't have a great track record with relationships, and I was pretty sure Jason had an even less impressive history. But for the first time in a long while I really wanted to try—maybe I'd finally met someone worth the effort. It had just taken us six years to get this far.

"Well, Mr. Roma," I told him, brushing my lips across his jaw, "tonight you've got me."

Another man might have settled for a quick kiss in the midst of so much company, but not Jason. He cupped my face in his hands and didn't think twice about sliding his tongue into my mouth. One hand tangled in my hair and the other pressed me closer. He wanted me to feel him, all of him, and I answered back by matching the hunger of his kiss.

"Get a room," a nearby deep voice bellowed, and we broke the kiss long enough for Jason to throw Dominic a dirty look. He floated by with Melanie and merely laughed when Jason followed up the dirty look with an obscene gesture.

I giggled and buried my face in Jason's collar, breathing the scent of his aftershave, enjoying the delicious pleasure of being so close to him. I nipped at his neck and felt his pulse quicken.

"It wasn't bad advice," I purred in his ear as my hand slid under the coat of his tuxedo and over the solid chest covered only by a thin shirt. Around Jason I felt more daring than I'd ever felt with anyone. At least while I was sober. There was a potent physical connection between us that couldn't be denied. Who would want to deny it? I wanted to revel in it.

Jason's hands moved to my hips. Through all our layers of clothes I could feel how hard he was. All of a sudden I was intensely eager to leave the party behind.

"I'm a step ahead of you," Jason teased.

"What does that mean?"

"It means check the left pocket of my pants."

I dipped my fingers down into his pocket and felt a sharp corner. "Is that a card key?"

"Yes."

"To what?" I asked, although I already had a pretty good idea.

"To a room upstairs."

"You were awfully confident coming into tonight."

Jason disagreed, shaking his head. "I haven't come at all yet, Audrey."

I gave him a playful smile and a light shove. "Thought you didn't just want me for my body."

"I don't," he said. "But it's definitely an appealing bonus."

We couldn't very well abandon the reception when it was barely half over, so instead we did the responsible thing. We returned to our table and made "fuck me" eyes at each other for the next two hours.

Once most of the guests began filtering out, Jason took my hand and led me on a round of farewells. Dominic had loaned his tuxedo jacket to Melanie, and from the looks they kept exchanging, it was obvious they couldn't wait to be alone together either.

"Thanks for being here, man," Dominic said to Jason, and gave his best friend a brotherly hug.

Melanie gave Jason a kiss on the cheek, offered me another friendly hug, and returned to the protective custody of Dominic's arms.

"I hope you guys aren't in the room next to ours," Jason mused. "I have a feeling the walls are thin in this place."

"Jason," I hissed, nudging him, because even though I tended to lose my inhibitions in his presence, I wasn't used to hearing my upcoming sexual activities broadcast in the company of near strangers.

"What?" Jason said innocently. "I just want to make sure the night doesn't turn out awkwardly for everyone."

Melanie and Dominic simply laughed.

"Good night, Jay," Melanie called as she wrapped her arms around her new husband.

"Good night, Mr. and Mrs. Esposito," Jason said as he led me away with a hand on the small of my back.

Finally, the doors of an impressive copper-faced elevator closed behind us.

Jason pressed the button for the fourth floor and slipped his arms around my waist. "So here we are," he said, kissing my right shoulder.

I turned my head and kissed him, living in the moment. I didn't stop until the elevator opened again.

"This is a nice place," I said, checking out the Prohibition-era décor as Jason led me down the corridor. "Lots of vintage stuff. You know, I remember hearing about this hotel. There was a big legal battle a few years back between the city historical society and a developer who wanted to raze the property and build condos. What was the name again?"

"What name?" Jason asked as he swiped the card key in the door.

"Of the developer. I'm pretty sure it's someone Lester & Brown has done business with. One of your projects, I think."

"Audrey." Jason backed me into the wall and peered down at me with a heated expression. "If you say the words *Lester & Brown* or anything remotely work-related at all for the rest of the night, I might have to punish you."

I grinned up at him. "Lester & Brown."

In a swift caveman move Jason heaved me over one shoulder. I didn't even have time to yelp as he hauled me into the hotel room and deposited me on the huge bed.

"Don't test my patience again," he warned cheerfully as he shrugged out of his jacket, threw it on the floor, and started unbuttoning the cuffs of his shirt.

I slipped my heels off and leaned back on the bed on my elbows, deliberately edging my leg out of the side slit. "I received good intel from the sales department that they're going to be bidding on a new gigantic cancer hospital in Scottsdale. What do you think about that?"

He knelt at the foot of the bed and parted my legs. "I think you haven't learned your lesson."

I batted my lashes at him. "Perhaps I need to be trained."

Jason thought about it as his hands dove under my gown. I closed my eyes and let my head roll back, smiling to myself as Jason sucked in a surprised breath.

"Fuck, no panties," he groaned.

"Nope. The lines would be visible through the gown. Can't have that."

Jason pushed all the satin fabric above my waist and seized my hips in his hands. "You could have worn a thong," he pointed out, offering a teasing flick of his tongue along the inside of my thigh.

"Let's just say you're not the only one who was nursing a few expectations about tonight."

His hot tongue teased the other thigh. "Is that so?"

"Yes, in fact. Oh, shit, Jason!"

Words were now out of the question because Jason's tongue had changed tactics and was now deep inside me. I clutched the thick bed comforter in my fists, sank all the way down to my back, and arched my body eagerly into his mouth. It didn't take long for the first wave of convulsions to threaten me with oblivion, but Jason had other ideas. When I was mere seconds away from climax, he withdrew. Feeling slightly thwarted and frustrated, I opened my eyes to find him sliding on top of me, quick and sure as a panther. His pants were down and his face was an open book of desire and triumph mixed with tenderness that showed in his eyes when he gently uttered my name.

"Audrey," he said, and a longing filled his voice like I'd never heard before.

I ran my hand over his cheek. "I meant it," I whispered. "You've got me, Jason."

"You're perfect," he said with gruffness, and I wasn't sure exactly what he meant. I just knew that I loved hearing the words.

They echoed in my mind as I moaned at the feel of him entering my body, and kept me company in my dreams.

CHAPTER SIXTEEN

"I haven't seen your house yet," I reminded Jason the Friday after Melanie and Dominic's wedding. We'd spent every night together this week, but always at my apartment. Of course, it made more sense because I lived only three miles from work while Jason's house was a twenty-mile commute over freeways. But I was curious about what kind of habitat Jason Roma had made for himself. And since we'd chosen to have dinner at a steakhouse all the way over by Arizona State, I knew we couldn't be too far away from where he lived.

He looked up from his plate of steak and potatoes. "We can stay there tonight," he said, sounding a little surprised. "It's actually a good thing, since I've been neglecting the place all week. I only stopped in for fifteen minutes here and there to grab some clothes."

I chewed my own steak over our late dinner and wondered if I shouldn't have said anything. Staying at my place would be easier tonight because I was planning to come into work early tomorrow despite the fact that it was Saturday. This week I'd been so preoccupied after spending all my time with Jason that, even with twelve-hour workdays, I was falling behind. A stack of subcontractor invoices sat on my desk needing to be approved or denied by Monday. Since spending influenced the project's bottom line, I verified each one with care. Jason had offered to take half of the pile off my hands, but he'd been busy all week running around to a variety of meetings, and our division of labor meant those invoices were my responsibility.

But Jason seemed pleased that I wanted to see his house, so I said nothing about work or invoices or the fact that I'd need a ride back from Chandler early in the morning.

We left the steakhouse after nine, and I yawned as Jason opened the passenger door of his car for me.

"Don't tell me you're worn out this early," he said.

I stood beside his car and stretched my arms. "We've been up since six, worked from seven a.m. to seven p.m., and we didn't exactly get eight hours of sleep last night."

"Or the night before." He grinned.

"Or the night before that," I added, blushing over a few naughty flashbacks.

"You complaining?"

I wrapped my arms around him and leaned in for a kiss. "Never."

Jason responded by grabbing my ass right there in the parking lot. "Good to know. I've got plans."

"What kind of plans?"

"You'll like them. Very low maintenance. You won't even need to wear clothes."

"Thank god," I quipped. "Clothes can be such an impediment. Now take me to your house and do bad things to me."

The town of Chandler, east of Phoenix, swarmed with stucco master-planned communities and shopping malls. Jason pulled into a neat but unremarkable neighborhood called Lake Cove.

"Where's the lake?" I asked.

"The lake is an artificially constructed giant puddle filled with recycled wastewater."

"Charming."

"Yeah. My neighbors like to zip around in there in paddleboats and pretend they don't live in the desert."

I laughed as he turned onto Beach Drive.

Jason's house was a typical one-story, two-car-garage tract home in a neat cul-de-sac. It seemed like the kind of quiet, comfortable place a growing family might choose. I was having some trouble picturing Jason here amid the boxy homes and neat front yards, but he opened the garage door and pulled in.

"I should have stopped by my apartment first and grabbed some clothes," I said as the garage door groaned shut at our backs.

Jason stroked my thigh. "I thought I told you that you wouldn't be needing clothes."

"You did." I opened the car door. "But first I'll go check out your house."

Jason unlocked the door and I walked into the dark kitchen. Maybe I was subconsciously expecting mirror balls and inflatable dolls or a variety of bachelor-pad trappings that would remind me he was only a very recently reformed party boy. But Jason turned on the light and I blinked at a kitchen—neat and clean and completely ordinary.

"You want a beer?" he asked as he opened the fridge. Then he winced. "Fuck, I'm sorry." He searched the fridge and removed a pair of cans. "Here. Let's each have a soda instead."

I sighed. "Jason, it's okay. I told you the other night at dinner you can drink whatever you want. Have a beer. Have two. I promise I won't rip it out of your hands."

He looked slightly embarrassed as he set the cans down on the counter. "A glass of water is healthier."

"Great. I'll have one too, in that case."

Jason started flipping on lights as we wandered into the living room with our glasses of ice water. The furniture looked as if he'd ordered it from an office supply store. Maybe he had, given our hours. A large television shone from one wall and a huge industrial-style clock from the other, but otherwise the living room walls were bare.

Jason fiddled with the television remote. "I've just got to run outside for a minute and check on the irrigation system."

Arizona heat never lets up. I smiled at him. "You care if I wander around in the meantime?"

He raised an eyebrow. "Not as long as you eventually manage to wander into my bed."

Jason exited through the back sliding-glass doors, and I took a walk. The master bedroom possessed a little more personality than the living room. The light green walls formed a nice contrast to the dark wood furniture. I ran my hand over the dark gray down comforter on his large firm bed, feeling a deliciously wicked thrill about the fact that we'd be defiling its surface shortly. On the wall hung several small paintings—vibrantly colored, almost dreamy landscapes. I looked at them more closely and felt a jolt of recognition, because I'd gone through an artsy phase before I discovered sex and alcohol.

In those days I'd been a great admirer of painter Maxfield Parrish. Apparently Jason was too, although I'd never heard him mention anything remotely art related.

The bathroom was surprisingly neat for a single man, only a razor and a toothbrush visible on the white marble vanity. The closet yawned just beyond the bathroom, but I didn't really want to go thumbing through his wardrobe.

Outside the master bedroom I found a linen closet with no linen, a half bathroom, a small study with a bare wooden desk and a half-empty bookcase, but at the other end of the hall appeared another bedroom with an adjoining bath.

This room held a smaller bed covered with a plain blue quilt. On the opposite wall stood a single chest of drawers with a folded red polo shirt on top. This room did have a television. And the walls were also decorated with several Maxfield Parrish paintings. I sat on the bed to admire the view of one that looked like a Technicolor rendering of the Grand Canyon.

I was still sitting there lost in the picture when Jason found me.

"Guest room?" I asked him.

He sat down on the bed beside me. "In a way."

I pointed to the print I'd been staring at. "We have similar tastes in art."

"Those are originals."

"You're kidding."

"Nope."

"All of them?"

He nodded and looked up at the paintings. "My father bought them decades ago. They used to hang throughout our house. The collection was larger but it was sold off, along with just about everything else after he lost his company."

I could tell the topic troubled him. "It was a construction company, wasn't it?"

"Yup. I was in college when it all went sour. Combination of the housing crisis and shitty management. Can't say that losing his fortune did anything to improve my dad's personality."

I remembered the terrible things Jason had said about his father the night we went to Esposito's. I picked up his big hand and moved it to my lap when he sighed.

"He was already in his mid-forties when I was born," Jason said, frowning. "Maybe he had more patience when he was younger, but I doubt it. He didn't ever plan on being a father. Telling me that was the closest he ever came to an apology, I guess. Like I should understand that by the time I came around, he was a proven motherfucker. He wasn't going to adapt for some snot-nosed kid who accidentally scratched his Ferrari while running by with a stick. His mood would turn on a dime, and when that man snapped, you either ran for the hills or you wound up bleeding."

"What about your mother?" I asked.

He shrugged. "She saw what she wanted to see and spent half her time at the spa. Anyway, she found another meal ticket when the money stopped coming."

"He lives close by? Your dad?"

Jason turned quiet, staring at one of the Parrish paintings. I could feel all the old hurt emanating from him in painful waves. My own heart ached as I pictured a vulnerable little boy at the mercy of a monster. As much as I hated thinking about certain episodes in my own past, I had never endured the kind of trauma Jason had.

Suddenly Jason made a funny sound, kind of a half-smothered laugh. "Maybe I turned into an extraordinary douchebag because I was expected to be one. Looking back, there's a lot I'm not too proud of, Audrey. I treated people carelessly, especially women. I think you're probably aware of that. And, except for Dom and his family, I sure as hell never let anyone get too close."

"Oh, Jason," I soothed, resting my cheek against his shoulder and hoping the contact helped him feel less alone. We sat like that for a few minutes in comfortable silence.

Jason coughed suddenly. "You asked me if my father lived around here," he said.

I turned his hand over in my lap and stroked the palm. "Does he?"

"This is his room."

I straightened up with surprise. "Your father lives with you?" I asked, seeing the room with new eyes now. Not a guest bedroom, but an elderly man's. It didn't make sense, though. There were hardly any personal belongings visible in the room, and I was sure I hadn't seen anyone who looked like he might be Jason's father while I roamed about the house earlier. "Where is he?"

Jason shook his head. "He doesn't live with me. Sometimes I bring him here to stay for a day or two if he's not under any medical watches. He lives in the nursing home two miles down the road."

"That's why you moved here to Chandler," I said, beginning to connect the dots. "To help take care of your father." If Jason moved close to where his father was living and brought him home whenever he could, they must have repaired their relationship. "I'm sure he appreciates it."

"He doesn't remember me, Audrey," Jason said abruptly.

I was startled. "What?"

"My father had a stroke three years ago that left him with brain damage. His dementia has advanced over time, and at this point he doesn't remember who I am. Doesn't remember he even had a son. As far as he knows, I'm just some nice kid who brings him home sometimes, feeds him ice cream, and lets him watch all the television he wants."

"My god."

He responded with a bitter burst of laughter. "He sure as hell doesn't remember what a bastard he was either. He's downright fucking cheerful most of the time. Always happy to see me, even though he couldn't separate my face from that of the orderly who changes his bedpan. It's impossible to even hate him."

I let Jason's words sink in.

I felt like I understood, or at least I was beginning to. Jason hadn't forgiven his father for his terrible mistreatment as a child.

But how do you hold a grudge against a man who has become helpless?

How do you hate someone who doesn't remember what he did or who he wronged?

Jason was doing the right thing. He was a much better son than his father deserved. All the times I had thought to myself that Jason Roma was nothing but a selfish, hedonistic prick, I had no idea what I was talking about. I had no idea who he really was.

"I sure as hell never let anyone get too close."

I leaned over to kiss his cheek. "Thank you," I whispered in his ear.

He looked at me oddly. "For what?"

"For letting me get close to you."

Jason's eyes softened and he tucked a strand of hair behind my ear. "Thank you for taking the chance, Audrey."

I stood up and faced him, placing my palm tenderly against his cheek. He pressed my hand to his face and then kissed it before rising. Wordlessly I led him down the hall to the master bedroom. Once we were there we undressed each other carefully, our breathing and movements growing increasingly frenzied as passion began to take over. We didn't usually make love gently and it wasn't gentle now. We collided with unrepentant force again and again, crawling beneath the covers only when we were too sweaty and spent to do anything else. There in Jason's bed I cradled his head on my breasts and stroked his hair, letting my fingertips wander over his skin, feeling the small indentation behind his shoulder where a terrible scar lived. He sighed in his sleep with contentment, but I stayed wide-eyed in the darkness of his room for a long time, thinking how much more alike we were than I'd realized.

I had also long been out of the habit of letting anyone get close to me. But as I kissed Jason's head while he slept, the thought occurred to me that I'd never felt this close to anyone.

The problem was I wasn't sure if that fact frightened me more than it thrilled me.

CHAPTER SEVENTEEN

My hands gripped the steering wheel as I kept an eye on the dashboard clock.

"Relax," Jason warned when I nearly blew through a four-way stop sign. "I guess I should have driven."

"My parents do not take kindly to tardiness at their dinner table."

"We'll be far tardier if you crash the damn car, Audrey."

I threw him a look and he held up a hand in the name of peace.

"I'm a little on edge," I explained.

"I noticed."

"I want this to go well."

He patted my leg. "Don't worry. I know how to impress people when I want to."

I was about to explain that Aaron and Cindy Gordon were a little tougher to please than the average pair of sixty-year-old parents, but I held my tongue. If anyone understood complex parental relationships, it was Jason.

Last weekend he'd introduced me to his father. The man was in his seventies now, but in his prime he must have been as good-looking as his son, because I could see the shadow of Jason in his smile. And he smiled a lot. He beamed at us all throughout lunch, although he wouldn't eat until Jason reminded him. Jason was planning on bringing him back to the house, but his father grew agitated after an hour at the restaurant and kept asking to see Sally. Jason had to explain to me that Sally was a woman his father had been briefly engaged to nearly fifty years earlier.

The elder Roma's mood improved when we returned to the nursing home. As we were departing a nurse prodded him, "Now say goodbye, Chris." Jason's father waved at us with childlike enthusiasm. "Goodbye, Chris!" he shouted.

I couldn't imagine how Jason felt. He must have gotten used to it by now, the fact that his father had forgotten him. Perhaps it was even a relief. I still struggled to hide my tears.

"Nice house," Jason remarked as I pulled into the circular driveway of my childhood home.

I sat there for a moment staring at the familiar sight of the imposing mini-mansion before I cut the engine. "Yeah."

My mother had surprised me with the invitation last week. She hadn't stopped dropping hints that Dole Closterman could still be talked into giving me a chance, so I decided to tell her the truth.

"I have a boyfriend," I told her.

"A real one?" she asked with obvious skepticism, perhaps having a flashback to when fictional baby-daddy Diesel was invented.

So I sighed and brought her up to speed on Jason. I left out the part about our three-week sex marathon six years ago, of course, as well as our more recent one. She was just pleased to hear that he existed, that he was successful, and that I hadn't managed to chase him away yet.

"You need to bring him to dinner," she gushed.

I'd never brought a man to my parents' dinner table before and I wasn't too fond of starting now. Jason knew about me, knew about my struggles with addiction and how I'd been a source of despair for my parents for years until I cleaned up and stayed that way. But he'd only ever actually witnessed the capable version, the Audrey who had her head screwed on straight, who was a competent adult and paid all her bills on time. Somehow I was uneasy about bringing him into an environment where I had lived at my lowest. I didn't want him to ever look at me the way my parents had.

I tried to delicately put her off. "Well, Mom, thing is we're both crazy busy with the courthouse project, working long hours. Maybe in a few months things will calm down."

"Next Saturday night," she said, as if I hadn't even spoken. "Your father will be thrilled."

I couldn't imagine my father being thrilled about anything unless it had to do with money or a rare bottle of vintage Scotch.

"Okay," I said weakly, thinking I could come up with an excuse before the day rolled around. It shouldn't be hard. Surely Jason wouldn't want to spend an evening in my childhood home getting grilled about his pedigree.

But Jason turned out to be enthusiastic. He said he couldn't wait to meet the people who had produced Audrey Gordon.

And that's what brought us here, ringing the doorbell of my parents' home on a beautiful Saturday evening five minutes late. I tried not to feel like I was bracing to face the Inquisition.

My mother opened the door with a smile. Her face looked smoother, likely the result of some timely Botox injections, and she accepted my kiss on her powdered cheek before holding out a manicured hand to Jason. "I'm Cindy Gordon. Welcome to our home." I didn't miss the way her eyes swept over him with distinct approval.

"Thank you for the invitation." He flashed her the smile that always made my knees wobble. Apparently Jason Roma's effect on women was powerful enough to transcend generations, because my mother actually blushed a little as she accepted the bakery box he handed over.

I took his arm as we followed my mother through the foyer and into the dining room with the hopeful thought that maybe this wouldn't be so bad after all.

"Aaron," called my mother in her airy soprano. "Audrey and Jason are here."

My father materialized with an empty highball glass in his hand and an annoyed look on his face. "Cindy," he boomed, "didn't you instruct the landscapers to rip out all that damn bougainvillea?"

My mother frowned and set the box—containing a gourmet Bundt cake—down on an antique sideboard in the dining room. "I think I mentioned to Luanne that she needed to inform them on their next visit."

"That was yesterday and nothing's been done." He shook his head and set down his glass, grumbling, "Someone explain to me why no one ever has any goddamn personal accountability."

"Hi, Dad." I spoke up before my father could launch into one of his usual tirades about the epidemic of incompetence.

He blinked at me and looked less annoyed. *Slightly* less annoyed. "Audrey. Didn't even see you there."

Story of my life.

My father patted my back absently when I hugged him. "Dad, this is my boyfriend, Jason Roma."

The two men shook hands, and I saw the way my father's shrewd eyes scanned Jason, trying to assess his character and abilities so he could be categorized rapidly and accordingly.

"How do you do, sir?" Jason said, guessing that my father was the type who appreciated deference.

"Fine, thanks," my father replied somewhat coolly.

"I'll just go check with Luanne and see if dinner's ready," my mother said, disappearing down the long hall that led to the kitchen.

"Can I get you a drink, Jason?" my father asked, bringing his own glass for another visit to the nearby liquor cabinet.

Jason glanced at me. "No, thank you."

My father filled his glass again and swirled the liquor around, a move I've seen him do since I was a child and never really understood the meaning of. When I was eight, I tried it myself. Then I hid under the vast table and sipped from the glass, grimacing as the searing liquid burned my throat. William arrived home from lacrosse practice and caught me under there. He warned me to never do it again, but he didn't tattle on me then. Maybe he should have.

"Ah, so you're like Audrey," my father said offhandedly, "also not a drinker."

"Jason's not an alcoholic, Dad," I snapped. "That's only me."

My father looked somewhat embarrassed for a few seconds, but he recovered. "You originally from the Phoenix area, Jason?"

"Yes, I was born here."

"And your folks?"

Jason looked a little uncomfortable, as he usually did when prompted to talk about his family. "My father is still local. Used to own a construction company years ago."

My father snapped his fingers. "Christian Roma. Right?"

"Yes."

"Well, isn't that something," he boomed. "Lost track of Chris years ago, but he used to have a seat on the Chamber of Commerce. We often golfed together. How's he doing these days?"

Still looking uncomfortable, Jason replied, "Actually he's living in a nursing home. After his stroke, his dementia worsened."

"Sorry to hear it," my father said with a grimace.

I wondered if we'd be sitting down soon. With my father standing on one side of the dining room table and Jason and me on the other, we were almost positioned to face off in battle.

"I appreciate that," Jason said, and I took his arm as a gesture of comfort.

"Now that I'm thinking about it, Chris often mentioned you, Jason," my father said slowly. "You were a teenager at the time. Seems you got into some trouble now and then."

"Nothing major," Jason said. I could hear the wariness creeping into his voice. "Though I could be a bit of a hell-raiser at times."

"That's putting it mildly," my father scoffed, never taking his eyes off Jason, seeming to revel in his discomfort.

I cleared my throat. "I guess we've all done things in our formative years we're not proud of."

My father tipped his glass to me. "And I guess the laws of attraction are correct. Like really does attract like."

There was no opportunity to dwell on the ramifications of that statement because my mother returned with Luanne in tow. Luanne Barrie had been working for my parents since I was thirteen. Her Scottish brogue still gave her words a burr even though she'd left her homeland some forty years ago. She was really getting too old to tend to a house this size, but I knew my mother would keep her on as long as she wanted to remain.

"Hello, my beauty," Luanne said, hugging me. "And this gorgeous lad must be Jason."

Luanne's sturdy body had locked Jason into a full embrace before he even knew it was happening. He didn't seem bothered.

The stubborn old Scottish woman refused our offers to help serve dinner and brought out all the food herself before she left for the evening to return to the small house she shared with her grown daughter.

The more I thought about my father's last sarcastic comment, the angrier I got. I tried to set it aside. He'd obviously had one too many drinks tonight, and in all probability one of his business dealings had gone awry, which always triggered a foul mood.

We ate a simple but delicious combination of roast beef, vegetables, and sourdough biscuits that were Luanne's specialty. My father didn't say much, but my mother was chatty and upbeat enough for both of them.

"How's the hospital?" I asked her.

She fluffed her hair and sighed. "Busy. Political. As always. I've decided to retire next year."

"You're kidding." I was stunned. My mother thrived on constant productivity.

"I'll still have my committees with the museum and the historical society," she said a little defensively.

"And it'll leave you plenty of time to help William kick off his campaign," my father added.

I spread a generous amount of butter on a hot biscuit. "Did you check with William about whether he was agreeing to run?"

"I'll never retire," my father announced from the head of the table as if my question had not been posed. "There's no daily purpose without work. The mind starts to atrophy." He pointed a steak knife across the table. "Don't you think so, Jason?"

"I don't think my father's stroke resulted from the absence of fourteen-hour workdays," Jason responded. "Work is a living. It's not your life."

My father didn't like that sentiment. "It's both," he said with gravity. "Or you're not doing it right."

"Audrey," my mother spoke up, "will you please run to the kitchen and get the Bundt cake from the refrigerator?"

I glanced at Jason, uncertain whether I ought to leave him out here with my father. Jason was busy devouring the last of his roast beef and didn't seem at all out of sorts, so I figured he could hold his own.

The key lime pie was easy to find in the neatly stocked fridge. I grabbed a silver pie server from a drawer and returned to the dining room to find my mother asking Jason questions about the office.

"I'm lucky to be working so closely with Audrey," Jason told her. "She's a natural leader."

I smiled as I set the pie down and began slicing it up. "I think we make a good team."

"I didn't realize you were managing the courthouse project together," my father said, staring at me with an expression I didn't really like. "I assumed you were handling it on your own, Audrey."

"Audrey oversees the lion's share of the management," Jason spoke up, and I felt bad as I recognized what he was doing, diminishing his own role in order to satisfy my father. If he knew my father better, he'd understand that it was probably an impossible goal.

"We both manage the courthouse project equally," I announced, and started handing out pie.

"That's good," my mother said. "Like a partnership."

"Exactly," I agreed.

An hour later my parents walked us to the door. My father had thawed toward the end of the meal as he and Jason found common ground discussing sports.

"Thank you for dinner," I told my mother as I hugged her goodbye.

"Thank you for coming," she said with a surprising amount of warmth. "We'll have to do this again soon. And we'll invite William next time. Audrey, I've been meaning to ask. Do you have any friends you could introduce him to? It hurts to think about how lonely he must be living in that condo. You know he only has the boys every other weekend."

"Mom," I said gently, "I don't believe William is interested in meeting anyone right now. His divorce only just became final."

"Some people move on from divorce quite well," she countered. "Just look at Jennifer."

I didn't want to start bashing Jennifer right now, so I just sighed and let the conversation drop.

"Good night, Dad," I said.

"Good night, Audrey," he said. "Appreciate the visit."

Somehow the words made me cringe. Maybe it was the formality, as if I were an outsider.

But then he and Jason were shaking hands in a manner that seemed friendly enough, so I figured I should probably put my paranoia to bed for the evening.

The door closed and Jason and I returned to my car. "That went okay," he said with enthusiasm.

"It could have been worse," I agreed. Then I started rifling through my purse. "Shit. I took my phone out earlier to check my email. I must have left it on the front table. I'm just going to run in and grab it, okay?"

"I believe I can entertain myself out here for a moment," Jason said and smiled.

I hesitated to ring the doorbell. I hated seeming inept in any way, even if it was just leaving my phone behind for two minutes. I tried the handle. It was unlocked. Chances were my folks had moved on to some other part of the house and I could dart in and grab my phone without an encore farewell.

As the door creaked open I peered inside slowly, feeling as if I were sixteen years old and attempting to sneak in at two a.m. There was no one in sight. My phone in its purple sparkly case was sitting on the table where I'd left it, winking beneath the overhead crystal chandelier. I felt ridiculous as I crept in, but in another five seconds I would have what I came for and I could run back to the car and to Jason.

Then I stopped.

Their voices carried from the dining room. I paused to listen even as I suspected I would soon wish I hadn't.

"He seems nice," my mother said a little defensively.

My father grunted. "He seems like someone she'd pick."

"Aaron," my mother warned. "Give him a chance."

"I know the type, Cindy. Charming, superficial, and worthless when it comes to practical matters. And the two of them are assigned to this courthouse project together? It's a disaster in the making. Audrey won't be able to handle the pressure, and we'll be picking up the pieces again when she backslides."

My mother murmured something that sounded argumentative, but I didn't stick around to hear it. I snatched the phone and left, closing the door quietly behind me.

"You okay?" Jason said when I got back behind the wheel.

I tossed the phone on the dashboard. "Absolutely."

When I was a mile away I suddenly wished I hadn't closed their front door with such care.

I should have slammed the fucking thing with all my might.

CHAPTER EIGHTEEN

The May sun glared already, but if construction work took a break for the heat, then nothing would ever get built in Phoenix. Jason handed me a water bottle from one of the coolers that were scattered around on-site. I took it gratefully as I listened to the foreman detail all the work completed this week.

"We're ahead of schedule," I said, pleased as I consulted my notes.

Barnes bobbed his sweaty head with a grin. "As of right now, yes."

"Great job," Jason told him, clapping a hand on his shoulder.

Barnes wasn't one to brag, though. "I'm only as good as the guys we hire," he said with a shrug.

"It gives us all a little bit of breathing room," Jason said. "That's something to celebrate."

"Guys," I broke in. "We can't afford to take anything for granted, not with a project of this scope."

Barnes nodded. He'd spent twenty years on construction projects. He understood. "Agreed," he said.

"But you earned the weekend off," Jason said. "So take it. I don't want to hear that your shadow was glimpsed within a mile of here."

"Sounds good to me," Barnes said. "My kid's got a Little League tournament tomorrow."

Jason and I left Barnes behind to finish the rest of his workday and we headed for Jason's car.

I pulled my hard hat off. "I'm sweaty."

Jason turned on the ignition and set his hand on my thigh. "You could be sweatier."

"Behave." I pushed his hand away because a half-dozen construction workers were milling around nearby on their lunch break. A month had passed since Dominic and Melanie's wedding, the night that always stuck out in my mind as the official beginning of our relationship. We weren't denying that we were together, but I also saw no reason to set tongues to wagging. Management had asked no questions and I doubted they would. They'd been forced to reconsider their tacit disapproval of employee relationships when the chief financial officer married a twenty-two-year-old clerk from the purchasing department. These days, as long as the situation didn't interfere with the job or result in any hysterical scenes beside the water cooler, it wasn't a problem. Even if the personal relationship rule hadn't been unofficially relaxed, The Man had been treading lightly around me ever since the Bracero incident, and I liked to believe he felt some remorse. There'd been some buzz around the office for a while, but now that it had died down I didn't believe The Man would be interested in turning my relationship with Jason into an issue.

Jason was navigating traffic on the way back to the office when he said, "I vote that Barnes shouldn't be the only one to receive a reward."

"Jason, it's daylight." I laughed. "I'm not putting my head in your lap right now."

"I'm not asking for a blow job."

"Then what are you asking?"

He flashed that irrepressible grin he knew I couldn't refuse. "Skip town with me for a few days."

I hesitated. "Why don't we just stay local in case anything comes up?"

Jason picked up my hand and kissed it. "No. Let's get out of here. Out of the heat and the dust and at least a hundred miles from anything that has to do with the damn courthouse."

"We could stay at one of the nearby resorts," I suggested. "Wild Spring is only ten miles away and it's so lavish it would be like being out of town."

"Audrey, we both need a few days off. Come on, let's just go. It's not like we can't be reached via cell phone. At this point in the process, any emergencies could wait until Monday."

I tried one more time. "I thought you wanted to see your dad this week."

"I did. I went to see him on Tuesday when you insisted on staying at the office late. We watched Bugs Bunny cartoons in the lounge for two hours and ate a bag of oatmeal raisin cookies."

Jason was pulling into the parking garage at Lester & Brown. He swung the car into an empty spot and set the brake. "Audrey," he said again, dipping into a serious tone.

I looked at him. Jason reached out and pushed a strand of hair behind my ear before running his knuckles along the side of my neck in just the right way to induce a slight shiver.

"Come away with me," he whispered, no longer smiling, his eyes fixed on me with all the promise of a secret getaway.

"Where would we go?" I asked, knowing I didn't have the power to refuse him. Not when he looked at me like that.

"Leave the details to me," he said with triumph. "Just knock off work at a normal hour and run home to pack a bag. Oh, and make sure you include some comfortable clothes and shoes."

For the rest of the afternoon I was guilty of letting my giddiness interfere with the long task list I'd set for myself first thing in the morning. At four o'clock I looked over the remaining items on the list, decided none of them were critical, and made the decision to take off early.

"Are you sick?" Marnie wanted to know when I told her I was leaving for the day.

"A little," I lied, coughing once for effect.

Marnie recoiled. "Hope you feel better," she said, already beginning to hastily wipe down the reception counter in case any of my germs had found a home there.

Jason had volunteered to drive to Mesa to pick up a minor part that was needed on-site. On the way back he planned to stop at his house to grab a few necessities. When I got to my apartment I texted him that I was ready and then I dashed around, tossing items into a rolling suitcase and feeling deliciously spontaneous.

"Ready?" he asked when I opened the door.

I jumped into his arms with a heated kiss. "Ready." I would have been glad to head for the bedroom before traveling anywhere, but Jason wouldn't be deterred from his plans. He broke contact and seized my bag from the floor.

"Let's get moving. It's a two-hour drive."

"What is?"

"Sedona."

The picturesque town full of towering red rocks and spiritualists was a favorite destination for both locals and out-of-state tourists. I wasn't a big believer in things like healing rocks and auras, but I couldn't deny the calming energy that hovered over the place and crept beneath my skin the instant we crossed into the Sedona city limits.

"Do you think there are really vortexes everywhere here?" I asked, peering through the windshield at a particularly majestic red rock formation just barely visible beneath the darkening sky. I snapped a photo with my phone. "Places where energy rises from the earth?"

"Don't know." Jason shrugged. "I've never been a student of New Age stuff."

"They say if you come across one you'll feel a wave of inner peace."

Jason gave me a sidelong glance. "If you want, I can offer you some inner peace in a few minutes, Audrey."

"I think your version is probably different."

"I think you're right."

Jason had booked a room in a resort outside the busy downtown mecca, nestled against the peaceful Oak Creek. Night had fallen, but as I stood on the balcony overlooking the wilderness, it was easy to imagine the beauty just beyond my reach.

I smiled when Jason came up behind me, kissing my neck. "I'm glad you talked me into this," I said.

"I'm glad you agreed," Jason said, gently turning me around for a more complete kiss.

I leaned into him, stretching up and pressing my body against his, reveling in the familiar arousal that surged every time we got close. We hadn't eaten dinner, yet another more urgent hunger claimed priority. Jason deftly unzipped my skirt and slipped his hands into my panties. I loosened his belt and began tugging on his pants, desperate to uncover the hard bulge within, my eagerness to feel him inside of me reaching a crescendo.

"Want you," I whispered, then moaned as his fingers pushed their way in, teasing me almost to the brink.

Jason laid me down on the bed before hastily stripping his clothes off. I admired the defined expanse of his smooth chest, the muscles coiling in his shoulders as he settled his body on top of me. I gripped his waist with my knees, anticipating the powerful thrust that I ached for, but he took his time, slowly unbuttoning my blouse, unhooking my bra with care, rolling his tongue over each nipple and then covering my right breast with his hot mouth.

"Jason," I panted, clutching his shoulders, bucking underneath him, ready to beg for satisfaction. "Please."

Only then did he pull his mouth away and cup my narrow hips in his strong hands to deliver the hard push we both needed. But, for a moment, he hovered there. "Audrey."

I looked up at him, getting lost in the dark eyes that could be playful and passionate all at once. This time they were neither. Jason looked at me with almost solemn reverence. We lingered in that peace for a moment and then, without warning, Jason drove himself in deep again and again. I welcomed every battering thrust and came with so much force a tiny scream ripped from my throat. Jason waited until I had my fill and then he convulsed with a string of curses and finished with a sigh into my neck.

"Every time," I whispered with wonder, stroking his sweaty back. "It's so good every time."

He kissed my forehead. "Always will be."

Eventually we did get hungry enough for a more practical meal. Jason ordered the most expensive room service items on the menu and we ate on the quiet balcony while listening to the music of the night.

Sleep came only after a few more energetic rounds of sex, and once I drifted off into unconsciousness in the shelter of Jason's arms, I did not awaken until sunlight flooded the room.

"Let's get out there," Jason suggested while I was still rubbing my eyes and yawning. "Look at that view. Maybe we'll run into one of those inner-peace-vortex things."

"I'll go anywhere with you if you just get me some coffee first," I promised, still yawning.

Once I was fed, showered, and properly caffeinated, I became more eager to leave the room. Jason wanted to go hiking and enjoy a picnic lunch on the trail. I was a little dubious because I hadn't been hiking in years, but to my relief he at least didn't have any grand ideas about scaling the towering red rocks. The picturesque trail in the woods had almost a fairy-tale quality with its babbling brooks and canopy of wispy vegetation. Here and there it was possible to get a glimpse of the stunning rock formations that loomed everywhere. We shared sandwiches and bottled water while perched atop a pair of large flat rocks overlooking a creek. I didn't know if the vortexes were real or if they really soothed the soul. People supposedly traveled to Sedona from all over the world in search of the opportunity to find out. But I did know inner peace was the most elusive human condition, and as I sat beside the creek in the company of the man I was crazy about, I thought this was about as close as I'd ever come to feeling it.

In a remarkable departure of habit, I didn't check my phone for hours that afternoon. I told myself there probably wasn't a signal this far into the woods anyway. That might have been true. Or if I had checked it sooner, I might have seen a message that would have crushed my delicate balance of harmony.

CHAPTER NINETEEN

The sun was beginning to drop over the horizon by the time Jason and I returned to our room at the resort.

"Let's eat downstairs at the restaurant tonight," I suggested, kicking off my sneakers.

He boxed me in against the wall and immediately ran his lips along my neck. "Personally I'd rather stay in again."

I giggled as his hands began roaming. "I'd like to eat my dinner wearing clothes tonight. Now let me shower."

"Let me join you."

"Then we'll never get out of here. Stay," I warned, slipping out of his grip.

Jason looked displeased, but he remained where he was while I dragged my bag into the bathroom with me.

After standing under the steamy shower spray for a few minutes, I began to regret keeping Jason away. But then my belly grumbled and I reasoned we'd have plenty of time after dinner to revisit the shower at a more leisurely pace. I toweled off and dried my hair quickly before slipping into a plain black cocktail dress that would suit nearly every occasion. The mirror was still steamed over, so I decided to grab my makeup bag and use the mirror in the room. Besides, Jason might be growing irritated over waiting so long for the shower.

I knew something was wrong as soon as I opened the door. Jason was sitting on the bed staring at his phone with a somber expression. He looked up and pasted a smile on his face when I entered the room.

"Hey there, gorgeous. You save some hot water for me?"

I threw my makeup bag on the bed. "What is it?"

Jason raked his hand through his hair and looked away. "You should check your phone."

"Tell me why."

He exhaled heavily before stating the bad news. "The county put a temporary halt on the project. They're saying they never received the right paperwork for the finalized architectural changes."

"What?" I shrieked, my heart pounding as I snatched his phone away so I could read the flurry of emails that had been exchanged this afternoon between Lester & Brown, the county, and the architectural firm Lukas worked for.

"I don't understand," I said, reading as fast as I could. "I don't understand at all. That paperwork was submitted over a month ago. They responded with an approval."

"Conditional approval," Jason corrected me gently.

As I skimmed through the email details, I understood what he meant. A finalized hard copy of the revised blueprints needed to be delivered to the county's downtown Phoenix office within thirty days of the conditional approval. I'd been handling all that communication regarding the architectural changes Lukas had designed, so that task fell to me. Somehow I'd overlooked that detail at the time I'd received that conditional approval. Jason had been copied on the communication, but following up was my responsibility. This was one hundred percent my fault.

The blood roared in my head as I scrolled through the rest of the messages. I heard myself speaking as if from far away. "So as of this afternoon all work on the courthouse project has been frozen. Oh my god, Jason. Oh my god." I dropped his phone and pitched forward with my head in my hands.

"Audrey, honey. Breathe." Jason's arm wrapped firmly around me. I might have fallen to the floor without it. "It will be all right."

Obstacles and constant challenges came with the territory when managing large-scale construction projects. I was used to that. Usually I could face them head-on with determination. But never had I personally fucked up in such a major way. It was galling to think I must have been so distracted in the throes of my exciting new love life that I hadn't thoroughly read the county's instructions.

Vaguely I heard Jason talking through my fog of panic.

"It's Saturday," he said. "There was only minimal work happening there today anyway. And tomorrow there's no labor on-site. We'll get this all sorted out on Monday morning."

I lifted my head. "We need to go back tonight, Jason. This can't wait until Monday."

He shook his head. "The county office is closed and will be closed tomorrow. Even if we left right now, by the time we get back to the valley it'll be almost ten. And like I said, it's Saturday night. Nobody will be available. We might as well stay here. We can call The Man to assure him that we're handling the situation and cc everyone on the chain, explaining the same thing." He gave me a comforting squeeze. "We'll handle it together."

I looked at him. "It's not your fault, Jason. It's mine. I'll let everyone know that."

He scowled. "We're partners in this, Audrey. I'm just as responsible for anything that goes wrong as you are." He tipped my chin up, and his eyes seemed to peer straight into my soul. "Didn't I tell you that I've got your back?"

I stood up and twisted my hands together as I paced. I felt nauseated and stupid and every ounce the fuckup my own father was convinced still lurked within me.

Worst of all, for the first time in years, I really, *really* felt tempted to take a drink.

My eyes landed on the small refrigerator tucked beneath the television. There had to be something containing alcohol in there. As the thought crossed my mind, a sudden ache blossomed deep within in a place I'd taken care to bury. It was the repulsively familiar desire to satisfy a destructive craving. And, like a volcano, it had only been dormant, not dead.

I smoothed my hands on my dress, more shaken over the thoughts that were racing through my head than over the courthouse debacle.

Taking my phone from atop the dresser where I'd left it, I said, "I'm going to call Marty."

"Put him on speaker," Jason ordered, coming to my side.

I paused. "He might wonder why we're hanging out together on a Saturday night."

Jason shrugged. "Then let him wonder."

The Man didn't wonder at all why Jason and I were huddled together in the same place or why we'd been unavailable all afternoon. He just wanted to hear that the problem would be solved with no significant delay.

"I will be there with the blueprints in hand when the county offices open on Monday morning," I promised.

"We'll take care of it," Jason added. "There will be no delay."

The Man sighed and told us we needed to draft an email to that effect so that everyone could breathe a little easier tonight.

After we ended the call, Jason showered while I wrote out an apologetic email ending with the assurance that everything would be resolved on Monday. Then I listened to make sure Jason was still in the shower and gritted my teeth while I did an unpleasant thing. I texted a message to Lukas Lund asking him for a favor.

Jason emerged from the bathroom with his pants undone. If I'd been a little less frazzled, I would have appreciated the way his wet hair dripped onto his muscled shoulders. I would have crept up to him and planted a kiss on the smooth skin just below the hollow of his throat.

"You shaved," I noticed.

He put a hand to his face and smiled at me in the mirror. "Beard was getting itchy."

"Are we still going to dinner?" I asked. I didn't really feel like eating.

"Sure," Jason said as he pulled a clean blue shirt on. "Everyone deserves dinner, Audrey."

He winked at me and I managed a small smile, remembering when he'd said those same words to me once before, the night we ended up at my apartment.

I could feel Jason's eyes on me as I carried my makeup bag to the mirror and quickly applied the basics.

When we were leaving the room, my phone buzzed with a new message. It was Lukas saying he'd be glad to help in any way he could in the wake of this misunderstanding. Jason was watching me as I read the message.

"Just my brother," I told him, and tossed the phone into my purse. Jason and Lukas had never really resolved their issues after their public brawl. I felt guilty over the lie, but to get this situation resolved quickly and painlessly, I needed Lukas's cooperation. I couldn't let anything get in the way of that.

With the restaurant fairly crowded, the hostess asked if we minded being seated beside the bar. I actually did mind, given my upset, but not enough to languish in the lobby until another table became available.

Jason, sensing I was hopelessly preoccupied, did a lot of the talking at dinner. He was trying to make me laugh, regaling me with stories about the kind of trouble he and Dominic used to find in their late teens and early twenties. I got the feeling he was leaving a lot of gaps in his wild tales.

"Sounds like you guys were quite the party animals," I commented, eyeing a bottle of wine that was being carried past.

When my gaze returned to Jason, he had a funny look on his face and I wondered if he had noticed, if he could tell that I had imagined grabbing that wine bottle and guzzling until I had to stop for breath. Then I decided I was being paranoid. Jason Roma possessed a wide range of talents but he couldn't read minds. And anyway, just because the thought flashed through my mind didn't mean I'd actually do it. I was in control. I was fine. One piece of bad news wouldn't change that. I'd had bad news before.

Our food arrived and even though it smelled delicious, I mostly picked at it, pushing pieces of chicken marsala across the plate.

"You want to try mine instead?" Jason asked, pushing his plate over. I shook my head. "No, thank you."

Jason got to his feet. "Need to go to the men's room, so feel free to change your mind in my absence." He smiled and tossed his napkin on the table.

I took a bite of my chicken after he left. I stared at the people cluttering up the space around the bar. They were mostly young and beautiful and full of laughter. Envy pricked at me as I observed the casual way they held their drinks. Like most adults, they were just indulging in fun, fully capable of stopping anytime they needed to. They probably weren't bound to their bad habits. Or maybe they were. Sometimes you couldn't tell.

With a sigh I took a sip of water and then looked up in time to notice Jason was returning. Abruptly his head whipped around in the direction of the bar as if someone had shouted his name. A second later I saw who it was. She couldn't have been a day over twenty-five. Her honey-colored hair reached halfway down her back, and the tight red dress she wore showed off every impressive feminine curve. She was approaching my boyfriend with her arms out and a wide smile parting her full lips. As she trapped Jason in an embrace, he glanced back at me with an apologetic look.

The girl's eyes dimmed when Jason edged out of her hug. They dimmed further as he spoke to her. She took a step back and her perfect features clouded as she touched his arm in farewell and then returned to the collection of people gathered around the bar.

"Did you find a friend on the way back from the bathroom?" I asked a little sarcastically.

He shrugged. "Gabby just came over to say hello."

"It appeared she intended to do more than that."

Jason gave me a puzzled look. "So what? I told her I was here with my girlfriend, Audrey. That was the end of it."

I sighed. "I didn't mean to sound jealous."

He grinned. "It's okay, it's kind of cute."

I looked toward the bar again and noticed that Gabby had been staring at us. She quickly snapped her head in the opposite direction when she saw me watching.

"How long did you guys date?" I asked Jason.

His eyes shifted. "I didn't say we dated."

"Okay, how long did you guys know each other?"

He shifted in his seat and stirred gravy into his mashed potatoes with a fork. "Not long. Met her at a mutual friend's Christmas party last year."

"That wasn't too long ago."

"I suppose."

"And you weren't dating her."

"No."

"Just fucking her."

He let the fork drop on his plate with a clatter. "What do you want to hear, Audrey? I was no angel and you know it." He grabbed my hand and gazed intently into my eyes. "She doesn't matter. All there is now is us."

I didn't know what had made me lash out other than the fact that I was distressed over the situation at work. Maybe I was searching for a way to not be the lone screwup today. In any case I had no right to take out my angst on Jason. I had no doubt that I was the only woman in his life. I covered his hand with my other one. "You're right. I'm sorry."

Jason smiled and kissed my hand like the prince he was.

Later we attacked each other as soon as we were back in the room. We screwed standing up against the wall and moved to the shower where I urged him to go harder, harder, and *fucking harder* still, even though my back would probably be sore the next day after knocking so forcefully against the wall tiles. Then I sank to my knees right there in the steam and finished him with my mouth. We retreated to the room and collapsed on the bed in an exhausted, wet pile, but I knew Jason had enough stamina to be ready again soon. He was. I climbed on top and rode him at a frenetic pace until I shook and came. Then he took charge, flipping me over and ending the job from behind.

We crawled beneath the covers sometime after one a.m. and Jason stroked my back. "Everything is going to be fine, Audrey," he soothed, undoubtedly trying to comfort me because he understood me well enough to know I wouldn't be able to stop worrying about my epic mistake.

"I know," I said, and wished I had a better talent for lying.

Jason was asleep when I slid out of bed and wrapped myself in his shirt before settling down on a leather armchair positioned opposite the television. There in the darkness with my boyfriend sleeping ten feet away, I drew my knees up to my chest and stared at the tiny refrigerator, wondering how the minibar was stocked. This was a classy resort. There might be an entire bottle of wine in there.

I never did open it to find out. But I did stare at the closed door for a long time before returning to bed.

CHAPTER TWENTY

On the drive home Jason mentioned that he planned on going to see his father later in the afternoon and take him out to eat, maybe bring him back to the house for a little while. He extended an invitation to me, but I said I was tired.

"I wore you out, huh?" he joked, placing a confident hand on my knee.

"Indeed," I said.

He carried my suitcase to my apartment door like a gentleman, and I kissed him tenderly before burying my face in his warm chest.

"Thank you for an amazing weekend," I murmured, wishing I could stay just like this for a few hours with my cheek pressed to his chest.

Jason's arms circled me. "The county offices open at nine. The architects open for business at eight. Why don't you get some rest and I'll meet you there in the morning? They can produce a clean copy of the plans, and then we'll drive straight over to the county office and drop them off. They'll lift the freeze and work should resume by the afternoon. I remember something like this happened once on a City of Surprise project I was working on. It's just bureaucracy, Audrey. It'll get sorted out."

"Okay," I said, feeling guilty because I had other plans, plans I couldn't tell him about.

He kissed me once more and started to walk away.

"Jason?" I called, with a sudden surge of panic that this moment right here was a turning point, that if I couldn't be honest with him right now, then I might lose him later.

He had turned around and was waiting to hear what I had to say.

"I'll see you in the morning," I said.

He grinned. "Yeah, you will."

Once I was inside my apartment, I went out to the patio and watched his car drive away. Then I immediately made a phone call.

"Can you still meet?" I said into the phone. "I don't mind coming to you. I really appreciate this."

Half an hour later I was knocking on Lukas Lund's door. He opened it almost immediately, wearing a white T-shirt, jeans, and a disarmingly friendly expression.

"Come in, Audrey," he said, standing aside.

I hesitated before stepping over the threshold. "I really do appreciate this, Lukas."

He nodded. "You mentioned that already."

"Well, I wasn't sure you'd be eager to help me after what happened the last time we saw each other."

"Eh." Lukas waved a hand. "Not my finest moment. I couldn't really blame the guy for getting territorial, and I wouldn't have pushed my nose in if I'd realized you and Jason were together." He paused. "You are together, right?"

"We are," I said, looking around his condo. The walls were covered with the baseball memorabilia I remembered seeing at his last place.

"Give me a second and I'll get what you need," Lukas said, disappearing down the hall.

The glass balcony doors were slightly ajar. I slid them open farther and took in the view of downtown Phoenix. Noise bubbled out of Chase Field next door, and I could see there was a baseball game under way.

I turned around when I heard the soft shuffle of Lukas's bare feet on the hardwood floor. He was holding a pair of rolled-up architectural plans for the county courthouse.

"Thank you," I breathed as he handed them over. "I'll get these turned in first thing in the morning, and hopefully they'll lift the halt right away."

"I'm sure they will," Lukas said to reassure me. "They want their courthouse built as much as you want to build it."

"Lukas." I tucked the plans under one arm and swallowed. "Thank you again. It would have been easy for you to throw me under the bus here."

He stared at me. "I wouldn't do that, Audrey."

The crowd at Chase Field roared and I looked over.

"Sounds like a home run," I observed, staring down at the sea of cheering people.

"Does he deserve you?" Lukas asked almost under his breath.

I looked up into his clear blue eyes. They weren't hurt or angry. Just curious.

"Yes," I said. "He does."

"Good," Lukas said. "Then please tell him I'm sorry for trying to sucker punch him."

I hugged the plans and moved away from the glass door. "I should let you get back to your Sunday afternoon."

He smiled. "I didn't mind the interruption at all."

"Goodbye, Lukas."

I went straight home after leaving Lukas's place. For a moment I considered texting Jason and offering to meet up with him and his dad. But I dreaded telling him I had been to see Lukas. Plus I wanted to spend the evening taking a second look at all my recent emails to make sure nothing else had slipped through the cracks. For the last month I'd been so consumed with all things Jason, it was no wonder I'd managed to screw up somewhere. Now wasn't the time for either of us to get used to goofing off. It was time to take stock of the things that were important.

By the time I was finished sorting through all my communications for the last month, it was close to midnight, and I fell asleep confident that I hadn't missed anything else. And I had no intention of missing anything in the future.

In the morning I awoke with a feeling of purpose. All I needed to do was be there at the county offices when they opened at nine, hand over the plans, and beg for the project to restart. I texted Jason at seven to let him know he didn't need to meet me at the architects' building to retrieve the plans. I nervously awaited his reply, figuring he would want to know why that portion of the plan had been scrapped.

He didn't want to know why. Somehow he already knew.

Jason: I heard.

I frowned over the message. But Jason didn't explain further, nor did he answer my next text when I let him know that I could handle the visit to the county offices myself.

I was the first person waiting in line for the county building to open, and as soon as I called my contact, Lacy Acker, to let her know that I was present with the plans in hand, she came down to the lobby and ushered me upstairs. After I presented the plans, I apologized for all this grief at least three times to every person I saw, even a roaming janitor, figuring it couldn't hurt. Lacy Acker left me waiting in her office while she personally obtained the go-ahead to resume work on the courthouse project now that this particular bureaucratic box had been checked off. I heaved an audible sigh of relief when Lacy made the call to The Man that the construction crews were free to return to the property. Before I left I shook the poor woman's hand so hard it nearly fell off, but I was jubilant, floating on air as I left the building, firing off a text to Jason to let him know all was well now. I even sang along to the car radio as I inched through downtown Phoenix traffic.

Walking into Lester & Brown I was still grinning like an idiot. I kept grinning until I got to my office.

Jason looked up from his laptop when I walked in. My first instinct was to run over and kiss him in celebration. But I could tell at once that he wasn't pleased about something.

"Don't tell me there's more bad news," I groaned, sinking into my chair. "We just got one major hassle resolved. It would be nice to enjoy at least twelve hours without another."

"*We* didn't get anything resolved," Jason said. He snapped the laptop lid closed.

Panic flared. "What are you talking about? I just came from Lacy Acker's office. The crews should be back on-site within an hour."

Jason stared at me for a long, silent moment. I had a feeling I wouldn't like whatever was going on behind his narrowed eyes. I was right.

"*We* didn't get anything resolved," he repeated. "You ran around and did it all yourself. Audrey Gordon, one-woman show."

I sighed. "Is that seriously what's bugging you? That I took care of this without your help? It was my fuckup, Jason. Of course I should be the one running around like my hair's on fire."

He crossed his arms over his chest. "And that's why you had to go to Lukas's place without telling me?"

How in the hell did he know about that? "He was willing to help out and get me the plans so I wouldn't have to worry about begging for them this morning. That's all it was, Jason."

Yet I knew my defense was a partial lie. I hadn't told Jason because I knew he'd object. The trouble between him and Lukas might have gotten in the way of my opportunity to obtain the blueprints and get a head start on fixing the mess I'd made. And I'd prioritized that above all else.

"I know," Jason said, but there was an ominous quality to his voice. "He told me."

"You talked to Lukas?"

"Yes, I talked to Lukas."

"So you're all pissed off I went to see him before you could go behind my back and do the same thing?"

He glared. "I was trying to spare you the chore of seeing him."

"It wasn't a chore. It took five minutes. Lukas was pleasant the entire time."

"He was *pleasant*? He's an ex who scared the shit out of you once, and I don't fucking trust the bastard."

"Jason, seriously, it was no big deal. He seemed glad to help. Anyway, what kind of conversation did the two of you have?"

"I gave him a call last night. Told him I wanted to clear the air between us and asked him if there was any possibility he might hand the plans over to me to give you one less thing to worry about. Turns out there was no need. You'd already been there to get them yourself."

I winced. "I know I should have mentioned it. But I thought you'd just worry. Or else you'd insist on coming along, and like I said, this was my fuck up. My mess to deal with."

Jason shook his head and looked away. "I don't get you, Audrey," he said in a wounded tone. "I thought we were on the same page. I assumed we were a team, in more ways than one."

"We are. It's just—"

"What?" he snapped.

"There's a lot at stake right now," I said, crossing my arms. "We've been so wrapped up in each other."

"And that's a bad thing?"

"It might be when we're trying to manage a two-hundred-million-dollar project together. Maybe we should cool it a little bit. Until the courthouse is done."

"That will be a year from now," he said quietly. "An entire goddamn year that you want to put us on freeze for."

"Jason," I choked out. None of this was coming out right. "You know how I feel about you."

"No, actually, I have no fucking idea how you feel about me, Audrey. But if you're interested, I'll tell you how I feel about you."

A sour taste filled my mouth and I had to bite my lip to keep it from quivering. I'd always prided myself on being a woman who didn't cry often. I've had macho assholes screaming in my face before and I didn't even blink. This was a different kind of pressure. Jason might say the kind of words that would actually make me crack.

"Are you interested?" he asked sharply when I didn't respond right away.

"Yes," I whispered.

Jason pushed out of his chair and crossed the small room. He pulled me to my feet before cupping my face in his hands and bending down a little so we were eye to eye.

"We're the same, Audrey, always have been. Both of us cut from the same damaged cloth. Both of us hell-bent on proving we're worth more than the sum of our past screwups combined. But in spite of all that bullshit bad history, I believe there's nothing we can't do together. You'd believe it too if you'd let yourself. And if that's not enough, then you should know that I'm absolutely fucking crazy about you."

I was crazy about him too. But those wild highs that surged through me when I was with Jason might prove to be a risk to my career, even my stability. I'd wrapped myself up too far in my job at this point, and I was afraid. I was afraid that work was the thing keeping me grounded, the thing that had defined the person I'd become. Without that constant focus I might flounder, I might backslide. My father hadn't been the one to plant the idea in my head. It was already there.

Plus, if Jason and my father were right, that we were essentially two sides of the same coin, was that really a good thing?

Even if I'm in love with him.

We were still eye to eye, still so close that anyone glancing in would know with certainty that we were lovers. Jason must not have liked what he saw in my face as my thoughts careened around, because he was already inching away when my phone started beeping.

"There's a meeting," I said, hating the lifeless sound of my own voice. "The weekly departmental meeting. That was the five-minute notification."

Jason took a big step away from me. I looked down. I didn't need to see his face to know I'd disappointed him. He'd asked me for optimism and I'd silently refused to have any.

I picked up a legal-sized notepad. I felt drained, ten years older than I had the moment I walked in here. The thought of losing Jason made me want to retch my guts out into the wire wastebasket.

My calendar reminder beeped again.

"Are you coming to the meeting?" I asked him.

He nodded without looking at me. "In a minute."

"I can wait for you," I said, watching his back. If he turned around now, I'd go to him. I'd run into his arms and tell him yes, that I believed we could do anything together. I'd tell him he was worth more than any job, any project, any career.

But Jason didn't turn around.

"Go ahead," he said. "I won't stand in your way."

He walked into the conference room a minute after I did. We sat on opposite sides of the table and avoided each other's eyes the entire time.

CHAPTER
TWENTY-ONE

"Are you and Jason fighting?" Helen asked over a lunch of wedge salads after she dragged me out of the office for a little while.

"We're not fighting at all," I said truthfully, because Jason and I weren't fighting. We'd scarcely spoken to each other in the four days that had elapsed since that emotional Monday morning confrontation, but I reasoned it couldn't be considered fighting if we communicated through terse work-related text messages. I hated the way things were right now between us, but the week had been hellish. It seemed the second work resumed on the courthouse site, a series of mishaps ranging from vandalized raw materials to a vanished crew of laborers had taken up the bulk of our attention. Jason had spent most of his time on-site this week and that might have been justified by the recent spate of disasters. Or it might have been because he was avoiding the tense atmosphere of our shared office.

On my end, I was bouncing between the jobsite and the office, clocking late hours as I tried to iron out some contract issues with our subcontractors. All week I'd been among the last to leave the building every night. I was sure Jason was working hard too, although he probably didn't go home and read through all the day's emails and texts one more time before collapsing into a brief, fitful sleep.

I missed him. I especially missed him at night. Sleeping alone is an empty feeling when you're yearning to have someone specific at your side. Even though I knew exactly where to find Jason virtually every minute of the day, a wide chasm yawned between us, and I was unsure how to cross it. The idea of losing him scared the shit out of me. Yet I didn't have the time or the energy right now to give him a more complete commitment.

"Audrey, earth to Audrey," said Helen, waving a hand in front of my face.

I blinked. "Sorry, what was the question?"

My coworker and friend raised an eyebrow. "No question, doll. You said that you and Jason weren't fighting, and then your eyes glazed over while you stared at that old man in the corner."

The old man in the corner turned out to be squeezing the contents of a salad dressing packet directly into his mouth.

"Purely unintentional," I said. "I must have blacked out for a moment."

Helen finished off the last of her food and gazed at me with a small frown. "Wouldn't surprise me, with all the hours you've been working. Do you ever sleep, Audrey? I swear you could stuff all your leftovers in those bags under your eyes," she claimed, pointing to my bowl of picked-over fried rice.

I raised my water glass. "Here's to friends who don't mince words."

Helen shrugged. "You should know I have no off switch. We've worked together for five years."

"Seven," I corrected her.

"Has it really been that long?"

"Yes."

"Shit," she swore. "I've got to find another job."

Helen didn't bring up Jason's name again, but she didn't let me leave the table without dispensing some advice.

"Give yourself a break now and then," she said. "The earth won't quit turning if you're not hovering over your laptop twenty hours a day."

Helen meant well, but our jobs weren't in the same category. When five o'clock on Friday rolled around, she could leave her desk and have faith that no accounting emergencies were likely to arise before Monday. She didn't bear my level of responsibility.

Surprisingly, Jason was at his desk when I walked into the office after lunch.

"Hey, you," I said, pleased to see him and hoping to clear the air between us.

He glanced up. "Hi."

I shoved my purse under my desk and sat down, checking out the blazer casually draped across the back of his chair. Jason usually dressed well, but a suit was uncalled for, especially if he'd spent the morning shuffling around in the dust at the courthouse site.

"Did I miss an important meeting or something?" I asked, realizing he wasn't going to do much to ignite the conversation.

"Not that I'm aware of."

"Then why the suit?"

He shifted in his chair. "I had an interview."

"What are you talking about? Like a job interview?"

"Exactly like a job interview."

I had to make a conscious effort to close my jaw and take a deep breath. Jason had never mentioned he was looking to move on.

"Jason." I eased out of my chair and crossed the room to perch on the edge of his desk. I wanted to touch him, but I would have had to lean all the way forward in order to reach his arm. "What's going on?"

He swiveled in his chair to face me. "It's not what you think," he said.

"What do I think?"

"That I'm having a temper tantrum in response to what happened this week."

"Are you?"

His lips thinned. "No."

I looked down at my nails. They were bitten down to the quick, an old, disgusting habit I hadn't realized I'd resumed. "But you're leaving."

"I didn't say that. I sent a résumé over to Barrow Brothers months ago, before the courthouse project was assigned, before we got together. They gave me a call on Tuesday out of the blue, so I figured it wouldn't hurt to go down there for an hour."

"And?" I asked, dreading what the answer would be.

Jason sighed and leaned back in his chair. "And the compensation package is competitive and the bulk of their projects are in the East Valley, which would cut down on my commute. It's a smaller company than Lester & Brown but family-owned, probably less bullshit office politics."

You're leaving me.

I lowered my head so he wouldn't see that I was a breath away from crying. "Are you going to take it?"

"I haven't decided."

It wasn't the most devastating reply he could have given, but it knocked the wind out of me a little.

Jason reached for me and I gladly went to him, allowing myself to be enveloped by the strong arms I loved so much. I raised my head and met his lips, softly at first, a kiss of tenderness and apology that quickly escalated. His hand crept beneath my blouse and my mouth moved to his neck, sucking the skin just enough to induce a soft moan from him.

"Fuck, I miss you," he growled, sliding his hand higher, underneath my bra.

"I'm right here," I whispered, kissing his neck, his chin, his cheeks. Jason was the man I wanted. I couldn't imagine feeling differently. I'd make it all up to him for being so immersed in work lately that I'd put him on the back burner of my life. It wouldn't always be this way. There would be time later.

"We'll go out tonight," he said with conviction as his palm playfully cupped my left breast. "I think it's time we crashed Esposito's again. Dom just asked me yesterday when we're planning on coming around. He's got some new menu items he wanted to test on a few guinea pigs." His thumb grazed my breast and his voice grew husky. "We'll make it an early night. My place or your place, doesn't matter. We've got a few nights of lost time to make up for." He teased my lips briefly with his tongue. "Be ready to go at five o'clock."

Every word out of his mouth was perfect. But I glanced over at my desk where a stack of subcontractor paperwork awaited. None of it was officially due until Monday, but I was determined to get through it before I left today. That would mean staying until seven. Or eight.

"I don't think I'll be ready by five," I said. "Why don't you go down to Esposito's and hang out with your friends and I'll let you know when I'm all done here."

He responded by taking his hands off me and heaving a mighty sigh of frustration.

I climbed off his lap, discreetly adjusting the bra he'd managed to displace.

"What's wrong?"

He threw me a look. "You know."

"Jason, I'm trying to come up with a solution that will work for both of us."

"This is not a project-management problem, Audrey. It's a night with your boyfriend. No analysis required."

I tucked my blouse back into my skirt. "This shouldn't be an issue. Of course I want to see you tonight. I'm just asking for a few extra hours."

"After you blew me off all week."

I glared at him. "Ditto, asshole. It's not like you were bending over backward to talk to me."

"I said what I needed to say. The ball was in your court, honey."

"Oh yeah? Well, there's been a hell of a lot of activity on the court, in case you haven't noticed." I was aware that I was dangerously close to yelling. I was also aware that the office walls were only marginally thicker than cardboard. "Jason, I'm up to my goddamn eyeballs in work right now."

"Because you don't like to share the responsibility. You'd rather go it alone."

I shook my head. "I don't understand why it's so painful for you to cut me a little slack."

He was standing now. "Goddamn it, this doesn't work that way, Audrey. You don't get to dictate the terms of a relationship when it's convenient for you."

"I'm not dictating. And when in the hell was *your* last relationship anyway?"

Jason stuffed his hands in his pockets and stared out the room's lone window, which had a lovely view of the parking garage. "We should knock this off for now. It's about to devolve into a shouting match."

"I think it already has. And since when is Jason Roma the voice of reason?"

He continued to stare out the window. "You want some help with that pile of paperwork on your desk?"

"I can handle it," I said. "I'm sure you've got work of your own to do."

I hadn't meant it to sound sarcastic, but I was aware that it came off that way.

Jason nodded and grabbed his laptop. "Conference room is empty. I'm going to go work in there for a little while and then I'll head over to the jobsite."

My heart hurt as I watched him heading for the door because he didn't want to occupy the same space as me.

"Are you going to take that other job?" I blurted.

Jason faced me and shrugged. "We can talk about it," he said. "I promise I won't finalize anything before we do."

He didn't return to our office for the rest of the afternoon. I made a deal with myself that if Jason returned, then I would leave with him at five. But the hours ticked past and eventually I heard the sounds of the staff departing for the weekend. Helen poked her head into my office long enough to order me to have a good one.

"You too," I said feebly.

The building hollowed out and the sky began to darken. I visited the vending machine shortly after seven and listened to the distant echoes of activity.

Rick Levin, one of the engineers, wandered into the break room and nodded at me. "Glad I'm not the only dumbass working late on a Friday." He shoved some change into the vending machine.

I crunched a potato chip. "I'll be leaving in a few minutes."

Rick grunted and his joints creaked as he bent to retrieve his soda from the dispenser at the bottom of the machine. "Be careful on the commute. Radio says there was an accident on the eastbound I-10. Pretty bad one. It's also turned traffic into one of Dante's circles of hell."

"Thanks, but I don't take the freeway. I'm just a few miles away."

Rick returned to his desk and I stood there alone in an empty room, licking potato chip salt off my fingers and wondering if this was to be my usual Friday night destiny. A pang hit me as I thought about how I'd spent last Friday night. In Sedona with Jason. Despite all the dramatic courthouse bullshit that sent me into a tailspin, it was still the most incredible weekend I'd ever had.

Did I bother to tell him that?

I tossed the potato chip bag into the trash and returned to my office. I looked at my comfortable chair and it occurred to me that I'd rather sit for a root canal than spend another minute in here tonight. Snatching up my purse and leaving paperwork strewn across the surface of my desk, I ran out of the room as if being chased by Freddy Krueger. Once I was out of the building and in my car, I felt slightly better. But not great.

I dug around in my purse for my phone and fired off a text to Jason. Where are you now?

As I awaited his answer, a smile spread across my face. I would ask if I could still see him tonight. I would offer to meet him anywhere. Esposito's or his place or my place or the freaking corner Walgreens. I just wanted to be wherever he was. Twenty minutes passed and he didn't answer. A call to his phone went straight to voicemail.

The parking garage after dark was really not an ideal place to hang out, so I drove out of there, feeling a little dispirited. Jason always had his phone with him. If he wasn't answering me, it was because he didn't want to. I thought about driving to his place in Chandler, but one glance toward the freeway told me Rick was right about the appalling state of eastbound traffic. It appeared to be backed up for untold miles, and a small shiver rolled through as I thought about why. Somewhere at the end of all those cars and lights was a tragedy.

Back in my apartment I cheered up a little when I discovered an unopened box of Girl Scout cookies in my pantry. Then I turned on the television to counter the empty silence of the apartment. I chewed my cookies and flipped to some show about homesteaders with substantial facial hair who lived off the grid in North Dakota. It was surprisingly addictive, and since the network was running a marathon, I watched four more episodes, devoured every last Girl Scout cookie, and obsessively checked my phone to see if Jason had responded yet. He hadn't.

At eleven o'clock I resigned myself to a lonely night in my bed and took a shower. As I toweled off I realized I hadn't even thought about work in hours, and the idea pleased me. Helen was right. A small break was in order now and then. I only wished Jason were here to enjoy it with me.

I set my phone on my nightstand as I always did and restlessly tossed in my bed.

A shrill ringtone awakened me from a sound sleep. Earlier I had turned the volume all the way up so I wouldn't miss Jason's call. Blearily I rubbed my eyes and tried to focus on the screen after noting the red numbers on my old alarm clock radio. A sense of fear built even before I focused on the name displayed on my phone. The thing bleated loudly once more. I picked it up.

"What happened?" A call this late could only mean terrible news was coming.

I was right.

CHAPTER
TWENTY-TWO

Dawn was just breaking, and the imposing, arched front door had never looked forlorn to me before this moment. But now I could swear there was a melancholy air in the way it seemed to frown at me as I rang the doorbell.

My mother answered the door with red, unfocused eyes. Her brassy hair was twisted in a careless ponytail and she seemed small in her leggings and bare feet.

"Audrey," she said with a rasp in her voice that came from too much crying. "Thanks for coming. You didn't have to."

I stepped over the threshold, slightly hurt that she thought I might not be here, that part of her still assumed I was the unreliable girl who wouldn't care enough to stand beside her family on a day like this.

"Where's William?" I asked, looking around the empty grand foyer.

She sighed and closed the door. "Your father's with him. The accident . . . well, it was gruesome. Her car was crushed, and they believe she died on impact. But someone needed to make a positive identification, and William wanted to see her. William already called Jennifer's mother in Portland."

Her voice broke a little over this last sentence and she put a shaking hand to her mouth, correctly figuring her own pain was nothing compared to that of the woman who would need to bury a beloved daughter.

I touched her arm in comfort. "Where are the boys?"

My mother pointed. "In the den. They're exhausted. I tried to get them to sleep but they don't want to."

I swallowed. "Do they know?"

She closed her eyes briefly and looked every day of her age. "They know." She twisted up a tissue in her hands and walked over to the big bay window. Her voice was little more than a whisper and I wasn't even sure if she meant to speak aloud. "No matter what I've said about her, I never would have wanted this. Never would have wanted this for those babies."

I struggled not to cry. "Nobody would have wanted this, Mom." After setting my purse down, I walked down the hall to the den, where I knew the lone television in the house was kept these days. The echoes of my footsteps on the marble floor seemed hideously loud to me.

The boys were sitting side by side on the huge cream-colored leather sofa. Their eyes tracked a garish collection of characters capering across the TV screen, but the sound was too low to hear what was going on. I doubted they were really watching the program. They looked too stunned.

"Leo?" I said softly. "Isaac?"

Leo turned his head and just stared at me, but Isaac's face crumpled and he shot off the sofa and into my arms. I picked up the heavy, heartbroken little boy and carried him over to an armchair. Leo watched us from the sofa, and I held out a hand to him, but he simply turned his eyes back to the television.

Isaac sobbed and I rocked him like a baby as my own heart broke thinking of what my nephews must be feeling right now. My mother had already told me the story on the phone.

When Jennifer hadn't picked up the boys by seven, the daycare provider called William, thinking something must be wrong. She was never this late when picking up her sons after work and she wouldn't have forgotten to call if something urgent came up. William told the babysitter he would come pick up the boys right away and then track down Jennifer. He was walking out to his car when a police officer, a friend of his, stopped him in the parking lot. The officer said he didn't know much, just that there'd been an accident. At that point William called my mother to ask her to please pick up Isaac and Leo. He wanted to make sure they were among family if the news about Jennifer was bad.

It had taken a long time to clear the scene of the accident because a fatality required an immediate investigation. I shuddered as I thought of how I'd casually glanced toward the freeway and saw the lines of unmoving traffic, never guessing the true and horrifying cause of it all.

For hours William languished in the hospital awaiting word on his ex-wife, the mother of his beloved sons. Maybe he held on to a tiny splinter of hope in all that time. Or maybe he understood that when she never reached the trauma center, it was because she couldn't be saved. The crack in my heart widened as I imagined my big brother's agony.

A shadow fell and I looked up to see my mother standing in the doorway. She watched me as I rocked the sobbing Isaac, then she sighed and went over to the couch to sit beside Leo. She'd never been naturally affectionate with her children or her grandchildren, but nothing was typical about today. After a moment the boy rested his head against his grandmother's shoulder and she slowly put her arm around him and kissed the top of his head.

My mother's eyes met mine and I knew we were thinking the same thing. The boys were so young. No matter how much love and support I gave Leo and Isaac, or how much my parents could even give, there would forever be a painful void where their mother should be.

Then I thought of Jennifer Kaufman Gordon, the pretty, vivacious girl who had clung to my handsome brother's arm on their wedding day.

Jennifer, the new mother, who stared down into the face of her first newborn baby with such an expression of serene awe and total love it was tough to look away.

Jennifer, the woman who beamed with pride every time her eyes landed on her sons.

Jennifer, who looked at me with pleading eyes and asked me not to despise her. I never had. She was my family and I loved her.

Goodbye, my sister.

The boys had been up all night, and now that the shock was wearing off, they agreed to try to get some rest. My mother tried to steer them to the guest room, but Isaac said he was afraid of the white filmy drapes so I brought them to my old bedroom instead.

Luanne had arrived at the house moments earlier and she brought me some extra pillows. Her broad, kind face looked on the boys with pity, and before she left the room, she told me not to hesitate to ask for anything else.

Leo was yawning as he kicked his shoes off, and he curled up into a ball, eyes already closed before I tucked the lavender comforter around his thin shoulders, while Isaac's bright eyes regarded me silently from the pillow beside his brother.

"Auntie Audi, will you be here when I wake up?" he asked.

I kissed his forehead. "I'll be here, Isaac."

"You promise?"

"I promise. You get some rest now."

He turned to his side, resting his chubby, tearstained cheek against the pillow. He didn't shut his eyes, though. "Will I see my mama there?"

"Where, baby?"

"In my dreams."

My throat threatened to close up with anguish as I searched for an answer. Who has the ability to explain life and death to a five-year-old? I didn't know how much he understood the finality of it all. But I knew that right now I could let him have a little hope that he might dream of his mother.

"Sometimes in our dreams we're able to see what we wish for the most," I told him.

Isaac was satisfied enough with that answer to close his eyes. I listened for a few minutes to the deep, even breathing of my nephews, and then I quietly turned on the ceiling fan and left the room.

After spending a few minutes searching all the predictable rooms where I might find my mother, I finally located her in my father's study. She was standing by the long narrow window and peering into the backyard.

"Are they asleep?" she asked without turning around.

"I think so."

"That's good." She set down the empty wineglass she'd been holding. "I think we'll need to refinish the pool after the summer."

I stood right behind her. "Mom?"

"I know no one cares about the pool right now, Audrey. I was just thinking out loud."

I wrapped my arms around her and squeezed for a solid ten seconds.

"What was that for?" she asked, twisting around and looking slightly bewildered.

"Because you're my mom and I love you."

Her face, pinched with grief and fatigue, relaxed into a smile. "I haven't heard you say that since you were a little girl."

A tear rolled down my cheek. "It never stopped being true."

She turned all the way around, opened her arms, and held me as I cried for Jennifer, for William, for the boys, for all the tragic and terrible things that can happen with no warning.

My father called a short time later to say that he and William were at the police station. He'd received word from one of his police department contacts that the driver who'd entered the freeway in the wrong direction and cost Jennifer her life was drunk at the time and would most likely be charged with vehicular manslaughter. He expected they might not be home for another few hours.

"Did he say how William was?" I asked my mother when she hung up the phone.

"He's in shock." She rubbed her eyes. "I think we all are."

"Did he mention anything about the funeral plans?"

"No. I'm not sure if he's even thought of it yet."

Luanne came into the room and softly asked my mother if she wanted to make a list of foods the boys might eat. She said she'd go out to the grocery store before they woke up. After the two women left the room, I sat in my father's armchair, which smelled of leather with a vague hint of lemon. My phone was in my back pocket so I made a call, unsurprised when voicemail picked up.

"Jason, it's me. You're probably still asleep. I need to take a few days off, which will of course leave you handling the courthouse project alone." I swallowed, choking a little on the next words. "My sister-in-law was killed in a car accident last night. Jennifer. She was the mother to two beautiful little boys. I'll send an email to management to let them know what happened, and I'll keep you updated. I'm sorry if all the extra work puts you in a tight spot. There's just one more thing I wanted to tell you . . . I really wish I'd gone home with you last night."

I ended the call on that abrupt note because I was having trouble talking now. The grief threatened to boil over in great heaving gasps, and I put my head down on my father's desk until I could breathe. I'd been a fool believing there would be time to reconcile old hurts, to show the people I cared about how I felt. I forgot that time is not required to cooperate. Time owes us nothing. If we don't seize those moments, then they might be lost forever.

"Audrey?" My mother's concerned voice hovered above me. I hadn't heard her return to the room. When I lifted my head, she gently pushed a strand of hair out of my face. "Why don't you go lie down?"

"I'm sure you're more exhausted than I am, Mom."

She shook her head stubbornly. People always said how much we looked alike, but I didn't see the resemblance often. It was only apparent to me at odd moments out of nowhere and for no reason. Like now.

"No," she said. "I don't want to sleep. There's nothing you can do right now. Might as well get some rest." She touched my cheek. "Please. It would make me feel better to know that at least one of my children is having a few moments of peace."

Reluctantly I agreed to go to my room and stretch out on the king-sized bed beside the boys. I promised Isaac I'd be right there for him when he woke up anyway. I curled my arm protectively across the sleeping bodies of my sweet nephews and pressed my cheek into the cool pillow. I didn't really mean to fall asleep, but the next thing I was aware of was that the light in the room had changed. The sun was sharper. I thought I heard male voices murmuring in the distance.

After peering carefully at the boys and feeling satisfied that they were both still sound asleep, I eased out of the bed, noticing how Isaac had burrowed against his big brother. I blew them a silent kiss before I left the room and hoped that they could feel that love wherever their dreams were taking them.

I followed the voices of my parents until I found them in my father's study. For once my father wasn't neatly shaved and composed. He leaned on the back of his desk chair with wisps of his gray hair falling aside to reveal a pink scalp. He looked old and uncertain. My mother stood beside him with her hand on his back. They had been discussing placing Jennifer's obituary notice in the largest local news outlet but stopped talking as soon as they heard me approaching.

"You okay, Dad?" I asked.

His face was a patchwork of wrinkles I couldn't remember seeing before. "I've been better, Audrey."

I would have gone to him and offered a hug if he'd moved an inch, but he just gazed at me as if wondering what I was doing in his study at this time of the day. William was nowhere in sight, and I was about to ask where I could find him when my mother spoke up.

"Jason was here," she said.

"Jason?" I was startled. "My Jason?"

She nodded. "He came to offer his condolences. I know he really wanted to see you, but when I told him you were sleeping, he didn't want to disturb you. He also said you shouldn't worry about work. He'll make sure everything gets taken care of, and you ought to take as much time off as you need."

My phone was on my father's desk where I'd left it earlier. I picked it up and saw that Jason had tried to call several times. "That was nice of him," I said, "to stop by like that."

A vague smile tilted my mother's lips. "It was, yes. Jason made me promise to let him know if there was anything he could do. I know it's just something people say in times like these, but he sounded sincere."

"I'm sure he was," I said. I shouldn't have been surprised to hear that Jason had shown up at my parents' door. I longed to talk to him, to be in his arms, more than anything. Every instinct begged me to dial his number and immediately connect to his voice. But there was someone else I needed to talk to before I could seek any comfort for myself.

"Where's William right now?" I asked.

My father answered first. "Probably still down in the kitchen. Luanne thinks she can solve his problems with some scrambled eggs."

"She's just trying to help, Aaron," my mother said.

He made a disgusted noise. "Yeah, everyone's trying to help. And no one really can." He sighed and walked over to the built-in cabinet where he kept a variety of liquor bottles. When I was sixteen he'd added a lock to it, a lock I knew how to pick if I was determined and hard up for a drink. It appeared that he didn't lock it anymore. Of course he wouldn't need to. I hadn't lived here in years.

"I'm going to find William," I said, and left the room.

He wasn't in the kitchen after all. He was wandering around the hallway near my bedroom looking like a confused, ashen-faced apparition.

"Hey there, Aud," he said as if we'd just run into each other somewhere, as if this wasn't the worst day of his life.

"I'm so sorry," I said, and my brother's face crumpled the way it did when he was eleven and I was six and he had to tell me that our puppy had run away from him on an evening walk and was attacked by a coyote.

I hugged him without hesitation and felt his shudder of grief before he pulled away.

"Where are the boys?" he asked.

I pointed. "Sleeping in my old room."

He nodded vaguely. "Good. It's good that they're sleeping. How are they?"

I answered honestly. "Crushed." I sighed. "What are you going to do about the funeral arrangements?"

He brushed the back of his hand across his face. "Jen told me once that she wanted to be cremated. She wanted her ashes returned to her hometown and scattered at sea."

"In Oregon?"

He nodded. "Small town on the coast called Lincoln City. The family still has a home there. Jen's mother told me over the phone that she'll plan a small service. I'll be bringing the boys, of course. They deserve a chance to say goodbye to their mother."

"When?"

William frowned. "Soon. I have a friend, an attorney, whose family owns a funeral home, who offered to expedite the cremation process. The paperwork has already been taken care of and the . . . uh, remains will be ready by Monday."

I winced over the way his voice cracked over the word *remains*. I couldn't even guess how painful this was for him. I touched my brother's arm.

"I'll come with you," I offered. "I can help with the boys. I want to be there. For all of you."

I wasn't lying. I wasn't just making a gesture out of grim obligation. All the work responsibilities I'd been prioritizing for so long had turned laughably trivial. My heartbroken family needed me, and there was nothing more important.

He stared at me for a moment. "Thank you, Audrey. I'd like that. And I know the boys would too."

William carefully opened the door to my old bedroom and stood at the foot of the bed staring at his sleeping sons, perhaps wondering how he was going to raise them singlehandedly from now on. I wanted to tell him that he'd never be alone. I would do anything for him, for them. But I hesitated to speak out loud and risk waking the kids, so I gently closed the door as William pulled a chair beside the bed to wait for his little boys to wake up.

On the other side of the closed door I stood for a moment, resting my forehead against the cool wood.

I found my mother in the library, but the glass doors were shut and she was speaking rapidly into her cell phone, perhaps making calls to distant relations to give them the awful news. She saw me standing outside the room and raised her eyebrows, the phone slipping from her ear. But I gave her a tiny smile to let her know that all was calm for the moment, and she returned to her conversation.

Distant sounds floated from the kitchen, but I knew I wouldn't find my father hanging out in there with Luanne. He was right where I'd left him in his study, in the middle of opening a bottle of Crown Royal. He looked up when I hovered in the doorway.

"You want a glass?" he asked, holding the bottle aloft. "If there was ever a day that warranted a drink, this is it."

"No, thanks," I said. "Wouldn't want to backslide."

He shrugged, apparently failing to realize that I was using his words, repeating what he'd said to my mother when I overheard their conversation the night I brought Jason to dinner.

"Suit yourself," he said, filling his own glass about halfway.

I cleared my throat. "Did William talk to you about Jennifer's funeral plans?"

My father took a sip, grimaced, and exhaled thickly. "Something about bringing her ashes to Oregon. It would be much easier to hold a service here. He should think of the boys."

"I believe he is thinking of the boys," I replied a little sharply.

My father ignored the comment and peered out the window at the vast and impeccable backyard.

"The thing to do," he said authoritatively, "is to ensure life returns to its everyday routine as soon as possible."

"Dad," I said wearily. "Nothing is ever going to be routine again, not for William or for Leo or for Isaac."

He took another sip from his glass. "I understand the heartbreak of Jennifer's death. We don't get to choose our challenges or tragedies, but we are able to choose how to respond. And at the risk of sounding clichéd, life does go on."

I hated his dismissive tone. "Yes, life goes on. But sometimes things happen that change the course of your life. And there's no shame in grieving."

He sounded annoyed. "Of course not. Don't twist my words, Audrey. Grieving is healthy. Wallowing is not. I would have thought you'd learned that by now." He snorted. "Lord knows you've had plenty of practice."

I was dumbfounded. "What are you talking about?"

His eyes were narrowed as he looked at me, and I shrunk back a little over the bitterness I saw there. "Do you have any idea what you put us through, Audrey? In and out of rehab, no respect for your family or yourself. You never had the courage or the character to pick yourself up, so the rest of us had to do it for you. It was exhausting."

I found myself leaning against the doorframe for support. All that struggle, all these years, and then sobriety and success. And yet in my father's eyes I was still a teenage fuckup who stole from his liquor cabinet and mortified the family at my high school graduation party. I'd already suspected as much. But hearing him say it to my face was something else.

"Aaron."

My mother's voice had come from behind me. Her face was flushed, her eyes two bright points of anger.

"Don't," she barked at him. "Not today."

He sighed and looked at her with some contrition as he set his glass down. "You're right, Cindy. I shouldn't have said that right now. I'm sorry."

It wasn't clear whether he was apologizing to me for his brutal words or apologizing to my mother for picking a scab off an old wound on a day that was already terribly painful. This wasn't even remotely the right time to have this conversation. It should have taken place years ago. But I wasn't willing to let the subject drop without saying my piece. I realized my hand had drifted up to touch my lip, right where it had split and bled the one and only time he had ever hit me in a fit of rage, after I told him to go fuck himself.

"You're one to lecture about wallowing," I said. "You've never been able to abandon your anger and disappointment. You've never forgiven me, Dad, no matter how hard I try. And now I know you never will."

He picked up his glass again and took another drink before answering. It was nearly empty. He'd need to refill it soon. When I searched my memory, it seemed there was hardly an occasion when he didn't have a goddamn glass of liquor in his hand.

The look my father gave me next wasn't exactly tender, but it was no longer hostile either. "You're my daughter, Audrey," he said sternly. "In spite of everything, I love you."

I digested his statement and nodded. "Well, if that's the best you can do, then I guess I'll take it. I love you too, Dad. Also in spite of everything. But while we're having an honest discussion about character, you may want to examine why in thirty years I've never known you to make it through a day without the aid of a drink. It can be genetic, you know. Alcoholism."

My father said nothing when I walked away, heading for the backyard, but my mother followed.

"Audrey."

I stopped at the French doors and turned around to face her. I was so used to seeing her in heels I'd forgotten that she was three inches shorter than me.

My mother touched a gentle hand to my cheek. Her lips parted as if she was on the verge of speaking, but no sound came out, and after a few seconds she took her hand away.

"Are you coming to Oregon?" I asked her. "I already told William I'd go."

A slight frown crossed her face. "I'm not sure I can be away from the hospital for that long."

"Of course," I said tightly, unsurprised by the answer. After all, we were Gordons. Even in the wake of disaster, work was still a priority.

"On second thought, I can justify taking a week off right now," my mother said after a pause. "After all, I'm retiring next year anyway, so they'll need to get used to functioning without me."

I smiled. "William will be glad. He's with the boys right now, but I'll talk to him in a little while and start making the travel arrangements."

She glanced behind me. "Were you going outside?"

"Yes. I need to call Jason."

Her eyes brightened. "I like Jason. I should have mentioned that."

"I'm happy you mentioned it now."

My mother bit the corner of her lip and crossed her arms over her chest as if she were either cold or nervous. "I'm proud of you, Audrey. I'm proud that you're my daughter. I should have mentioned that too."

The words surprised me. I hadn't realized how much I'd been longing to hear them all these years.

"Thank you for telling me, Mom," I said, trying to suppress the quaver in my voice.

She smiled up at me. "Go call Jason. I'm sure he's sitting by the phone."

My mother might have been right about Jason waiting to hear from me. He picked up on the first ring.

"Sorry I missed seeing you earlier," I told him as I sat down on a stone bench in the orchard, appreciating the shade offered by the dense citrus trees.

"I could come back," he offered.

I glanced across the yard at the house, staring at my closed bedroom window where William was waiting for his children to wake up. "It's probably not a good time. The boys will be awake soon, and I need to start making travel arrangements."

Jason paused. "Where are you going?"

"Oregon. To Jennifer's hometown. She told William once that she wanted her ashes scattered in the sea. We'll be leaving as soon as possible." I swallowed and ran my fingers along the rough surface of the bench. "Jason, I can't say for sure when I'll be back at work. I'll try to return by Thursday."

"To hell with work."

"But we've got all that subcontractor paperwork to approve and a big progress report to hand over to the county this week and—"

"And I'll handle it," he said tersely. "I'll make sure it all gets done, Audrey. Just be with your family."

I sighed. "Okay," I said with some reluctance. "Give me a call if you have any questions or if you have trouble finding the documents you need."

"I'll do that." He paused. "I really wish I were coming with you."

I was startled. It hadn't occurred to me that Jason would want to accompany me on this sad mission. Of course it was out of the question.

Someone had to stay behind and manage the courthouse project. In spite of this heartbreaking tragedy, there was still a job to do.

"I wish that were possible," I told him, and meant it as I suddenly ached to be enclosed in the comfort of his arms.

"How about if I flew out just for a day?" he suggested.

"Better not," I said, thinking of the long task list for the upcoming week. "There's too much to do at work. You need to be there, not hanging out with me in Oregon. This is the point where you thank me for delegating, Jason."

Jason's exhale sounded slightly exasperated. "Whatever you want," he said.

I picked at the frayed knee of my jeans. They were a really old pair. I'd thrown on the first clean thing I could find this morning. "My mother likes you," I said. "She told me."

"Yeah?" He sounded pleased.

"Yeah," I said softly. "I like you too."

"It does feel good to be liked," he said with a touch of wryness. Then his voice changed, deepened. "And Audrey, you already know I'm over the fucking moon about you."

I closed my eyes. "Jason? I have another favor to ask."

"What's that?"

I opened my eyes and took a deep breath. "Please don't fall in love with anyone else while I'm gone."

"Don't worry," he said, and now it sounded like he was smiling. "I haven't yet come across a woman who could compete with Audrey Gordon."

CHAPTER TWENTY-THREE

There was an earthquake.

Or else a poltergeist was causing the bed to vibrate so hard my teeth rattled.

"Auntie Audi."

I cracked an eye open. Neither an earthquake nor a supernatural entity was responsible for disturbing my sleep. It was my five-year-old nephew.

Isaac, surprisingly strong for a kindergartener, stopped trying to shake me awake and smiled triumphantly. He'd lost his first two teeth a few weeks ago, and I couldn't help but smile back at the gap-toothed, tousle-haired little demon who had decided to deprive his poor old aunt of some much-needed rest.

I yawned and rolled over. "What's wrong, buddy? You need something?"

"I need to go to the beach and get some seashells."

A glance at my phone told me it was barely six thirty. "Right now?"

"Grandma says the best time to go is early in the morning before the bee combs come out."

"The what?"

He looked impatient. "The people who come to visit and take all the shells."

"You mean the beachcombers?"

Isaac shrugged his thin shoulders.

I yawned again and sat up, trying to rub the sleep out of my eyes. "Why don't you go get dressed and I'll get you some breakfast?"

"I am dressed," he insisted.

I checked him out. "That's your underwear, Isaac."

"I didn't bring a bathing suit."

"You remember what your daddy said. Water's too cold to go swimming anyway. Now go get dressed, and if you're quiet, I'll take you down to the beach after you eat some breakfast."

My nephew hopped off the bed and began rummaging through his suitcase, presumably in search of clothes. I peered at Leo, who was stirring in the other bed. Since rooms were limited in the beach house owned by Jennifer's family, I was sharing a guest bedroom with the boys. They'd been squeezing into one twin bed while I occupied the other. William insisted on taking the couch and leaving the other two bedrooms for our mother and Jennifer's mother.

The rest of the house was quiet, meaning everyone else was likely still asleep. Yesterday had been an emotional day as we said our farewells to Jennifer.

A family friend, a diminutive elderly fisherman who had known Jennifer's father before he died of colon cancer six years ago, had taken us out on his creaking boat. In the tranquil waters several miles from shore, we said our sad, unfairly early farewells to Jennifer Kaufman Gordon. Leo cried in his father's arms. My mother kept her arm around Jennifer's mother, who was bereft over the loss of her only child. Isaac asked for my help when he wanted to toss a piece of paper overboard. It was a careful crayon drawing of his mother, beaming with a blue mouth and long blue hair beneath a bright orange sun. Isaac's drawing fluttered on the sea breeze and settled atop the water, and the real sun shone directly on Jennifer's blue smile before the paper bobbed away in the waves.

I tied my hair up, grabbed some comfortable clothes out of my own suitcase, and tiptoed into the bathroom to change. When I returned to the room, Isaac was now wearing a red sweatshirt with green shorts, and Leo was sitting up in bed blinking at us with a frown.

"We're going to have a quick breakfast and take a walk along the beach," I said. "Why don't you come with us?"

I thought he'd refuse. Leo had been quiet. He'd been quiet the day of his mother's death, he'd been quiet on the plane to Portland and quiet on the drive to Lincoln City. Then yesterday, as his mother's ashes blended with the ocean, he'd unleashed the most inconsolable wail I'd ever heard and sobbed on William's shoulder until we returned to land.

But this morning Leo nodded and swung his legs around the side of the bed. "Okay, I'll come."

In the kitchen I tried to be as noiseless as possible as I put a pot of coffee on and opened a box of muffins someone had been kind enough to bring over yesterday. Throughout the afternoon old friends and family had stopped by to pay their respects. The house itself had been in the family for generations and was jointly owned by Jennifer's mother and her three sisters. Now it was mostly used as a vacation place, since most of the family had moved away from town. Jennifer's mother lived in Portland and planned to return home today. She ran her own business, a small bakery, and indicated she couldn't be gone long. But she said she liked the idea that we would remain at the beach house with the boys and encouraged us to stay as long as we wanted.

I heard the shuffle of footsteps and looked up to see my mother wandering into the kitchen. I held up the pot of coffee and she nodded, so I poured her a cup while she veered toward the living room where William slept on the couch. She leaned over and touched his face with a gentle sigh before approaching the breakfast bar to retrieve her coffee.

"Did you sleep well?" she whispered.

I hadn't really. Isaac had woken me up twice during the night because he needed to use the bathroom and was afraid to go down the hall himself. And the mattress I slept on had felt as if it had been stuffed with hard potatoes instead of foam and springs.

"I slept fine," I whispered back.

She smiled and sipped her coffee. My father had not accompanied us to Oregon. Something about a big deal one of his companies was finalizing on a coveted piece of property in Scottsdale. I pictured him coming home late to that big, empty house and brooding in his study with a half-empty bottle on his desk. It was not a nice picture.

Isaac and Leo jostled their way into the kitchen, shoving each other halfheartedly. I put a finger to my lips before giving them each a muffin and a glass of juice.

"We're going to walk along the beach and look for shells," I murmured to my mother.

"Otherwise the bee combs will get it all," Isaac hissed as he kicked his legs on the high stool.

My mother nodded seriously. "I see."

"You should come too, Grandma."

She smiled. On the plane to Oregon she had confided that she had decided to retire even sooner than expected. William would need help with the boys, and his extremely demanding job complicated the situation.

"All right," she said, getting to her feet. "Let me go change and I'll come along."

The old cottage was only steps away from a stretch of pristine beach. The area was nearly empty this early, the soft waves of the Pacific Ocean gently splashing the hem of the sandy beach.

"Don't go in the water!" my mother shouted as the boys took off running.

A handful of seagulls had been pecking in the sand at the water's edge. As the boys whooped and sprinted close to the shore, the gulls took flight in a shrill explosion of indignant calls that sounded for all the world like some heavy-duty bird cussing.

Leo picked up a stick and poked at something in the wet sand while his brother squatted down and stared intently.

"I hope it's not a washed-up jellyfish," I said to my mother.

My mother looked alarmed. "Boys!" She clapped her hands to get their attention. "Please be careful."

I sat down on the sand, but my mother hesitated.

"We should have brought a blanket," she said, looking at her white linen pants.

"Come sit, Mom." I tugged at the pretty patterned shawl she had wrapped around herself in case the ocean breeze was cool.

After a few seconds of fretting over her spotless clothes, she gave up and eased herself primly onto the sand beside me.

We watched as Leo picked something up, dangling it by two fingers. Isaac shouted, "It's a crab!" and they both shrieked while Leo flung the poor creature somewhere in the sand. Then they started laughing and I had trouble deciding which one looked more like William.

My mother must have been having the same thought. "They look so much like their father."

"Yes, they do."

"But I can also see Jennifer," she admitted.

"Um, Mom?" I struggled for the words to approach a delicate topic. I didn't want to anger her, but something needed to be said, and I wanted to spare William the chore of saying it.

She turned to me with a cocked head, waiting for me to speak.

I took a breath and looked at my nephews capering around on the sand. "The boys only have memories of their mother now. We have to be mindful of that. And we have to be careful what we say in front of them."

In other words, don't go bashing Jennifer anymore.

Luckily she understood what I was saying and nodded thoughtfully. "I know. I will never again utter a cross word about their mother."

"What about Dad?"

"I'll talk to him."

Leo and Isaac flapped their arms, pantomiming the seagulls circling overhead.

"He's not a bad man," she said. "Your father. He's just bad at opening up his heart sometimes, bad at letting the people he loves know that he gives a damn."

I thought about Jason, about the way he was always the one to say how much I meant to him. Had I ever said it back? I couldn't remember.

"I'm bad at that too," I confessed. "Something else I inherited, I suppose."

My mother circled her arm around my back. "No," she said. "No, you're not like that, Audrey. You were such a loving little girl and you've grown into a kind, caring woman."

She dropped her arm and stared out at her grandsons. They both had sticks now and they were scratching pictures in the sand.

"We should have come to places like this when you and William were kids. Instead we hardly took vacations. Lord knows we had the money. Your father and I just always had work, always had other priorities. And we allowed time to slip away."

When she grew quiet I realized she'd stopped staring at the boys and was now staring at me with a mournful expression.

"I should have been there more," she said. "For you. You were desperate for attention. You deserved attention. Instead you became so lost."

"Mom, it wasn't your fault I started drinking myself into oblivion every chance I got."

She sighed. "But the fact that I refused to deal with it was my fault. You were still a child, Audrey. I couldn't face the fact that you needed help. I couldn't face what it said about my failures as a parent. I'm sorry for that."

A breeze lifted my hair, and I breathed in the clean salt air. The boys were still determinedly carving up the sand with their sticks.

"Maybe someday we can all take that vacation together," I said. "Perhaps we can even convince Dad to come along with us."

She grinned. "I'm pretty sure I can persuade him."

"Grandma!" Isaac shouted. He jumped up and down and held an object up high in his left hand. "It's a shell! It's a shell!"

"Ooh, let me see," she exclaimed, and got to her feet, brushing sand off her palms. The spot we were sitting on had been a little damp, and my mother walked away with wet sand clinging to the backside of her white pants. Mentioning such things would have ruined the moment, though, so I said nothing. I just watched as Cindy Gordon laughed and played on the beach with her grandsons.

My knees were getting stiff, so I stood up and stretched, wishing I'd brought my phone with me so I could take the opportunity to check in with Jason. With so many people around all the time for the last few days, I hadn't had the chance to talk to him much. He assured me repeatedly that the project was running smoothly, probably because he figured that's what I would be most worried about. Yet what I longed for even more was to hear his voice drop into a sexy whisper and say something outrageous, something that would get me turned on or cause me to dissolve in a swirl of romance. Every hour I was away from Jason, I missed him even more.

I was bending my torso back and forth, trying to relieve the knot in my back that came from sleeping on the terrible mattress, when I saw William standing about twenty feet behind me wearing nothing but a pair of gray sweatpants. From the look of his hair, he'd literally just rolled out of a deep sleep on the couch and stumbled outside.

"Morning," I said, shaking off some sand and approaching him.

He'd been gazing at Leo and Isaac, who were now kneeling down and digging in the sodden sand beside their grandmother. Apparently she'd given up all concern for her white pants, because she was crouched right down there with them.

"Good morning," William answered politely but tonelessly. Like Leo, he'd been quiet since Jennifer's death. I knew he was trying to be strong for the boys, but there were moments when he looked as if he might not have the strength to keep standing. This was one of those moments.

A broad piece of driftwood had been abandoned nearby, probably dragged up this far to serve as a natural bench. I sat down on the edge, hoping my big brother would get the picture, and he did, easing his tall body down on the driftwood with a thick sigh.

"They're having fun," I said, pointing to the boys with a smile.

William nodded absently. "Good."

"Is Lisa still leaving today?" I asked, referring to Jennifer's mother.

He scratched his head. In childhood his hair had been as light as his sons', but it had darkened as he grew up. For the first time I noticed a little bit of gray around his temples. "I think so. I haven't seen her yet this morning."

"When were you thinking of leaving?" I asked him.

"I don't know. Tomorrow maybe," he said. "You really don't have to stay, Audrey. I know you have important things to get back to."

There was no bitterness in William's voice. He thought he was just stating a fact, that the demands of my job would be occupying my thoughts. But nothing could be further from the truth. I didn't care if I returned to Lester & Brown tomorrow or three weeks from now. I wasn't going anywhere until William and the boys were ready.

"Hey." I touched his bare shoulder so he would look at me. "There's nothing more important than being with all of you."

William's eyes, a rich hazel, looked so tired. I had never seen my brother look as tired as he'd looked these past four days. "I didn't mean to sound ungrateful," he said. "I'm so glad you're here. You and Mom."

"Lisa let me know there's no hurry for us to leave. She also said the family would love it if you brought the boys back here now and then."

William looked out toward the horizon. The ocean appeared so endless from here. It was easy to imagine why people had once thought it stretched into infinity.

"This was her favorite place in the world," he said wistfully. "We came here for a week the summer we got engaged. And then again the year we got married and several years after that. She was pregnant with Isaac the last time I was here. She brought them a few more times after that but I didn't come along. I was too busy. Too busy working."

A small wave crashed as if to emphasize William's last statement, which he'd spat out with a tone of disgust. The beach occupants squealed and scattered as the cold water crept toward their ankles.

"It wasn't her fault, Audrey," he said.

"The accident? Of course it wasn't her fault. It was a goddamn drunk driver who got on the freeway in the wrong direction."

He shook his head. "That's not what I meant. The end of our marriage wasn't her fault."

"It makes no difference now," I said uneasily, thinking about how Jennifer had cheated on him and shattered their family. William was just so heartsick he was taking responsibility for everything.

"I let her go," he said, narrowing his eyes at the horizon. "Worse than that, I pushed her away. I was so hell-bent on becoming the greatest legal superstar the Gordon name had ever known that I neglected the most important thing in my life. I forgot birthdays, ignored anniversaries. Jen tried. She tried for years. Hell, I think she had that damn affair as a last-ditch effort to get my attention. But even when we were at our worst, we were determined to give the boys a good life. We were learning how to make this new normal work, how to share the responsibility of our sons. In time, I think we would have been friends. I can't believe she won't get to see them grow up."

William had always been like Superman to me. Perfect, invincible, indomitable. Hearing him confess to his failures and his anguish tore me up in a way that nothing else ever had. I didn't even know what to say. The only thing I could do for him was remain at his side and listen.

"I'm going to step down from the bench," he said. "I sacrificed far too much to get there. It all feels hollow now." He looked at me, his handsome face full of torment. "What the hell is the point of grabbing for the fucking brass ring if you wind up letting go of everything that really matters in the process?"

I had no answer. "I don't know, William. I really don't."

My brother let out a snort of laughter that had no humor in it. "I heard someone say once that when a man's gasping his last breath, the one thing he won't be thinking is 'Damn, I wish I'd put in more time at the office.' I didn't really appreciate that warning until recently. Now I get it. Of course, now it's too late."

I nudged my brother's arm and pointed toward the beach. Our prim and proper mother had sunk down to her knees in the middle of the beach, laughing with abandon as her two young grandsons tickled her with glee.

"It's not too late," I told him. "You have two miraculous reasons to wake up every morning and be the best damn father on the planet. And you'll do it. I know you will. You're already their hero. And you've always been mine."

He looked at his boys running around, tiptoeing to the surf and then shrieking when the water chased them back to the sand. For the first time in days a real smile lit up his face.

"Thanks, sis," he said softly, and stood up.

Leo and Isaac noticed him then and they both came running. William laughed gently as the boys collided with his legs, then he lifted them each in one strong arm and carried them over to where our mother waited with her hands on her hips, her hair all over the place, her expensive clothes a disaster. She didn't seem bothered, though. She hugged William when he set the boys down, and they all began scouring the shoreline for elusive shells.

I stood and watched them for a few minutes, then drifted closer to where the dry sand had been soaked by the waves when they crept ashore and then receded. I could still see the animal shapes the boys had been drawing with their sticks earlier. They'd even written their names side by side.

I picked up one of the abandoned sticks and carefully scratched some words into the wet sand. I was standing back and admiring them when Leo approached to check out what I was doing.

"Who's Jason?" he asked, looking down at what I'd written.

"My boyfriend," I answered with a smile.

"Why did you write that you love him?"

"Because I do."

My nephew looked doubtful. "I've never met him."

"You will." I took his hand. "Come on, let's go see if we can hunt down some more shells before the bee combs find them."

CHAPTER TWENTY-FOUR

On our way to the airport on Friday William promised the boys he'd take them back to Oregon soon to see their mother's family and stay at the beach house.

"Can Grandma come?" asked Isaac.

"Of course."

"And Auntie Audi?" Leo wanted to know.

My brother glanced at me and smiled. "Auntie Audi is always welcome."

Leo turned to me. "Are you going to bring Jason?"

William was confused. "You met Jason?"

"No, he hasn't met Jason," I explained. "I happened to mention him a few times."

"*Are* you going to bring Jason?" my mother wanted to know.

"I suppose that's up to Jason," I told her, starting to feel a little restless about getting home. Thanks to a hurricane on the East Coast, flights all over the country were delayed, and we wound up waiting for a connecting flight in the Denver airport for over four hours. When we were finally called to board a flight to Phoenix, I texted Jason to let him know I was on my way and would love to see him tonight. It was close to five o'clock by that time and he was probably busy wrapping up the workday. At least that's what I told myself when he hadn't answered by the time the plane took off.

On the flight to Phoenix I wound up wedged between my two nephews. Leo flipped through a comic book. Isaac fell asleep and drooled all over my left arm. I didn't mind.

As the plane touched down, a tremor of excitement rolled through me. Not so much because I had a deep and abiding love for my home-town but because every nerve in my body was instantly awake with the sense that I was getting closer to Jason.

"Why are you smiling so much?" Leo asked me with a little suspicion.

"I'm just happy to be home," I said.

Isaac suddenly lurched right out of a sound sleep. "My shells!" he cried. "Where are my shells?"

"In my purse." I patted it in my lap. I'd bought a new one before we left Lincoln City. My fancy name-brand purse hadn't contained enough room for Isaac's pile of seashells that had been carefully wrapped in paper towels and stowed in a plastic shopping bag. He was afraid they'd get crushed or lost, so I offered to take custody of them. My new bag was bright pink, possessed no designer labels, and contained plenty of space for a beloved nephew's seashell collection.

I was like a little kid squirming around in my seat as the plane seemed to take forever to taxi to the gate and allow us to exit.

"We ought to get the boys some dinner," my mother said, checking her watch as we traveled down the escalator toward baggage claim. "I'm sure your father sent a car over, but it shouldn't be a problem to make a stop."

"Sounds good," William said, and yawned tiredly. "I wouldn't mind eating."

"Audrey?" my mother prodded. "Will you be coming with us?"

"No, I don't think so," I said hastily. My stomach could wait. I was already calculating how soon I'd get to see Jason. He might be at home in Chandler unless he needed to work late. The minute I was off this damn endless escalator, I'd call him.

"But thank you for asking," I added.

My mother seemed surprised. "Of course I asked you. When have I ever not asked?"

I bit my lip to subdue a smile. "You're right," I told her. "You do always ask."

"Why is Grandpa down there?" Leo wanted to know.

"Where?" I followed the boy's pointing finger and received my first surprise in the form of my father. Rather than sending a hired car to the airport to greet his family, he'd come himself. It was admittedly a small step, very small, but it was something. It was more than I had been willing to give him credit for a moment ago.

The second surprise jolted me much more deeply.

Standing beside my father was Jason Roma.

And what's more, they appeared to be talking to each other in a way that seemed friendly, at least from a distance. Also standing down there by the luggage carousels, looking happy, if a little confused, was Jason's father.

"Aaron!" my mother called with a frantic wave, and I knew from the broad grin on her face that she was enormously pleased he'd shown up himself.

Jason stopped talking to my father and looked up as we approached the bottom of the escalator. Immediately he broke into the smile that had always cast a powerful spell on me, whether I wanted to admit it or not. In that smile was kindness and passion and friendship and a promise that it was all for me. It was a good thing I was stepping off the escalator, because I was in imminent danger of swooning.

Instead I hopped off the final step and ran to him with my arms out. Unfortunately, in my haste to leap into the arms of my sexy lover, I forgot that I was wearing cheap flip-flops. An instant after the rubber toe of my left shoe caught on the ugly airport-terminal carpet, I rolled my ankle and tumbled forward.

What might have been a lovely romantic moment ended somewhat gracelessly with me sprawled on the floor beside a revolving baggage carousel.

"Audrey!" Jason reached me first, hovering with worry written all over his face.

I touched his bristly cheek. "Your beard is back."

He grinned. "There's this girl I like, and she decided she has a thing for beards."

"Lucky girl," I said, and then winced as I let Jason help me up to a sitting position.

"Would it be unrealistic to assume that no one saw my airport swan dive?"

He considered. "A little. I saw a few cell phones out, so I'm pretty sure you'll find it on YouTube within an hour if you want to revisit the event."

I groaned and buried my face in my hands. When I looked back up, my entire family had gathered and were staring at me.

"Are you hurt?" my mother asked.

"You fell so hard!" Isaac exclaimed. He smacked one palm into the other for emphasis. "Just like that."

"I almost tripped on this damn carpet myself earlier," my father declared, and glowered at a passing pilot as if he must be responsible for the floor that had so carelessly injured his daughter.

"You're very beautiful," announced Jason's father.

"I think you might have sprained your ankle," William said sympathetically.

"Who's he?" Leo asked, pointing to Jason. "Is this your boyfriend, Auntie Audi?"

Everyone looked at Jason.

He raised an eyebrow at me. "What do you say, Auntie Audi? Am I still your boyfriend?"

"If you help me up off the floor, the job remains yours."

Jason responded by lifting me into his arms as if I weighed no more than a bed pillow. I curled my arms around his neck and relished every second, even if my ankle was throbbing like a son of a bitch.

Jason had already met William and my parents, but there were two very curious, very important people who were staring up at him with some awe as he effortlessly carried their aunt in his arms. Fortunately, an airport employee appeared with a wheelchair, and Jason set me down carefully.

I beckoned to my two nephews and put a hand on each of their thin shoulders as I introduced them. "Jason, this is Leo and Isaac, otherwise known as the best nephews ever. Boys, this is Jason."

"He's strong," Leo observed shrewdly. "That must be why you love him."

Jason gave no sign that he heard my precocious nephew. He hunkered down to the boys' level. "I've been looking forward to meeting you guys."

"Do you like baseball?" Isaac asked.

"I like baseball," Jason assured him.

"Our mom liked baseball," Leo said in a small voice. "She used to take us to Diamondbacks games all the time."

Jason put a hand on the boy's shoulder. "She sounds like she was a great mom," he said, his voice quivering just a little.

Leo nodded as if in thought. "She was."

Some movement caught my attention, and I looked up in time to glimpse the astonishing sight of my father embracing my brother in the middle of the bustling airport terminal. For all my father's devotion to his son, he'd never been an openly loving man, and I couldn't recall a time when I'd ever seen them hug.

My father patted William on the shoulder after he released him. My brother looked as if the grief had caught up to him again. Maybe it was being back home or hearing Leo mention his mother. That's probably how things would be for him and the boys, at least for a while.

Life would go on as life does, but at certain times, the dreadful loss of Jennifer would hit them fresh and raw. In time the sharp pain would fade to a dull ache, but it would always be there.

"Are we still getting ice cream?" Chris Roma wanted to know.

"Yeah, Dad, we'll get ice cream soon," Jason assured him.

"You're getting ice cream?" Isaac said a little enviously.

Chris beamed. "Yes."

William wiped a tear from his eye and smiled down at his little boy. "I'll get you some ice cream after dinner. In the meantime, I believe that's our luggage making the rounds on Carousel Four."

Once we had all our bags and headed out to the parking garage, it was time to part ways, William and the boys going with my parents. Both my father and William shook hands with Jason, and my mother actually gave him a hug.

"I'll call you tomorrow," I promised my brother after I kissed the boys goodbye and relinquished Isaac's bag of shells. I wanted William to remember that he wasn't facing life alone, that I would be there for him and for Leo and for Isaac. We were family and that wasn't replaceable.

William looked at me gratefully. "Thanks again. Thanks for everything."

My mother wanted to fuss over my stupid ankle, but I assured her I would survive and asked if we could perhaps never again discuss Audrey's Airport Adventure.

"Fine. But put some ice on it," she ordered before bending down and kissing me on the cheek.

My father seemed uncertain as he approached me. We hadn't really spoken since our disastrous last encounter in his study.

"Went to a meeting this week," he said in a low voice, glancing over to where my mother was peppering Jason with instructions on how to care for my grievous injury.

"A meeting?" I asked, puzzled as to why my father would be discussing his business with me out of the blue.

He nodded and coughed once. "Four days sober."

I couldn't have been more astonished if he told me he'd started taking tap dancing lessons. "Must have been a good meeting," I said.

"It was. Maybe we could go together sometime," he said, and I saw in his eyes the apology that he couldn't quite express in words.

"That would be nice, Dad," I said, and reached out to squeeze his hand. I hadn't been to an Alcoholics Anonymous meeting in years, but remembering the way I'd stared at that hotel liquor cabinet still made me break out into a sweat. Perhaps talking about it among people who understood would do me some good. There was nothing wrong with accepting a little help. Even my father had arrived at that understanding.

When my parents left with William and the boys, Jason's dad attempted to follow them as well, but Jason caught him and steered him back to the car.

Jason settled his father in the backseat as he returned the wheelchair.

"How are you, Chris?" I asked, swiveling around from the passenger seat to see him.

"Are we friends?" he asked me curiously.

"Of course we are," I answered, and he smiled.

"We're out of here," Jason said as soon as he was back in the car.

I touched his arm. His shirtsleeve had been rolled above the elbow, and I let my fingers travel over his skin. "I can't believe you came here without telling me."

"I know," he responded. "You were so stunned you literally fell all over yourself."

I groaned. "I'm not going to live that down."

"Nope."

"But I didn't tell you what flight I was on. Pretty sure I didn't even mention the name of the airline."

"You didn't. I had to call your dad to squeeze that information out of him."

"The two of you looked pretty friendly, chatting down there in baggage claim."

Jason nodded. "It's possible I managed to win him over."

My fingertips explored the smooth, solid muscles along his forearm. "I'm well aware that you can be fairly charming, Mr. Roma. When you're not being vulgar."

"I believe you appreciate vulgarity as much as you appreciate charm, Audrey."

I smiled. "You might be right."

Jason's hand landed on my thigh. "You haven't asked me a thing about work yet."

"That's right, I haven't."

"Can't believe you're not dying to know every detail about what's happened at the courthouse this week."

I moved my hand over his. "And I can't believe you haven't kissed me yet."

Jason turned back to his father. "Hey, Dad, cover your eyes for a second."

Christian Roma obediently placed his palm over his face.

Jason moved his seat back and patted his lap. "Come here."

It was a chore trying to crawl across the front seat to him, but he scooped me up with tenderness and helped me the rest of the way. The instant I was in his lap, I never wanted to be anywhere else.

Jason's breathing quickened as his hand went to the back of my neck, pulling me in for a searing, deep kiss that took my breath away and might have led to more erotic activities if Jason's father hadn't complained from the backseat that he was tired of holding his hand over his face.

Jason broke away from my mouth and kissed my neck, his hot breath close to my ear.

"Is this a better greeting?" he asked.

I tightened my arms around him. "Much better."

CHAPTER
TWENTY-FIVE

I was sitting on Jason's couch idly flipping channels with a bowl of popcorn in my hands and a frozen bag of sweet corn on my ankle when he returned from dropping off his father at the nursing home. Jason had asked Chris to stay overnight in the guest bedroom, but the man started growing agitated shortly after we arrived at Jason's house following dinner and began demanding to go home. Jason told me that had been happening more and more lately.

"How's the ankle?" he asked, walking through the front door and promptly tossing his keys on the coffee table.

"Pretty sure I wasn't lying to my mother when I told her I'd live." I plucked the ice pack off and examined my swollen ankle. Then I winced and replaced the cold compress on the sprain. "I'll probably be limping around the jobsite all next week, though."

"We can go to your place if you'd be more comfortable."

"I'm extremely comfortable right here, thank you."

"You sure look comfortable," he said as his eyes scanned my body. In his absence I'd changed out of my sloppy yoga pants and T-shirt into a short blue sundress that I'd packed in my suitcase but hadn't worn on the trip.

Jason sat down on the couch and gingerly picked my feet up, setting them in his lap, displacing the cold bag of sweet corn, and gently running his broad thumb over my injured ankle. "Does this hurt?"

"Actually it feels a little better when you touch it."

A deviously sexy look came over him and his hand traveled higher. "In that case, can I touch other things too?"

"You're incorrigible," I said, although I parted my knees to give him better access.

But instead of taking advantage, he grew serious. "And you're beautiful."

I swallowed. "I missed you so much."

He took my hand. "I missed you too."

"I'm sorry I didn't call you more often. I was always with the boys, and it was an emotional week."

He nodded solemnly. "How are they doing?"

"They're children. With that comes a certain amount of resilience, but I expect this will be a wound that will never quite heal. And William is devastated. He'll always love Jennifer."

"I'm sure he will," Jason said.

My throat tightened as I remembered the conversation my brother and I had on the beach. "He told me things I didn't know. He blames himself for the divorce because he spent all his time chasing professional success and neglected his family. You know what my brother said to me?"

"What?"

"William said no one ever died thinking, 'Damn, I wish I'd put in more time at the office.' It's true. It's absolutely true. Jason, I don't want to do that. I don't want to sideline the things in my life that matter and someday look back with terrible regret."

Jason had leaned back and was peering at me intently. "And what matters to you, Audrey?"

I picked up his hand and kissed the broad palm. "You matter to me. I should have told you this sooner instead of pushing you away. I want to be with you, Jason. I want to be with you more than I've ever wanted anything."

He smiled. "I think your nephew already spilled the beans on that topic."

"I don't know what you mean," I said, blushing and knowing full well he was talking about Leo and what he'd blurted out in the airport.

"He's strong. That must be why you love him."

Jason Roma was strong in more ways than I had ever guessed. Calm in the face of pressure, protective when confronted by any perceived threat, and generous enough to forgive a dying parent who could no longer remember the terrible things he'd done. No wonder I'd fallen for him.

"You know exactly what I mean," Jason accused. He seized me around the waist and pulled me into a straddle across his lap, taking care not to jostle my ankle. Then he reached up and traced my lower lip.

"Say it," he whispered.

I swallowed hard and took the plunge. "Jason, I love you."

He didn't say anything immediately, so I felt the need to continue.

"You're brilliant and loyal and kind and so goddamn ridiculously gorgeous I can hardly breathe every time I look at you. I've closed myself off for so long, but I like who I am when we're together. I love you not just for you but for bringing out the things in me I couldn't admit I was missing. And—"

"I love you too," he interrupted, curling his arms around my body and reminding me of the most practical feature of his strength. "And in case there's any doubt in your mind, I want you to know those aren't words I've ever said to any woman before."

He kissed me quickly, then fiercely whispered, "I love you, Audrey Gordon."

I touched the rough bristle that was growing in across his jaw. "You're everything to me. You're more important than all the two-hundred-million-dollar courthouse projects in the world."

He grinned. "I'm pretty sure that's the most romantic statement ever uttered."

"I'm serious." I paused before I made the next statement. "And Jason, if you want to take that other job, you have my full support. I mean that."

"Nah," Jason said. "I'm afraid you're not getting rid of me."

I smiled. "No?"

He shook his head for emphasis. "No. Pissing you off is too much fun."

I playfully swatted at him, but he caught my hands and pinned them behind my back. Now that we'd voiced our heartfelt feelings, it seemed more-physical desires were going to claim priority. I was ready. I wanted him more than ever.

Jason's kisses turned aggressive and I pressed my body against him, loving the feel of my breasts being crushed against his hard chest. But suddenly he broke away.

"What's wrong?" I asked breathlessly, ready to start tearing clothes off and get wild.

Jason released my wrists and looked around the tidy, if understated, living room. "This isn't exactly a downtown penthouse suite."

"I like it," I said, nibbling on his neck and wondering when he was going to get back to business. Jason was never one to hold back when it came to sex.

He plucked at the right strap of my dress and slowly eased it over my shoulder. "Do you really?"

I ran my hands all over his chest. "Yes. It's a nice house. Quiet neighborhood." I pulled the hem of his shirt up, admiring the smooth, tanned expanse of his muscled belly. I smiled when he sucked in a sharp breath as I moved lower, toying with his belt. "And most important," I continued, loosening the leather strap, "you're here."

"Do you think you'd want to be here too?"

I stopped messing with his belt and looked at him. "What?"

Jason's smile was somewhat shy. "You mentioned your apartment lease is up at the end of the summer."

I vaguely recalled telling him that I needed to find a new apartment soon because my apartment complex was converting to condos next year. I didn't like the place enough to make a permanent investment. But since there were still several months left of my lease term, I hadn't made any plans.

"That's true," I said.

Jason slid the left strap of my dress down. "I'd love to have a roommate," he said, and gently kissed the top of each breast. "If you wouldn't mind living out in the stucco suburbs and commuting on the freeway in rush hour traffic."

I hadn't expected Jason to ask me to move in with him. But it took less than five seconds of consideration before I had an answer.

"We could commute together," I suggested, returning to the job of getting his belt out of the way.

"And make better time using the carpool lane," Jason agreed.

He let out a small groan when my fingers triumphed over the belt and began working on his zipper.

"Jason, I'd love to live here with you."

His face lit up and I loved knowing I was the reason. We were in love. We made each other happy. There might not be any such thing as perfect when it comes to relationships, but I was determined to keep working at it. This kind of work was the real success in life. The things we did in exchange for a paycheck could never measure up.

After we kissed tenderly for a few minutes, Jason was delighted to discover that I wasn't wearing panties beneath my dress. As he lifted me in his arms and carried me to bed, I told him the same thing I'd already told him. There was no such thing as saying it too much.

"I love you."

EPILOGUE

ONE YEAR LATER . . .

"Oh my god, I'm starving," I groaned, leaning against Jason and pretending to wilt into a faint.

He circled an arm around my waist to prop me up. "I've got a solution for that," he said confidently.

I glanced up at him. "Are you talking dirty?"

"No, I'm talking about pizza. Dominic said we should come down and celebrate when we're done here."

I eyed the collection of sweaty, overdressed people who were still milling around in the shadows of the newly completed courthouse. "Are we done shaking hands with half of Phoenix?"

"I hope so. That was exhausting—I don't know who the fuck half of these people are."

"County officials, local businessmen, and a lot of local politicians pretending to be eager about meeting the team responsible for the new courthouse."

"In that case I'm glad I pretended to be eager to meet them back," Jason said.

"Yes, although we should probably make it a point to locate some hand sanitizer before eating lunch."

"Good idea," Jason mused. "Davis Brown's handshake felt a little wet. I don't really want to think too hard about why."

I gagged.

The Man approached with a big smile and an orange hard hat above it.

"There's my dynamic duo," he crowed, pumping our hands for about the tenth time today.

I couldn't blame our boss for being pleased. The largest construction project in the company's history had been completed on schedule and within budget. In this industry, that counted as an astounding victory.

"I don't think you need this anymore," Jason said good-naturedly, pointing to the hard hat. The courthouse was no longer an active construction zone and precautionary measures were not necessary, but The Man's eccentricities were well known. He was the only person in sight wearing a safety hat.

The Man removed the hard hat with some reluctance. "Can never be too careful," he said, scanning the sky in case a rogue crane was about to drop a brick on his head. In the next instant his name was called by a trio of men who looked like members of the aforementioned political class. The Man wordlessly handed his hard hat to Jason and scurried over to the men who had summoned him.

Jason held the thing aloft. "What am I supposed to do with this?"

I considered. "Let's keep it as a souvenir."

He nodded. "I can stick it in the garden to scare away the crows."

"Jason, we don't have a garden."

"Then what's all that green shit in the backyard?"

"Weeds."

He laughed and tried to lead me away. "Let's get out of here, gorgeous. Ceremony's over. Courthouse is open. We're no longer needed."

Just before Jason and I walked away hand in hand, I glanced up to see a familiar tall blond head. The man attached to it saw me at the same time. Of course it made sense that he would be present for the ribbon-cutting ceremony since he was the chief architect. Jason and I waved, and Lukas Lund smiled at us before waving back.

"Want to walk or drive?" Jason asked.

"Drive," I said immediately, fanning myself with a program that had been handed out for the ceremony. "It's too damn hot to walk."

"It's Phoenix, Audrey. It's always hot."

"Then we should always drive."

Jason's car was on the first floor of the new parking structure beside the courthouse. He opened the door for me with a gallant flourish and I paused to kiss him before ducking inside.

"You hear from William this week?" he asked on the short drive over to the quaint old downtown neighborhood where Esposito's Pizzeria was located.

"He's having a blast at the beach with the boys. And you know my folks flew in yesterday. They're all excited that we're coming to visit next week."

William was in the middle of a long-term sabbatical from the court. Working as a legal consultant gave him the flexibility to do things like take Leo and Isaac on a one-month vacation to the beach house on the Oregon coast. He knew Jennifer would have wanted him to bring the boys there to spend time with her side of the family.

"That's going to be one crowded house next week," Jason commented.

"Yes, crowded," I agreed, "but fun. Full of family and love."

At the mention of family, I thought Jason looked a little wistful. Christian Roma had died in his sleep only a month ago. Jason's father never did remember us from one visit to the next, but he always seemed thrilled whenever we came by, believing we were friends he was just meeting for the first time. His grin spread a mile wide during our small, intimate wedding three months earlier, and I knew Jason had been glad to have his father there. The fact that he was no longer himself had been what made it possible for Jason to absolve him in the first place. The terrible father Christian Roma had been was dead long before his body gave out.

"Hey." I put my hand on Jason's knee.

He looked at me.

"I love you."

My stunning husband smiled. "I love you too, baby."

I squeezed his knee. "Then feed me some pizza."

Dominic and Melanie were full of hugs the second we entered the restaurant. Since we'd gotten into the habit of hanging out with them often, Melanie and I had become quite close. It was nice to have a girlfriend outside of work, and Melanie, a little spitfire, always made me laugh.

As the pair of them watched us bite into the custom pizzas they'd prepared in anticipation of our arrival, Dominic stood behind his wife with a protective arm across her petite shoulders. Melanie absently rubbed her growing belly with a small smile on her face.

"Sit down," I said, scooting over.

"Can't," said Dominic. "Got to return to the kitchen."

"The lunch crowd will be descending any minute," Melanie agreed.

"I'm proud of you guys, though," Dominic said. "I passed the courthouse this morning. The place kind of gives new meaning to the word *impressive*. And now every time I hear that a crime has been committed, I'll think of you."

Jason snorted. "Thanks, buddy. That's a hell of a tribute."

Dominic shrugged. "I do what I can," he said before he retreated to the kitchen, where he would happily slave away in front of the giant brick ovens hour after hour.

"I'm proud of you too," Melanie said, and pecked each of us on the cheek before heading over to help at the takeout counter, which was already starting to get busy.

I finished off a slice of pizza and reached across the table to take Jason's left hand in mine.

"You were right to pick the platinum bands," I said. "I like the way they look together."

He picked up my hand and kissed the knuckle beneath the ring. "I like the way *we* look together." He set my hand down on the table and lightly ran his fingertips across the back. "You ready to embark on our next adventure, Audrey Roma?"

"I thought you promised me a lifetime of adventures."

"And I plan to deliver. But I was specifically talking about the business side of our relationship."

"Oh, that." I smiled at him. "I'm ready. I think it's high time to stop working for someone else."

He nodded with approval. "Time to call all our own shots."

Jason and I had decided our days at Lester & Brown were numbered. Just this week we'd filed the necessary paperwork to incorporate Gordon Roma Construction. Jason had always dreamed of having his own construction firm, and even though I'd never thought about it much, with Jason at my side I wasn't short on optimism. We planned to start small, bidding for projects out in the East Valley where construction was booming. My father heard about our plans and pledged to offer any additional financial support we might require. Although I was grateful, I told him we really didn't need any favors. Aaron Gordon frowned and told me it was no favor. He believed in me. Moreover, he believed Jason and I made a hell of a team. That was about as remarkable an endorsement as we could ask for.

"The Man's liable to shit bricks when we tell him we're both leaving," I said, cheerfully taking a bite of pizza.

Jason waved a hand. "Might be good for the guy to shit bricks. He's always been bunched up too tight. All that pressure has to crack sometime."

I snorted into my iced tea glass over the imagery. "You're nasty."

He winked at me. "I could be nastier."

"Don't I know it."

A few minutes later I noticed Jason was looking me up and down in a very familiar way.

"What?" I teased.

"Are you finished eating?"

"Are you in that much of a hurry to get back to the office?"

"To hell with the office. They're not even expecting us back this afternoon."

"How do you know that?"

He leaned forward. "Because this morning before the ceremony I called and ordered Marnie to inform everyone we'd be at a meeting and unavailable for the rest of the day."

"What meeting? With whom?"

Jason's hand touched my knee under the table, slowly creeping higher under my skirt. "With each other," he said in that slow, sexy voice that left no doubt about exactly what he had in mind.

I held up one finger. "Check, please."

"Get out of here, you guys," Melanie scolded as she walked by carrying a basket of garlic bread. "You know your money is no good in this establishment."

Jason took two twenties and tossed them on the table anyway.

"Let's get the hell out of here before Dom comes roaring out and yells at me for paying," he said, pulling me to my feet.

I laughed and held on to him as we stepped outside into the brilliant sun. We had to pause at the corner and wait for the light to turn green. When it did, Jason glanced my way, raised an eyebrow, and we crossed to the other side hand in hand.

ACKNOWLEDGMENTS

A ton of gratitude to my family for their steadfast support of my long working hours, lackluster housekeeping skills, and insatiable appetite for Red Vines.

Thank you to my lovely agent, Kimberly Brower, for her constant encouragement and honest feedback.

To the dedicated Montlake team, who are tireless in their efforts to help me produce the best story possible, I am indebted to you.

Most important, to all the wonderful readers who flatter me enormously by asking for more stories, every word was written for you.

ABOUT THE AUTHOR

Cora Brent was born in a cold climate but escaped as soon as it was legally possible. These days she lives in the Arizona desert with her husband, two kids, and a prickly pear cactus she has affectionately named Spot. Cora's closet is filled with boxes of unfinished stories that date back to her 1980s childhood, and someday she fully intends to finish her first masterpiece about a pink horse that plays baseball. But in the meantime, she's consumed with her romance novels. The author of the Gentry Boys books and the Worked Up series, which includes *Fired*, Cora feels blessed to have appeared on the bestseller lists of both *USA Today* and the *New York Times*. Visit her at www.corabrent.com, or connect on Facebook at www.facebook.com/CoraBrentAuthor.